Women of Worth

SALZWASSER
VERLAG

Anonymous

Women of Worth

Reprint of the original, first published in 1863.

1st Edition 2022 | ISBN: 978-3-37500-356-2

Verlag (Publisher): Salzwasser Verlag GmbH, Zeilweg 44, 60439 Frankfurt, Deutschland
Vertretungsberechtigt (Authorized to represent): E. Roepke, Zeilweg 44, 60439 Frankfurt, Deutschland
Druck (Print): Books on Demand GmbH, In de Tarpen 42, 22848 Norderstedt, Deutschland

WOMEN OF WORTH.

WOMEN of WORTH

A BOOK FOR GIRLS

ILLUSTRATED BY W. DICKES

MRS FRY READING TO PRISONERS IN NEWGATE 1812

NEW YORK:

1863.

As when the night its highest noon attains,
And not a cloud o'ercasts the blue serene,
The stars diffused through all the ethereal plains,
And all arrayed in living light are seen;

So in this night of time what patterns rise,
Rich in celestial lustres to adorn
And bless our world, till from those lower skies
Shine the full glories of that promised morn,

When Jesus rising, like the orient sun
Shall drown these stars in his superior rays,
And all these saints, their race nocturnal run,
Alone on his unrivalled beauties gaze.

But till this day shall break, how much we owe
To those divine examples that illume
Our journey through this vale of sin and woe,
Direct our steps and half dispel our gloom.

Ye fair, heaven's kindest, noblest gift to man,
Adorned with every charm and every grace,
The flame your forms inspire let virtue fan,
And let the mind be lovelier than the face.

Daughters of Eve, or in your silver hairs,
Or flourishing in youth's auspicious bloom,
The soul, the immortal soul, demands your cares;
Oh live as heirs of endless life to come!

Well weigh your various characters, fulfil
All your relations both to God and man,
Press to be perfect, high, mount higher still;
Crown, crowd with blessings your contracted span.

CONTENTS.

LIST OF ILLUSTRATIONS.

PREFATORY NOTE.

THE RELATION OF BIOGRAPHY TO EVERY-DAY LIFE.

"It is the divinest thing to be good."—JOHN FOSTER.
"Goodness is beauty in its best estate."—MARLOWE.
"The true mark of a good heart, is its capacity for loving."—
MADAME DE SEVIGNE.

THE following Biographical Sketches form, it is believed, a book which a woman of any age may take up with pleasure and profit; while to the young—it may be of unformed character—the work is calculated to be more specially useful, in so far as it serves to show how those who were of "The Excellent of the Earth" walked amongst us.

After a careful examination of the numerous books which treat of the lives and works of notable women, it may be sufficient to remark that if the editor of the present volume has made even an approach to the standard kept in view, this publication will be found to present elements of character and examples of action in a manner likely to exercise a wholesome influence while it possesses a distinctive tone.

In conjunction with this pervading spirit it has been an object to combine in one cheap volume, brief, graphic, and suggestive sketches, not only of those already famous in the annals of female worth, but of those whose lives, from having been spent in the midst of us, or at least within the memory of a still-existing generation, have thus, to some extent, been overlooked in previous collections of a somewhat similar character. The aim has therefore been to record "deeds which should not pass away, and names that must not wither."

With respect to the materials of which the book is composed a few words are necessary. The more lengthy sketches are original, enriched by a little fresh information from private sources. Of the shorter lives, the majority are taken from the third era of Sarah Josepha Hale's "Records of Women."* The interesting account of the labors of Sarah Martin is gathered from the pages of the "Edinburgh Review;" and the sketch of Mrs. Elizabeth Rowe is derived from Miss Kavanagh's "Women of Christianity."

Every life here given has at least its one phase of excellence; but not a few of them are worthy of contemplation under many aspects, and of imitation in several ways. In all we see blended the fruits of that labor, patience, truth, trust, and love which are the crown and glory of woman.

There are not here many names of the great and

---

* Woman's Record; or Sketches of all Distinguished Women from the Creation to A. D. 1854. By Sarah Josepha Hale. New York: Harper Brothers.

titled. All honor to those who, with all the weakness of our common humanity, have borne meekly and bravely the trials of prosperity and high station: the full cup needs a steady hand. It has rather been designed to draw lessons from more commonplace people, and to show something of the poetry and charm of every-day life—from a notion that thereby the book will be more impressive to the majority of readers. Perhaps it may serve to soothe, encourage, and sustain, as well as to warn and guide. For, as good old Jeremy Taylor has well put it, good books, and the examples of good lives, are amongst the thousands of excellent arts which it has pleased God to use to win us.

It is no doubt often a difficult matter for an enthusiastic young woman to settle into the harness of every-day life. It seems so easy and so fine to act gracefully or grandly upon grand occasions, amongst people who are to one's taste. It is often very hard for a time (we use the words of a piquant and thoughtful writer) to learn that "fellow-mortals, every one, must be accepted as they are: you can neither straighten their noses, nor brighten their wit, nor rectify their dispositions; and it is these people—amongst whom your life is passed—that it is needful you should tolerate, pity, and love; it is these more or less ugly, stupid, inconsistent people whose movements of goodness you should be able to admire—for whom you should cherish all possible hopes, all possible patience. . . . . . . In this world there are so many of these common, coarse people, who have no picturesque sentimental wretchedness! It is so needful we should remember their existence, else we may happen to leave them quite out of our religion and philanthropy, and frame lofty ideas which only fit a world of extremes. . . . . There are few prophets in the world; few sublimely beautiful women; few heroes. I can't afford to give all my love and reverence to such rarities: I want a great deal of those feelings for my every-day fellows, especially for the few in the foreground of the great multitude, whose faces I know, whose hands I touch, for whom I have to make way with kindly courtesy."

And so it will be a good thing if this gathering of exemplary lives will teach some to study to be kind, and others to be quiet, and all to be cheerful.

THE EDITOR.

WOMEN OF WORTH.

THE ILLUSTRIOUS MATRON,

MARY WASHINGTON,

THE mother of George Washington, the hero of the American revolutionary war, and the first president of the United States, claims the noblest distinction a woman should covet or can gain, that of training her gifted son in the way he should go, and inspiring him by her example to make the way of goodness his path to glory.*

Mrs. Mary Washington was descended from the very respectable family of Ball, who settled as English colonists on the banks of the Potomac. Bred in those domestic and independent habits which graced the Virginia matrons in the old days of Virginia, this lady, by the death of her husband, became involved in the cares of a young family, at a per'.- when those cares seem more especially to

* This b\ .aphy was written by George W. P. Custis, grandson of Mrs. Martha Washington.

claim the aid and control of the stronger sex. It was left for this eminent woman, by a method the most rare, by an education and discipline the most peculiar and imposing, to form in the youth-time of her son those great and essential qualities which gave lustre to the glories of his after-life. If the school savored the more of the Spartan than the Persian character, it was a fitter school to form a hero, destined to be the ornament of the age in which he flourished, and a standard of excellence for ages yet to come.

It was remarked by the ancients, that the mother always gave the tone to the character of the child; and we may be permitted to say that, since the days of old renown, a mother has not lived better fitted to give the tone and character of real greatness to her child, than she whose remarkable life and actions this reminiscence will endeavor to illustrate.

At the time of his father's death, George Washington was only ten years of age. He has been heard to say that he knew little of his father, except the remembrance of his person, and of his parental fondness. To his mother's forming care he himself ascribed the origin of his fortunes and his fame.

The home of Mrs. Washington, of which she was always mistress, was a pattern of order. There the levity and indulgence common to youth were tempered by a deference and well-regulated restraint, which, while it neither suppressed nor condemned any rational enjoyment usual in the spring-time of life, prescribed those enjoyments within the bounds of moderation and propriety. Thus the chief was taught the duty of obedience, which prepared him to command. Still the mother held in reserve an authority which never departed from her, even when her son had become the most illustrious of men. It seemed to say, "I am your mother, the being who gave you life, the guide who directed your steps when they needed a guardian; my maternal affection drew forth your love; my authority constrained your spirit; whatever may be your success or your renown, next to your God, your reverence is due to me." Nor did the chief dissent from these truths; but to the last moments of his venerable parent, yielded to her will the most dutiful and implicit obedience, and felt for her person and character the highest respect, and the most enthusiastic attachment.

Such were the domestic influences under which the mind of Washington was formed; and that he not only profited by, but fully appreciated their excellence and the character of his mother, his behavior toward her at all times testified. Upon his appointment to the command-in-chief of the American armies, previously to his joining the forces at Cambridge, he removed his mother from her country residence to the village of Fredericksburg, a situation remote from danger, and contiguous to her friends and relatives.

It was there the matron remained during nearly

the whole of the trying period of the revolution. Directly in the way of the news, as it passed from north to south, one courier would bring intelligence of success to our arms; another, "swiftly coursing at his heels," the saddening reverse of disaster and defeat. While thus ebbed and flowed the fortunes of our cause, the mother, trusting to the wisdom and protection of divine providence, preserved the even tenor of her life; affording an example to those matrons whose sons were alike engaged in the arduous contest; and showing that unavailing anxieties, however belonging to nature, were unworthy of mothers whose sons were combating for the inestimable rights of man, and the freedom and happiness of the world.

When the comforting and glorious intelligence arrived of the passage of the Delaware (December, 1776), an event which restored our hopes from the very brink of despair, a number of her friends waited upon the mother with congratulations. She received them with calmness, observed that it was most pleasurable news, and that George appeared to have deserved well of his country for such signal services; and continued, in reply to the gratulating patriots (most of whom held letters in their hands, from which they read extracts): "But, my good sirs, here is too much flattery—still George will not forget the lessons I early taught him—he will not forget *himself*, though he is the subject of so much praise."

During the war, and indeed during her useful

life, up to the advanced age of eighty-two, until within three years of her death (when an afflictive disease prevented exertion), the mother set a most valuable example in the management of her domestic concerns, carrying her own keys, bustling in her household affairs, providing for her family, and living and moving in all the pride of independence. She was not actuated by that ambition for show which pervades lesser minds; and the peculiar plainness and dignity of her manners became in nowise altered, when the sun of glory arose upon her house. There are some of the aged inhabitants of Fredericksburg who well remember the matron, as seated in an old-fashioned open chaise, she was in the habit of visiting, almost daily, her little farm in the vicinity of the town When there, she would ride about her fields, giving her orders, and seeing that they were obeyed.

Her great industry, with the well-regulated economy of all her concerns, enabled the matron to dispense considerable charities to the poor, although her own circumstances were always far from rich. All manner of domestic economies, so useful in those times of privation and trouble, met her zealous attention; while every thing about her household bore marks of her care and management, and very many things the impress of her own hands. In a very humble dwelling, and suffering under an excruciating disease (cancer of the breast), thus lived this mother of the first of men, preserving, unchanged, her peculiar nobleness and independence of character.

She was always pious, but in her latter days her devotions were performed in private. She was in the habit of repairing every day to a secluded spot, formed by rocks and trees, near her dwelling, where, abstracted from the world and worldly things, she communed with her Creator, in humiliation and prayer.

After an absence of nearly seven years, it was at length, on the return of the combined armies from Yorktown, permitted to the mother again to see and embrace her illustrious son. So soon as he had dismounted, in the midst of a numerous and brilliant suite, he sent to apprise her of his arrival, and to know when it would be her pleasure to receive him. And now mark the force of early education and habits, and the superiority of the Spartan over the Persian school, in this interview of the great Washington with his admirable parent and instructor. No pageantry of war proclaimed his coming, no trumpets sounded, no banners waved. Alone and on foot, the marshal of France, the general-in-chief of the combined armies of France and America, the deliverer of his country, the hero of the age, repaired to pay his humble duty to her whom he venerated as the author of his being, the founder of his fortune and his fame. For full well he knew that the matron would not be moved by all the pride that glory ever gave, nor by all the "pomp and circumstance" of power.

The lady was alone, her aged hands employed in the works of domestic industry, when the good news was announced; and it was further told that the victor chief was in waiting at the threshold. She welcomed him with a warm embrace, and by the well-remembered and endearing name of his childhood; inquiring as to his health, she remarked the lines which mighty cares and many trials had made on his manly countenance, spoke much of old times and old friends, but of his glory—*not one word!*

Meantime, in the village of Fredericksburg, all was joy and revelry; the town was crowded with the officers of the French and American armies, and with gentlemen from all the country around, who hastened to welcome the conquerors of Cornwallis. The citizens made arrangements for a splendid ball, to which the mother of Washington was specially invited. She observed that, although her dancing days were *pretty well over*, she should feel happy in contributing to the general festivity, and consented to attend.

The foreign officers were anxious to see the mother of their chief. They had heard indistinct rumors respecting her remarkable life and character; but, forming their judgments from European examples, they were prepared to expect in the mother that glare and show which would have been attached to the parents of the great in the old world. How were they surprised when the matron, leaning on the arm of her son, entered the room! She was arrayed in the very plain, yet becoming garb worn by the Virginia lady of the olden time. Her address, always dignified and imposing, was courteous, though reserved. She received the complimentary attentions, which were profusely paid her, without evincing the slightest elevation; and, at an early hour, wishing the company much enjoyment of their pleasures, observing that it was time for old people to be at home, retired.

The foreign officers were amazed to behold one whom so many causes contributed to elevate, preserving the even tenor of her life, while such a blaze of glory shone upon her name and offspring. The European world furnished no examples of such magnanimity. Names of ancient lore were heard to escape from their lips; and they observed that, "if such were the matrons of America, it was not wonderful the sons were illustrious."

It was on this festive occasion that General Washington danced a minuet with Mrs. Willis. It closed his dancing days. The minuet was much in vogue at that period, and was peculiarly calculated for the display of the splendid figure of the chief, and his natural grace and elegance of air and manner. The gallant Frenchmen who were present, of which fine people it may be said that dancing forms one of the elements of their existence, so much admired the American performance, as to admit that a Parisian education could not have improved it. As the evening advanced, the commander-in-chief, yielding to the gayety of the scene, went down some dozen couple in the contra-dance, with great spirit and satisfaction.

The Marquis de Lafayette repaired to Fredericksburg, previous to his departure for Europe, in the fall of 1784, to pay his parting respects to the mother, and to ask her blessing.

Conducted by one of her grandsons, he approached the house, when the young gentleman observed, "There, sir, is my grandmother." Lafayette beheld, working in the garden, clad in domestic-made clothes, and her gray head covered in a plain straw hat, the mother of "his hero!" The lady saluted him kindly, observing: "Ah, marquis! you see an old woman—but come, I can make you welcome to my poor dwelling, without the parade of changing my dress."

The marquis spoke of the happy effects of the revolution, and the goodly prospect which opened upon independent America; stated his speedy departure for his native land; paid the tribute of his heart, his love and admiration of her illustrious son; and concluded by asking her blessing. She blessed him; and to the encomiums which he had lavished upon his hero and paternal chief, the matron replied in these words: "I am not suprised at what George has done, for he was always a very good boy."

In her person, Mrs. Washington was of the middle size, and finely formed; her features pleasing, yet strongly marked. It is not the happiness of the writer to remember her, having only seen her with infant eyes. The sister of the chief he perfectly well remembers. She was a most majestic woman, and so strikingly like the brother, that it was a matter of frolic to throw a cloak around her, and place a military hat upon her head; and, such was the perfect resemblance, that, had she appeared on her brother's steed, battalions would have presented arms, and senates risen to do homage to the chief.

In her latter days, the mother often spoke of her own *good boy;* of the merits of his early life; of his love and dutifulness to herself; but of the deliverer of his country, the chief magistrate of the great republic, she never spoke. Call you this insensibility? or want of ambition? Oh, no! her ambition had been gratified to overflowing. She had taught him to be *good;* that he became *great* when the opportunity presented, was a consequence, not a cause.

Mrs. Washington died at the age of eighty-seven, soon after the decease of her illustrious son. She was buried at Fredericksburg, and for many years her grave remained without a memorial-stone. But the heart of the nation acknowledged her worth, and the noble spirit of her native Virginia was at length aroused to the sacred duty of perpetuating its respect for the merits of its most worthy daughter. On the seventh of May, 1833, at Fredericksburg, the corner-stone of her monument was laid by Andrew Jackson, then the President of the United States. The public officers of the general government, and an immense concourse of people from every section of the country, crowded to witness the imposing ceremonies. Mr. Barrett, one of the monument committee of Virginia, delivered the eulogy on Mrs. Washington, and then addressed the President of the United States. In his reply, General Jackson paid a beautiful tribute to the memory of the deceased, which, for its masterly exposition of the effect of maternal example, and of the importance of female influence, deserves to be preserved. We give a few sentences:

"In tracing the recollections which can be gathered of her principles and conduct, it is impossible to avoid the conviction, that these were closely interwoven with the destiny of her son. The great points of his character are before the world. He who runs may read them in his whole career, as a citizen, a soldier, a magistrate. He possessed an unerring judgment, if that term can be applied to human nature; great probity of purpose, high moral principles, perfect self-possession, untiring application, an inquiring mind, seeking information from every quarter, and arriving at its conclusions with a full knowledge of the subject; and he added to these an inflexibility of resolution, which nothing could change but a conviction of error. Look back at the life and conduct of his mother, and at her domestic government, and they will be found admirably adapted to form and develop the elements of such a character. The power of greatness was there; but had it not been guided and directed by maternal solicitude and judgment, its possessor, instead of presenting to the world examples of virtue, patriotism, and wisdom, which will be precious in all succeeding ages, might have added to the number of those master-spirits, whose fame rests upon the faculties they have abused, and the injuries they have committed.

"How important to the females of our country, are these reminiscences of the early life of Washington, and of the maternal care of her upon whom its future course depended! Principles less firm and just, an affection less regulated by discretion, might have changed the character of the son, and with it the destinies of the nation. We have reason to be proud of the virtue and intelligence of our women. As mothers and sisters, as wives and daughters, their duties are performed with exemplary fidelity. They, no doubt, realize the great importance of the maternal character, and the powerful influence it must exert upon the American youth. Happy is it for them and our country, that they have before them this illustrious example of maternal devotion, and this bright reward of filial success! The mother of a family who lives to witness the virtues of her children, and their advancement in life, and who is known and honored because they are known and honored, should have no other wish, on this side the grave, to gratify. The seeds of virtue and vice are early sown, and we may often anticipate the harvest that will be gathered. Changes, no doubt, occur, but let no one place his hope upon these. Impressions made in infancy, if not indelible, are effaced with difficulty, and renewed with facility; and upon the mother, therefore, must frequently, if not generally, depend the fate of the son.

"Fellow-citizens: at your request, and in your name, I now deposit this plate in the spot destined for it; and when the American pilgrim shall, in after ages, come up to this high and holy place, and lay his hand upon this sacred column, may he recall the virtues of her who sleeps beneath, and depart with his affections purified, and his piety strengthened, while he invokes blessings upon the mother of Washington."

This monument bears the simple but touching inscription, MARY, THE MOTHER OF WASHINGTON.

THE TRUE WIFE,

MARTHA WASHINGTON,

WIFE of General George Washington, was born in the county of New Kent, Virginia, in May, 1732. Her maiden name was Martha Dandridge; at the age of seventeen, she married Colonel Daniel Parke Custis, of the White House, county of New Kent, by whom she had four children; a girl, who died in infancy; a son, named Daniel, whose early death is supposed to have hastened his father's; Martha, who arrived at womanhood, and died in 1770; and John, who perished in the service of his country, at the siege of Yorktown, aged twenty-seven.

Mrs. Custis was left a young and very wealthy widow, and managed the extensive landed and pecuniary concerns of the estate with surprising ability. In 1759, she was married to George Washington, then a colonel in the colonial service, and soon after, they removed permanently to Mount Vernon, on the Potomac. Upon the election of her husband to the command-in-chief of the armies of his country, Mrs., or Lady Washington, as she was generally called, accompanied the general to the lines before Boston, and witnessed its siege and evacuation; and was always constant in her attendance on her husband, when it was possible. After General Washington's election to the presidency of the United States, in 1787, Mrs. Washington performed the duties belonging to the wife of a man in that high station, with great dignity and ease; and on the retirement of Washington, she still continued her unbounded hospitality. The decease of her venerated husband, who died December 14th, 1799, was the shock from which she never recovered, though she bore the heavy sorrow with the most exemplary resignation. She was kneeling at the foot of his bed when he expired, and when she found he was gone, she said, in a calm voice: "'Tis well; all is now over; I shall soon follow him; I have no more trials to pass through." Her children were all deceased—her earthly treasures were withdrawn; but she held firm her trust in the divine mercy which had ordered her lot. For more than half a century, she had been accustomed to passing an hour every morning alone in her chamber, engaged in reading the Bible and in prayer. She survived her husband a little over two years, dying at Mount Vernon, aged seventy.

In person Mrs. Washington was well-formed, though somewhat below the middle size. A portrait taken previous to her marriage, shows that she must have been very handsome in her youth; and she retained a comeliness of countenance, as well as a dignified grace of manner, during life. In her home she was the presiding genius that kept action and order in perfect harmony; a wife, in whom the heart of her husband could safely trust. The example of this illustrious couple ought to have a salutary influence on every American family; the marriage union, as it subsisted between George and Martha Washington, is shown to be the happiest, as well as holiest, relation in which human beings can be united to each other. The delicacy of Mrs. Washington's nature, which led her, just before her decease, to destroy the letters that had passed between her husband and herself, proves the depth and purity of her love and reverence for him. She could not permit that the confidence they had shared together should become public; it would be desecrating their chaste loves, and, perhaps, some word or expression might be misinterpreted to his disadvantage. One only letter from Washington to his wife was found among his papers; the extracts we give from this letter indicate clearly the character of their correspondence.

"PHILADELPHIA, June 18th, 1775.

"MY DEAREST,—I am now set down to write you on a subject which fills me with inexpressible concern; and this concern is greatly aggravated and increased, when I reflect upon the uneasiness I know it will give you. It has been determined in Congress, that the whole army raised for the defence of the American cause shall be put under my care, and that it is necessary for me to proceed immediately to Boston, and take upon me the command of it.

"You may believe me, dear Patsy, when I assure you, in the most solemn manner, that, so far from seeking this appointment, I have used every endeavour in my power to avoid it, not only from my unwillingness to part with you and the family, but from the consciousness of it being a trust too great for my capacity, and that I should enjoy more real happiness in one month with you at home, than I have the most distant prospect of finding abroad, if my stay were to be seven times seven years. But as it has been a kind of destiny that has thrown upon me this service, I shall hope that my undertaking it is designed to answer some good purpose.

* * * * *

"I shall rely, therefore, confidently on that Providence, which has heretofore preserved and been bountiful to me, not doubting but that I shall return safe to you in the fall. I shall feel no pain from the toil or the danger of the campaign; my unhappiness will flow from the uneasiness I know you will feel from being left alone. I therefore beg that you will summon your whole fortitude, and pass your time as agreeably as you can. Nothing will give me so much sincere satisfaction as to hear this, and to hear it from your own pen."

* * * * *

He then goes on to say, that as life is always

uncertain, he had had his will drawn up, and inclosed the draft to her; by this will he gave her the use and control of all his estates and property during her life-time, which will was observed at his decease. Such was the love the greatest man the world ever saw cherished toward his wife; and she worthy of his love. What higher celebrity could a woman desire?

THE WORTHY DAUGHTER,

CHARLOTTE BRONTÉ.

In the central region of Yorkshire, which, from its elevation, forms the rivershed of that portion of Great Britain, where wold and moor, beck and force, deep scooped-out valleys, and tier after tier of high-rounded hills running up into mountains, prevail, was born, and lived, and died, Charlotte Bronté. The region is rough and unsightly—no trees, no velvety soft verdure, no golden crops, no nestling hedges, consequently few birds to wake the echoes, save the lark and the more common of the freemen of the air—a naked, cold, and barren tract, where, however, the treasures below the surface largely compensate for the absence of picturesque beauty above, and where, "as the soil is, so the heart of man," rough in the husk, rich in the core. Iron and coal, and lime and freestone, abound in these bold and hilly masses, and in the depressed flats between them; but without, the soil is cold and peaty, its chief vegetation being coarse pasturage, sundry heaths and mosses, and other components of the moorland Flora.

In one of the least attractive spots of this district, hard by the rising manufacturing town of Keighley, stands the village of Haworth, rather high upon the moors, which, nevertheless, seem to stretch illimitably above and beyond it, till they border the sky. The village street runs straight up the hill, and can be seen for miles' distance. The cottages are all of that plain two-story, rough aspect, which is common in this part of Yorkshire and the corresponding section of Lancashire, built of the grit which abounds in the neighborhood, and which furnishes the stone dykes that demark the fields; those stony fences conveying the impression that, like the material of which they are built, they are more useful than ornamental. With the same material the steeply-ascending street is pitched, the edge of the stones projecting sharply to give footing to the tripping horses, the whole seeming the very coarsest contrivance of an imperfect civilization, and in singular keeping with all around. The church stands at the top of the street, with nothing of architectural decoration to recommend it, and behind it, still nearer the bleak moor, at the further end of the churchyard, is the plain, primitive, two-storied parsonage, where the author of "Jane Eyre" spent her early days, and where, at the end of thirty-nine years, she rendered up her breath to the Great Giver; a house gloomy in its position, gloomy in exterior aspect, and in all its conditions gloomy—the only cheerful thing which the manse and the village can boast being the fires which, summer and winter, the abundance of coal and the habits of the people bid sparkle in almost every apartment. The parsonage looks out on a churchyard, paved throughout with tombstones, the singularly-ugly fancy predominating here, as throughout the whole factory region, of hiding the verdure with flat stones, while headstones would admit of the green sod growing over graves, and are every way more appropriate and pretty. But this uncouth and neglected look is in harmony with the appearance of every thing around: not poverty-struck, far from it, but a carelessness about arrangements which are not demanded by the necessities of existence.

And this is very characteristic of the manly and primitive population that abound in such districts, who in manner seem somewhat repulsive, from their frankness and independence of bearing, and in speech scarcely intelligible, from their broad provincialisms and abounding Saxon phraseology. A visitor must expect to be *thee*-and-*thou'd* by them as sturdily as by any follower of George Fox, while *thorpe* and *fored*, and *t'oud un*, and a thousand peculiarities more, sufficiently proclaim the native affinities of their tongue. But they are faithful and affectionate, thoughtful and religious; old Tabby, the servant of the Brontés, who died under their roof after a thirty years' residence, being an instance of the one, and the abounding of church and chapel, well supported and well attended, together with a deference for revealed religion, being proof of the other. The contamination which springs from crowded factories, high wages, and the impulsive life of competition, is kept very steadily in check, in the part of Yorkshire of which we speak, by the earnest and successful efforts at evangelization made by Christians of all persuasions, and no district of the country is full of more lively promise for the future, on the score of morality and religion.

They have a shrewd and racy humor, too, these blunt and downright fellows, with an amazing fund of plain common sense. As a sample of their Yorkshire Doric, and, at the same time, a spice of their caustic jokes, we quote a paragraph from their classic annual, the "Pogmoor Olmenack," which will give a better idea of their style of thought and speech than an express dissertation. They call this screed of satire the "Dumestick Tutor."

Long Division.—T' curns in a baker's cake.

Short Division.—T' space atween a miser's purse an hiz heart.

Cumpaand Addishan.—An oud laidy at tacks snuff, an hez hur cloaze scented it bargan.

Propoarshun.—A womman lettin hur waist grow summut like natur intended it, an not squeaze it wal its na thicker then t' neck ov a champaine bottle.

Exchainge.—Two wimmin differin, and tellin wun anuther all they naw.

Discaant.—A milk seller tackin t' cream off, an

then warmin' t' oud milk up and sellin hiz customers it for new.

Invoices.—A womman at tawks more indoor then aght.

Profit an Loss.—A man at swaps a good horse for a bad an, an gies summat ta booit.

Promiscuous Examples.—A man tackin hiz bairns to a plaice a warship nobbat when t' fit tacks him.

Evolushans.—A man goin raand abaght ta get into hiz nabor's affairs.

Rule-a-three.—A lodgin-hause bed.

Single Posishan.—An oud meaid—poor thing!

Book-keepin.—Borrain wun ov a friend, an nivver tackin him it back agean.

Weight an Measure—

Ov Trubbles.—A regular weight.

Ov Sorrow.—A full cup.

Time—

Fast.—A slander fresh slipt off an a womman's tongue.

Slaw—A snail wauk wi' good deed on it back.

The same dialect prevails in the language of the old woman whom Miss Bronté met on the moor, and who accosted her in a way which further illustrates the natural frankness and independence of the natives of the West Riding. "How! Miss Bronté! Hey yah seen owt o' my cofe (calf)?" Miss Bronté told her she could not say, for she did not know it, when the old woman proceeded to describe it· "Wall! yah knaw its gettin up like nah between a cah (cow) an a cofe, what we call a stirk, yah know, Miss Brontë: will yah turn this way if yah happen to see't, as yah're going back, Miss Brontë; nah *do*, Miss Brontë!"

Amid such a people and such scenery was Charlotte Brontë ordained to spend the greater part of her mortal life, her father, the Rev. Patrick Brontë, A.B., of St. John's College, Cambridge, having obtained the perpetual curacy of Haworth in the year 1820. Previous to this, while curate of another place in Yorkshire, he married his wife, a Cornish lady, who was possessed of an annuity of £50 a year, and on the slender means of both proceeded to set up house in 1812. After the birth of his six children, he received the small benefice of Haworth, and thither he transported his household gods in the year before named—a delicate wife, a swarm of little ones to be provided for, and scanty resources; an unusual plain dietary and almost total seclusion from society being the result. Just one year after their arrival in the place, Mrs. Brontë died, leaving her six motherless children the inheritance of a consumptive constitution and a morbid tendency, which was probably heightened by the eccentric notions of their father on the subject of early education. His wish was to make them hardy, he himself having been reared amid the stern penury of an Irish peasant's home. Other eccentricities of his, which dictated an almost total seclusion of himself from the orphans, such as having his meals alone, a custom observed by him throughout life, were not favorable to the cheerfulness of spirits, nor consequently to the good health of the little ones.

About a year after their mother's death, a prim maiden aunt, their mother's sister, came to reside in the parsonage, and took charge of the helpless family. She was a rigid domestic disciplinarian, understanding how the work of a house should be done, and having it performed by her nieces and the servant, like so much clockwork. Every menial office in the establishment was exacted of the children, not more as matter of necessity than of duty, and Charlotte continued to discharge them all until the year before her death, with the force of habit and the *penchant* of liking. Grates were scoured, furniture scrubbed, beds tossed, floors washed and swept, bread baked, and all sorts of plain cooking done by these little, quiet, heartbroken-looking children, who did every one of the same things daily after they became celebrated women. To afford them, however, advantages of education superior to those which home supplied, the two elder sisters of Charlotte were sent, in the year 1824, to a school for the daughters of the clergy, which had been opened shortly before at no great distance from Haworth. This is the school, the graphic description of which is one of the main features of "Jane Eyre." In the same year, at a later period, Charlotte, the third child, and Emily, her still younger sister, were sent to the same school. The failing health of the whole party led to their removal in the autumn of next year, during which (1825) Charlotte lost her two eldest sisters by consumption, and became by this dispensation the eldest of the survivors.

The education of the family was now conducted in the most homely way in their aunt's bedroom, papa occasionally assisting with lessons in his study. Nevertheless, except that such volumes as were in the house were at their disposal, these remarkable children were to a great degree self-taught. Society they had none beyond the walls of their own home; but their father was a man of books, and this, and their seclusion, probably furnished the strong impulse toward a creative literature which the surviving members of the family so early exhibited. When Charlotte had reached only her thirteenth year, she had, assisted in some small degree by younger members of the family, filled volume after volume of MS. with tales, romances, plays, and poems, indicative of the most extraordinary bent toward literature, and ease and variety in composition. Before she was sixteen, the following verses fell from her pen:

"THE WOUNDED STAG.

"Passing amid the deepest shade
Of the wood's sombre heart,
Last night I saw a wounded deer
Laid lonely and apart.

"Such light as pierced the crowded boughs
(Light scatter'd, scant, and dim),
Pass'd through the fern that formed his couch,
And centred full on him.

"Pain trembled in his weary limbs,
Pain fill'd his patient eye,
Pain-crush'd amid the shadowy fern
His branchy crown did lie.

"Where were his comrades? Where his mate?
All from his death-bed gone!
And he, thus struck and desolate,
Suffer'd and bled alone.

"Did he feel what a man might feel,
Friend-left and sore distrest?
Did pain's keen dart and grief's sharp sting
Strive in his mangled breast?

"Did longing for affection lost
Barb every deadly dart?
Love unrepaid, and faith betray'd,
Did these torment his heart?

"No! leave to man his proper doom!
These are the pangs that rise
Around the bed of state and gloom
Where Adam's offspring dies!"

These surely are not common verses, either in thought or style of expression, for any young person of her age, and are the more remarkable in her, the half of whose time was spent in the kitchen, in companionship with as uncultivated a specimen of Yorkshire old-womanhood as Yorkshire could supply, the before-named Tabby.

In the year 1831, Charlotte was sent to a private school, under more favorable auspices than her former venture. Her appearance was that of a very small girl, quaintly dressed, with large and plain features, and with such strange nearness of vision, that her ordinary expression was that of a person assiduously seeking something. She seemed a regular scarecrow to most of the young people around her, avoiding their society, never joining in their plays, and being not seldom the butt of their ridicule, as the old-fashioned daughter of a poor tory country clergyman, while they were the blooming daughters of wealthy dissenters. But, while she secured the esteem and regard of the proprietor of the school, she also made one or two fast friendships, which continued through life. In one year she left this school, and then devoted herself at home to the instruction and charge of her younger sisters, whom she tenderly loved, and carefully watched over. Their life was spent in the house or on the moor, never mustering courage enough to face the stare of the village street, except at some call of duty. Charlotte taught regularly in the Sunday school.

Besides the extreme seclusion of their home, and the sensitive pride fostered by their father, both in a measure the result of narrow circumstances, but both aggravated by that eccentricity which in his children took the form of genius, the girls had anxieties and sorrows arising from their brother, a youth of great talent and lively conversational powers, next in age to Charlotte. His tastes inclined him to adopt the profession of an artist; and in order to furnish the means sufficient for his residence in London while studying in the Royal Academy, whither it was projected he should go, the family circle must be broken up, and Charlotte become a governess. She returned to her last school in that capacity on the smallest possible remuneration, and had one of her sisters with her as pupil in the establishment. Here her whole time was devoted to teaching, to anxieties about her sisters' health, who were both delicate, to her own personal troubles, which were not few, and were aggravated by the sensitiveness of her nature, and to painful solicitudes regarding home and her brother. Branwell had begun to exhibit a tendency toward vicious society and dissolute habits, which was, of all things, most repulsive to his pure-minded and self-denying sisters. The year in which Charlotte, under the influence of the most lofty motives, first left home to be a governess, her brother was only eighteen years of age, and yet even then his face was as familiar at the Black Bull Inn, at the head of the village, as at home. The good humor of the lad, his high spirits and rare conversational talent, made him an acceptable visitor within the bar of the Taurine hostel; and the habit of conviviality, which began in fun, ended, as it has often done before, in sad earnest.

From the hour in which he took to segars and the taproom he was a lost man, for he lacked that seven-fold shield of virtue which his sisters possessed, in their indomitable feeling of pride or self-respect, which would descend from its sphere for the sake of no indulgence whatsoever, and, above all, that high sense of duty which made Charlotte's exertions through life a daily martyrdom, with her weak frame and her tremblingly susceptible soul, that rendered to her things which others cared not for, as if she "had been touched with hot iron." Pride and principle he lacked, and the consequences were to himself ruin, and to his family the unspeakable misery of many years.

To help this ungrateful boy and reduce the family expenditure, after a short interval spent at home, poor Charlotte has to turn out again in search of a situation, home being peculiarly home to her, because it gave her leisure for the cultivation of literature, because, too, her person was so little attractive, her diffidence so painful, and her acquisitions, on the scale of accomplishments, so deficient, that she could only occupy a subordinate position among teachers. The immortal author of "Jane Eyre" never got above being a kind of nursery governess, with £16 a year, and endless tasks of sewing to do. Her experiences of governess-work were not of an agreeable kind. When twenty-two years of age she writes thus of her employer, and in no complaining mood, but simply describing the facts of the case: "She cares nothing about me, except to contrive how the greatest possible quantity of labor may be got out of me; and to that end she overwhelms me with oceans of needlework; yards of cambric to hem, muslin nightcaps to make, and, above all things, dolls to dress. . . . . I see more clearly than I have ever done before, that a private governess has no existence, is not considered as a living rational being, except as connected with the wearisome duties she has to fulfil." In conversation at a later period she said: "that none but those who had been in the position of a governess could ever realize the dark side of 'respectable' human nature." If this be so, as this retiring woman, of no inordinate expectations, and the most modest pretensions, avers, God help our governesses, and speed their emancipation from the thraldom of the taskmasters of their own sex. Men have some conscience how they tyrannize over their servants, and in any case dread the vengeance of their over-goaded victim; but female tyrants are alike destitute of shame and fear, in their treatment of their female subordinates. Some of Charlotte Bronté's employers appear to have been of this character. Poor girl! well might she write to her sister from that situation: "I could like to be at home—I could like to work in a mill—I could like to feel some mental liberty." The roughest country girl in a Yorkshire mill was not worked half so hard, and dared not be treated ill, while she received larger wages than this refined, shrinking, upright, and most gifted child of a reputable clergyman in the neighborhood. However, even governess-ships end, and there is an exodus from the house of bondage of the most unbending female Pharaoh. Miss Brontë left this uncongenial family in 1837, but not before the constant strain upon her strength and spirits had seriously affected her health. When this delicacy became apparent in palpitations and shortness of breath, it was treated as an affectation, and the summary prescription of her considerate mistress, who was reckoned agreeable in society, was—a good scolding. Well might the emancipated girl enjoying the freedom of her home, write to a friend, describing their doing without a servant: "Emily and I are sufficiently busy, as you may suppose; I manage the ironing, and keep the rooms clean; Emily does the baking, and attends to the kitchen. . . . Human feelings are queer things; I am much happier blackleading the stoves, making the beds, and sweeping the floors at home, than I should be living like a fine lady anywhere else. . . . . I intend to force myself to take another situation when I can get one, though I *hate* and *abhor* the very thoughts of governess-ship. But I must do it; and therefore I heartily wish I could hear of a family where they need such a commodity." There spoke the brave, heroic soul which sustained this delicate, shy, home-loving woman through many a scene of painful endurance from which stouter natures have shrunk.

But there was an alternation to governessing abroad, and that was teaching school at home.

But this required capital, and capital they had none. So Charlotte reverts of necessity, to seeking a situation again: "Verily, it is a delightful thing to live here at home, at full liberty to do just what one pleases. But I recollect some scrubby old fable about grasshoppers and ants, by a scrubby old knave yclept Æsop: the grasshoppers sang all the summer, and starved all the winter." Thus no distaste, no suffering, ever made her shrink from any course which she believed it her duty to engage in. Hence, we find her again in a place where at least she was treated with the civility of a Christian, although even here "the tale of the bricks," in the matter of sewing, was also exacted. The task was tenfold severe to Charlotte, as the infirmity of her vision made a redundancy of such occupation particularly trying. No wonder she writes under the pressure of many *désagreéments:* "What dismays and haunts me sometimes, is a conviction that I have no natural knack for my vocation. If teaching only were requisite, it would be smooth and easy; but it is the living in other people's houses—the estrangement from one's real character—the adoption of a cold, rigid, apathetic exterior, that is painful."

Once more at home—this is now the close of 1841. What art thou projecting now, with thy genial and loving sisters, thou stout and unyielding, and yet intensely feminine heart? The project of a school for the three girls is recurred to again and again, somewhat more hopefully now;

for that maiden aunt, who has been the presiding deity amongst their Penates so long, has certain savings that may be reckoned on to help. But would not something more in the shape of accomplishment on the part of the teachers, be an acquisition, and a great aid to success? Doubtless, and on the really good and kind, but somewhat rigid aunt's money, a sojourn in Brussels was secured for a few months to the two elder girls, in order to qualify themselves in French for the task of keeping school. In February, 1842, Charlotte and Emily Bronté entered that domicile in Brussels made famous in "Villette," and, therefore, concerning which we need say no more. We did not positively know this to be true before; but we know Brussels, and could have sworn that a *pensionnat* in French style could not have been described as in that remarkable novel, except from personal experience. Our dictum may require some little abatement, inasmuch as romance may have invested reality in colors gayer than truth, nevertheless, it is scarcely going beyond the due license of expression to affirm that that novel is historically true.

Here, for the first time in her life, Charlotte Bronté was in a position that she liked, where her only business was to improve herself, and where she employed the means of improvement. Her mind rapidly developed under the system of acquisition pursued by an intelligent teacher. As learner first, and afterward as teacher, Charlotte spent two years at Brussels, and left that city in 1844, an accomplished French scholar, to begin the battle of life earnestly at home.

All that was now wanting to these good girls was pupils; but how to get them was the rub. They fixed their terms low, and sought far and wide for the means to live, offering really superior advantages; but where ignorant pretenders acquire fortunes, these meritorious persons might have starved. Month after month rolled away, till 1845 itself had passed into eternity; and while they hoped for good tidings with every post, after the hour of delivery, the upshot was a daily disappointment—not one pupil ever arrived. And it was almost a relief, so came they in their sorrow to think; for their brother, who should have been their stay, and would have been their pride, became, from his folly and wickedness, their shame and their curse. Driven with ignominy from a situation which he disgraced, he sought refuge at home, where, till his death, his days and nights were interchanged between the fiery passions of a hell-cat and the stupor of a sot. His language, his habits, his very appearance, were contamination, and yet the aged parent and the suffering sisters afforded him an asylum, paid his drunken debts over and over again, to keep him out of jail, bore as patiently as they could what was all but intolerable, and at last laid the churchyard mould over his shame, when he died in 1848, at the early age of thirty misspent years. We shall not recur to this subject again; for far beyond poverty, or dependence, or natural disappointments, was this guilty relative a misery, a daily eyesore, a gnawing heartache, to this struggling and high-souled family. For three weary years, the trial and the degradation growing worse and worse, did this great wrong continue. During all that time it only became more aggravated. At the close of 1845, Miss Brontë writes to a friend: "No sufferings are so awful as those brought on by dissipation. Alas! I see the truth of this daily proved. . . . . It seems grievous, indeed, that those who have not sinned should suffer so largely." Again: "Branwell declares that he neither can nor will do anything for himself; good situations have been offered him, for which, by a fortnight's work, he might have qualified himself; but he will do nothing except drink, and make us all wretched."

In addition to this sorrow, her aged father had been becoming gradually blind from the access of cataract, and to read and write, and care for him, especially to comfort and cheer him, under this sore privation, became her leading concern. Her own health, too, ever delicate, was a source of constant suffering to her, and her sisters were no less invalids. Their old servant, Tabby, the unpolished but faithful domestic, was paralytic and almost helpless; for the girls would never consent that she should be dismissed, and nursed by others than themselves. The old creature, to the last, persisted in doing all those offices of kindness for the young ladies in which she fancied she excelled, one special task in which she prided herself, being her skill in peeling potatoes for table. With a delicate sense of kindness, which Charlotte ever displayed after Tabby's eyes failed her, and she did most imperfectly what she fancied she had accomplished in her best manner, her young mistress used to steal away the dish from beneath her purblind vision, complete the process, and replace them on the dresser, as though no amendment had been made of the old attendant's botch-work. Had Tabby been the grandmother of the family, she could not have received more touching attentions from these admirable women; and when she died from their midst at eighty years of age, and was buried by their care, they mourned as a loss what their affectionate kindness had made a voluntary burden of nursing and maintaining for years. The regard maintained for the worn-out domestic, after infirmity had robbed her of her capacity of usefulness, speaks volumes for the merits of both parties, and, as much as their unusual endowments, endears the names of Charlotte, Emily, and Anne Bronté to posterity. We write this sentence with no measured feelings of admiration and respect.

But even in this valley of tribulation all is not unmingled woe, and the desert itself is coated here and there with its oasis of verdure. This melancholy year, 1845, witnessed the first venture in literature of the three girls under their now well-known pseudonyms of Currer (Charlotte), Ellis

(Emily), and Acton (Anne) Bell; names so chosen as to leave the sex of the parties denominated in doubt. The volume of poems which they launched, while meeting with a sufficiently friendly reception, gained little notoriety, and entailed considerable loss on the writers.

Correspondence about this small venture, and devotion to prose composition occupied the year 1846, during which our heroine completed the "Professor," a prose tale, and "Jane Eyre," and her sisters "Wuthering Heights," and "Agnes Grey." The "Professor" went the round of the publishers in London, and was universally rejected; but "Jane Eyre," after frequent rejections (and the same fate befell her sisters' tales), was accepted, as well as theirs. How enthusiastic was its reception, and how fully public opinion indorsed the judgment of the publishers, it were an old tale to tell. Genius struggled against difficulties, and in this case at last met with its reward. While composing this extraordinary fiction, of which the largest portion is fact, Miss Brontë had to nurse her father, now seventy-one years of age, through an operation for cataract, and the long season of helplessness which preceded and followed it. But for the strong sense of filial duty which bound her to her father's side, amid these and other trials, again and again would Charlotte have sought another home, under more congenial auspices, her qualifications for tuition now entitling her to more adequate remuneration and more respectful treatment. Her inducements to go were strong, for her proficiency in French had hitherto been turned to no account, and to let this and other qualifications lie idle pained her; but she silenced every selfish consideration by the mandate of duty: "Whenever I consult my conscience, it affirms that I am doing right in staying at home, and bitter are its upbraidings when I yield to an eager desire for release. I could hardly expect success if I were to err against such warnings." Her success was reserved for 1847, in the October of which year she received complete copies of "Jane Eyre" from her publishers, and startled and delighted the world by a style of composition so novel, so fresh, so natural, so simple, and yet so redolent of undoubted genius, that it forms an era in the history of fictitious literature.

There is, it must be owned, something like caprice in the taste and judgment of the reading public, and of those who cater for them, the publishers. In the joint volume of the poetry of the three sisters, Emily's verses were pronounced superior to Charlotte's; and again, when they volunteered their three tales together, hers was the only one returned in MS. But when she published her "Jane Eyre," her popularity was immense and immediate, while the tales of her two sisters made no impression upon the public mind. Her distinguished success must have been a source of pure satisfaction to the timid author; but it neither altered her habits, nor overcame her dislike and shyness of company, nor very materially affected the condition of her home. It gave her two or three pleasant friendships and acquaintances, and it supplied her with an impulse to employ her pen; but otherwise effected scarcely any change in her views and pursuits. Home was still home, and its meanest cares imperative duties. The time of the author of "Jane Eyre" was mainly devoted to the offices of a housemaid and nurse, for the health of all the family required constant attention, and her own weakness of sight enforced an almost total abstinence from the use of the pen. In the year 1848, the wretched brother was called away to his last account; and, alas! the threefold cord of the beloved sisterhood lost two of its strands; for first Emily, and next Anne, was taken to a better home, leaving Charlotte, at the age of thirty-three, the only surviving child of the family. The pain rested with the survivor, for the death of these excellent persons was a Euthanasia, and they passed into the world of spirits with words of peace, resignation, and hope. The last expressions of Anne were, "Soon all will be well, through the merits of our Redeemer. . . . . . Take courage, Charlotte, take courage." Charlotte had a heavy time of it, but knew where to resort for present help in trouble: "I do not know how life will pass, but I do feel confidence in Him who has upheld me hitherto. Solitude may be cheered and made endurable beyond what I can believe." Again, giving way to her sorrow, she writes: "My life is what I expected it to be. Sometimes when I wake in the morning, and know that solitude, remembrance, and longing are to be almost my sole companions all day through; that at night I shall go to bed with them; that they will long keep me sleepless; that next morning I shall awake to them again—sometimes, Nell, I have a heavy heart of it. But crushed I am not yet, nor robbed of elasticity, nor of hope, nor quite of endeavor. I have some strength to fight the battle of life. I am aware, and can acknowledge, I have many comforts, many mercies. Still, I can *get on*. But I do hope and pray that never may you, nor any one I love, be placed as I am."

Throughout 1849 she had the greater part of the house work to perform herself, being in the most delicate health, and to wait on her father and helpless old Tabby, who were both invalids. Well might the old crone say, two years afterward, to Mrs. Gaskell, in her homely Yorkshire way, referring to Charlotte Bronté's care of her: "Eh! she's a good un—she *is!*"

After the publication of "Shirley," Miss Bronté went to town, but lived in a state of almost entire seclusion at her publishers'. She met the author of "Vanity Fair" by invitation, and says of him: "Thackeray is a Titan of mind. His presence and powers impress one deeply in an intellectual sense."

Edinburgh received a flying visit from her in the midsummer of 1850, and of that grandly-sited city she says: "Edinburgh, compared to London, is like a vivid page of history compared to a large dull treatise on political economy; and as to Melrose and Abbotsford, the very names possess music and magic."

She was only two days in Scotland. In the same strain she writes to an English gentleman: "I always liked Scotland, as an idea; but now, as a reality, I like it far better; it furnished me with some hours as happy almost as any I ever spent. . . . . . . My dear sir, do not think I blaspheme, when I tell you that your great London, as compared to Dunedin, 'mine own romantic town,' is as prose compared to poetry, or as a great rumbling, rambling, heavy epic, compared to a lyric, brief, bright, clear, and vital as a flash of lightning. You have nothing like Scott's Monument; or, if you had that, and all the glories of architecture assembled together, you have nothing like Arthur's Seat; and, above all, you have not the Scottish national character—and it is that grand character, after all, which gives the land its true charm, its true greatness."

The author of "Jane Eyre" read freely the best French writers of the day. Her expression of disgust at Balzac's novels is striking. "They leave such a bad taste in the mouth." To Madame Dudevant she is more indulgent: "Fantastic, fanatical, unpractical enthusiast as she often is—far from truthful as are many of her views of life—misled, as she is apt to be, by her feelings—George Sand has a better nature than M. de Balzac; her brain is larger, her heart warmer than his." On one of the works of the poet-laureate, she says—ourselves avowing of the self-same volume that it is amongst our hid treasures: "I have read Tennyson's 'In Memoriam,' or, rather, part of it; I closed the book when I got about half-way. It is beautiful —it is mournful—it is monotonous." We can understand this in the author of "Jean Eyre," while our personal feeling toward that choicest volume of modern poetry is exactly the reverse. We find it hard to drag ourselves away from it, dip into it where we will.

Of Dr. Arnold her judgment is mingled: "Dr. Arnold, it seems to me, was not quite saintly; his greatness was cast in a mortal mould; he was a little severe, almost a little hard; he was vehement, and somewhat repugnant. . . . . . Afterward come his good qualities: about these there is nothing dubious. Where can we find justice, firmness, independence, earnestness, sincerity, fuller and purer than in him? But this is not all—and I am glad of it. Besides high intellect and stainless rectitude, his letters and his life attest his possession of the most true-hearted affection. *Without* this, however one might admire, we could not love him; but *with* it, I think we love him much. A hundred such men—fifty, nay, ten or five—such righteous men, might save any country, might victoriously champion any cause."

Writing of Miss Martineau, during a visit to that lady at Ambleside, Miss Bronté declares: "Of my kind hostess I cannot speak in terms too high. Without being able to share all her opinions, philosophical, political, or religious; without adopting her theories, I yet find a worth and greatness in herself, and a consistency, benevolence, perseverance in her practice, such as win the sincerest esteem and affection. . . . . . . She seems to me the benefactress of Ambleside, yet takes no sort of credit to herself for her active and indefatigable philanthropy. . . . . . . Her servants and her poor neighbors love as well as respect her."

Of Ruskin her judgment is generous: "The 'Stones of Venice' seem nobly laid and chiselled. How grandly the quarry of vast marbles is disclosed! Mr. Ruskin seems to me one of the few genuine writers, as distinguished from book-makers, of this age. . . . . . . He writes like a consecrated priest of the abstract and ideal."

In 1851 Miss Brontë saw the Great Exhibition in Hyde Park, but with no great interest. "It is a marvellous, stirring, bewildering sight—a mixture of a genii palace and a mighty bazaar; but it is not much in my way." More in her way was it to hear D'Aubigné preach, and Thackeray lecture, and the terrible Rachel declaim. We are disposed to believe that, in her judgment of the French tragedienne, she unconsciously allowed herself to be drawn into the error of identifying the actress with the parts she performed—the very injustice which she herself complained of when Charlotte Brontë was pronounced to be Jane Eyre.

"Rachel's acting transfixed me with wonder, enchained me with interest, and thrilled me with horror. . . . . . . It is scarcely human nature that she shows you; it is something wilder and worse —the feelings and fury of a fiend. The great gift of genius she undoubtedly has; but I fear she rather abuses it than turns it to good account." Now, with all deference to Miss Bronté's judgment, the wrong lies not at the door of the actress who represents a Phædra or Potiphar's wife with a startling resemblance to reality, but in that state of public morals which takes such a theme for a dramatic composition, and tolerates its exhibition on the stage.

To the touching power of Kingsley's drama on St. Elizabeth, she bears testimony: "I have read the 'Saint's Tragedy.' As a work of art, it seems to me far superior to either 'Alton Locke' or 'Yeast.' Faulty it may be, crude and unequal, yet there are portions where some of the deep chords of human nature are swept with a hand which is strong even while it falters. . . . . . . Seldom do I cry over books; but here my eyes rained as I read. When Elizabeth turns her face to the wall, I stopped—there needed no more."

Her notion of the political characters of 1852 is amusing: "Disraeli was factious as leader of the Opposition; Lord John Russell is going to be factious, now that he has stepped into Disraeli's shoes. Lord Derby's 'Christian love and spirit is worth three-half-pence farthing."

On Miss Kavanagh's "Women of Christianity," she passes the following just strictures: "She forgets, or does not know, that Protestantism is a quieter creed than Romanism; as it does not clothe its priesthood in scarlet, so neither does it set up its good women for saints, canonize their names, and proclaim their good works. In the records of man their almsgiving will not, perhaps, be found registered; but heaven has its account as well as earth."

The happiness which our heroine had long looked for, by a release from an irksome solitude, at last made its appearance in a union with a Mr. Nicholls, who had for years been the observant witness of her virtues in his position of Mr. Bronté's curate. But her draught was brief; for nine months thereafter, after protracted weakness and suffering, she laid down the load of life in the parsonage at Haworth, and departed to be forever with the Lord. No more satisfying testimony to the purity of her wedded bliss can be required, than that furnished by her last unpremeditated words to her husband: "Oh, I am not going to die, am I? He will not separate us, we have been so happy!" But, alas! the sentence had gone forth, and, early in April, 1855, all that was earthly of Charlotte Nicholls, *née* Bronté, was committed to the dust, and sleeps with the sleepers in Haworth Church, awaiting the resurrection of the just.

The impression left upon our mind by the perusal of this fascinating history is one of unutterable sadness, arising from sympathy with the heroine, and of the highest admiration of her stainless character and career. Every thing was against her through life—plainness of person, poverty, a solitude and sensitiveness of soul that no one could appreciate, and disappointment of almost every expectation and wish. Yet she nobly struggled on—her watchword DUTY, and her reliance Heaven. Such is the testimony of her life-long friend, who, in an extract given at the close of her memoir, writes thus: "She thought much of her duty, and had loftier and clearer notions of it than most people, and held fast to them with more success. It was done, it seems to me, with much more difficulty than people have of stronger nerves and better fortunes. All her life was but labor and pain; and she never threw down the burden for the sake of present pleasure." This is a true record, and justified by a thousand incidents in Miss Bronté's correspondence and history. We should be doing an injustice to the memory of this singularly-excellent person, did we not present, in connection with this sketch, a letter to a young friend written in 1846, which clearly exhibits her own principles of action:—

"I see you are in a dilemma, and one of a peculiar and difficult nature. Two paths lie before you; you conscientiously wish to choose the right one, even though it be the most steep, straight, and rugged. But you do not know which is the right one; you cannot decide whether duty and religion command you to go out into a cold and friendless world, and there to earn your living by governess-drudgery, or whether they enjoin your continued stay with your aged mother, neglecting, *for the present*, every prospect of independency for yourself, and putting up with daily inconvenience, sometimes even with privations. I can well imagine that it is next to impossible for you to decide for yourself in this matter; so I will decide it for you; at least I will tell you what is my earnest conviction on the subject—I will show you candidly how the question strikes me. The right path is that which necessitates the greatest sacrifice of self-interest, which implies the greatest good to others; and this path, steadily followed, will lead, I believe, in time, to prosperity and happiness, though it may seem at the outset to tend quite in a contrary direction. Your mother is both old and infirm; old and infirm people have but few sources of happiness, fewer, almost, than the comparatively young and healthy can conceive: to deprive them of one of these is cruel. If your mother is more composed when you are with her, stay with her. If she would be unhappy, in case you left her, stay with her. It will not apparently, as far as shortsighted humanity can see, be for your advantage to remain at ——, nor will you be praised and admired for remaining at home to comfort your mother; yet probably your own conscience will approve, and, if it does, stay with her. I recommend you to do what I am trying to do myself." The pure soul of the writer of this letter contended successfully through her whole life against selfish instincts and unfriendly circumstances, as the broad river of Egypt, in its beneficent march to the sea, has resisted, from age to age, the sandy incursions of the desert; and, beneficent as the fertilizing Nile, none approached Charlotte Brontė whom she did not bless.

THE NEWGATE SCHOOLMISTRESS.

ELIZABETH FRY.

MRS. ELIZABETH FRY was the third daughter of the late John Gurney, of Earlham Hall, near Norwich. Her childhood was characterized by strong affection and great mental vivacity. She early evinced an angelic disposition to alleviate the cares and soothe the sorrows of all those around her who needed sympathy and aid. As she increased in years, her inclination and powers of doing good extended and strengthened, the youthful stirrings of benevolence gradually became principles of philanthropy, and the kind and spontaneous actions of her juvenile years were performed in her opening womanhood from a sense of Christian duty. She took especial pleasure in organizing and superintending a school upon her father's premises for the indigent children of Earlham and the surrounding parishes, and the effect which her mild authority and judicious instructions produced upon these hitherto-neglected little ones, was a powerful illustration of the potency of gentle means, when employed to guide the young in the path of learning, or to raise them from moral debasement. Notwithstanding this and several other similar benevolent pursuits, Miss Gurney's attachment to worldly pleasures was not compatible with that gravity of deportment and subdued mildness of manners common to the members of the persuasion to which she subsequently belonged, her natural vivacity, and the companionship of those who made pleasure their pursuit, having a tendency to divide her mind with the practical and holy operations of benevolence. But "infinitely higher and better things than the follies and vanities of polished life, awaited this interesting young person," says the writer of her obituary, in the "Friends' Annual Monitor." She was affected by a disease which assumed a serious character, and she thus became awakened to a true sense of the instability of human life and the vanity of those inferior pleasures which have not their source in the higher principles of our nature, but depart with our capabilities of enjoying them. Soon after her illness she was powerfully awakened to a knowledge of her relation to God, and of her relation to mankind in their character of brethren in Christ, through the ministry of an American friend, the late William Savery. She forsook the pleasures which had hitherto divided her mind and time, and in the bosom of her family cultivated those social and endearing qualities which render home a temple of the affections, make woman a priestess of love, and elevate the hearth into an altar of peace and unity. She became the joy and comfort of her widowed father and of her ten brothers and sisters; and in her own family she schooled her heart to that abandonment of self, and anxiety for the good of others, which inspired her with a Christian philanthropy scarcely paralleled, and a courage which was superior to obstruction, danger, or immoral obduracy, and rendered her an invincible conqueror in her crusade against vice in its most hardened and appalling forms.

In the year 1800, when she was twenty years of age, Miss Gurney became the wife of Mr. Joseph Fry, a banker in London, and settled in a house connected with her husband's business, in the very heart of the Great Babylon. It may easily be supposed that, in the metropolis, objects and scenes of especial interest would frequently be presented to this benevolent lady, and that her active philanthropy and holy aspirations for human weal would not be blunted in consequence of her new relations as a beloved wife and tender mother. The poor found in her an untiring benefactress and a willing friend. She visited their lowly homes, and, if she found them worthy, their wants were effectually relieved.

Shortly after her marriage, Mrs. Fry became impressed with the opinion "that it would be required of her to bear public testimony to the efficacy of that divine grace by which she had been brought to partake of the joy's of God's salvation;" and when she had reached the thirtieth year of her age, she began to speak in the religious meetings of the Friends. Her exhortations were marked by peculiar humility and much persuasive sweetness of manner, and she was early engaged with the unity of the monthly meeting to which she belonged, in paying religious visits to Friends and others of various denominations. And now we have arrived at the most remarkable era of her life—at that period which begins the history of her glorious career of reformation, when, strong in faith and charity, she entered the receptacles of the outcast and impious, and bore to the hearts of the demoralized criminals human sympathy and heavenly hope. Newgate, that grave of pollution, whose name we were taught to associate with all that was dark and fearful, was visited about 1812 by Mrs. Fry, who was induced to inspect it by representations of its condition made by some members of the Society of Friends. The prison had been constructed to hold about four hundred and eighty prisoners, but eight hundred, and even twelve hundred, had been immured within its walls. Mrs. Fry found the female side in a most deplorable and indescribable condition. Nearly three hundred women, sent there for every species and gradation of crime—some untried, and therefore presumably innocent—others under sentence of death—were promiscuously huddled together in the two wards and two cells which were afterward appropriated to the untried, whose numbers were even inconveniently large for the limited space.

Here the criminals saw their friends and kept their multitude of children, and here they also cooked, washed, took their victuals, and slept. They lay down on the floor, sometimes to the number of one hundred and twenty in one ward, without even a mat for bedding, and many of them very miserably clad. They openly drank ardent spirits, and their horrible imprecations broke upon the ears of this pure-minded and noble lady, mingled with offensive and disgusting epithets. Every thing was filthy and redolent of disgusting effluvia. No prison functionary liked to visit them, and the governor persuaded Mrs. Fry to leave her watch in his office, assuring her that his presence would not prevent its being torn from her; and as if to illustrate the frightful extent to which vice and wretchedness can sink our nature and deaden our feelings, two women were seen in the act of stripping a dead child for the purpose of clothing a living one. It must be recollected that this is no exaggerated picture of that den of pollution, Newgate, in those days. Mrs. Fry's own simple, yet powerful testimony is before us, and she thus expresses herself: "All I tell thee is a faint picture of the reality; the filth, the closeness of the rooms, the ferocious manners and expressions of the women toward each other, and the abandoned wickedness which every thing bespoke, are quite indescribable." We do not know which quality most to admire in this magnanimous woman—the exalted sympathy which recognized in these outcasts a common humanity, or the heroic courage which supported her in her ministrations of love and mercy. She clothed many of the children and some of the women, and read passages of the Bible to them in such soft and silvery tones, that latent feeling awoke in their bosoms, and the big tear started into many an eye. She left that prison with a strong conviction that much might be done; but circumstances intervened for three years to render efforts on her part inoperative.

About Christmas, 1816, she resumed her visits, and found that much improvement had been made by the jail committee; especially the females had additional accommodation conceded to them; they were provided with mats, and gratings had been erected to prevent close communication between the criminals and their visitors. Still, the chief evil remained unremedied—all the women were playing cards, reading improper books, begging, or fighting for the division of the money thus acquired; and a fortune-teller was imposing upon the credulous and ignorant prisoners with her absurd divinations. There were continual complaints of want of employment, and declarations that profitless idleness had only been substituted for active vice. Mrs. Fry's first undertaking was the education of about seventy children, who, in this abode of iniquity, were wandering about unheeded, which was no sooner proposed, than the most abandoned mothers thanked her with tears in their eyes for her benevolent intentions, and young women crowded round her, and prayed in pathetic eagerness to be admitted to her projected school.

Application was now made to the governor of Newgate, sheriffs of London, and the reverend prison ordinary. These gentlemen cordially approved of her intentions, but they intimated "their *persuasion that her efforts would be utterly fruitless.*" So little zeal did they manifest in furtherance of this scheme of piety, that an official intimation informed Mrs. Fry that there was no vacant place in the prison fit for school purposes. But she was not disheartened; she mildly requested to be admitted once more alone among the women, that she might investigate for herself. *She* soon discovered an empty cell, and the school was opened the very next day. Mrs. Fry was accompanied by a young lady, who had visited Newgate for the first time, and who had generously enlisted under the banner of philanthropy, to assist in the work of reclamation so gloriously begun by her exalted friend. When they entered the prison school, the railing was crowded by women, many of whom were only half-clothed, struggling for front situations, and vociferating most violently. The young lady felt as if she had entered a den of wild beasts; and when the door closed and was locked upon her, she shuddered at the idea of being immured with such a host of desperate companions. The first day's work, however, surpassed the utmost expectations of Mrs. Fry, and the only pain she experienced was that of refusing numerous pressing applications from young women, who prayed to be taught and employed. The assurances and zeal of these poor forlorn creatures, induced Mrs. Fry and her companion to project a school where the tried women should be taught to read and work. When this idea was first expressed to the friends of the projectors, it was declared to be visionary and impracticable. They were told that the work introduced would be stolen; that women so long habituated to crime and idleness were the most irreclaimable of the vicious; that novelty might, for a time, induce apparent attention and a temporary observance of rule, but that the change would not be lasting. In short, failure was predicted with almost oracular confidence. Nothing could induce the ladies, however to abandon their forlorn and almost unsupported enterprise: from earth they turned their eyes to heaven, and when men forsook them, they asked aid of God and took courage. They declared if a committee could be found who would share the labor, and a matron who would engage to live in the prison night and day, they would undertake the experiment—that is, they would *find employment* for the women; they would procure funds for the prosecution of their scheme till the city could be induced to relieve them of the expense; and they promised to become responsible for the property intrusted to the prisoners. Volunteers for this glorious service immediately presented themselves; the wife of a clergyman and eleven members of the Society of

Friends declared their willingness to suspend every other engagement and calling, and to devote themselves to this good work, and faithfully they did their self-imposed duty. They almost entirely lived amongst the prisoners; not a day or hour passed but some of them were to be found at their posts, sharing the employments and meals of their protégées, or abstemiously instructing their pupils, from morning till long after the close of day. Yet all their toils, and the progress of those for whose advantage they labored, were insufficient to eradicate the skepticism of some who viewed their exertions. The reverend ordinary admired their intrepid devotion; but he assured Mrs. Fry that her designs *would inevitably fail*. The governor cheered her with words of sympathy, but those who possessed his confidence were accustomed to hear him declare "that he could not see the possibility of her success." But that charity which "hopeth all things, and believeth all things" was strong within her; she looked to the goal, and not to the impediments in her path; she looked beyond the means to the consummation; she was wiling souls from the meshes and snares of sin, and she sought under God to lead her erring sisters into the fold of grace. She presented herself to the sheriffs and governor, and nearly one hundred women were brought before them, who solemnly engaged to yield the strictest obedience to all the regulations of their heroic benefactress. A set of rules was accordingly promulgated, and the vices which the prisoners had formerly fostered were discarded and disclaimed. After a month's private exertion, the corporation of London was invited to behold the effects of these noble women's labors. The lord mayor, sheriffs, and several aldermen attended. The prisoners were assembled, and, in accordance with the usual practice, one of the ladies read a chapter in the Bible, when the prisoners proceeded to their various employments. What a change was here to the accustomed tumult, filth, and licentiousness of former days! Their attention to the reading of the Scriptures; their modest deportment, obedience, and respectful demeanor; and the cheerfulness visible on their faces, conspired to excite the wonder and admiration of all who beheld them. They were no longer a herd of irreclaimable creatures, whose sympathies with the world were destroyed, and for whom the world had no longer any sympathy. Kindness had awakened reciprocal sentiments in their breasts, and mankind could no longer deny the possibility of their reclamation to the ranks of humanity. The prison had ceased to be a nursery of crime; its cells no nger resounded with the laugh of women dead to hope and shame; the bitter imprecation and the scoff of hardened hearts had died away; and peace, cleanliness, and order, reigned under the influence of those true sisters of charity—Mrs. Fry and her assistants. The magistrates, to mark their appreciation of this system, incorporated it with the Newgate Code of regulations. They empowered the ladies to punish the refractory by temporary confinement, undertook to defray part of the matron's sustentation, and loaded the ladies with thanks and blessings.

A year passed away, and still the little band of philanthropists was cheered by progression; infidelity fell before indubitable truth; and success, confirmed by so long a trial, at last forced conviction on those who had doubted and predicted failure, and all who beheld the vast change which had been effected, expressed their satisfaction and astonishment at the great improvement which had taken place in the conduct of the females. Mrs. Fry did not confine herself to the amelioration of prisons exclusively; she visited lunatic asylums with the same high and holy purpose. It was her habit, when she did so, to sit down quietly amongst her afflicted fellow-mortals, and, amidst the greatest turbulence, begin to read in her sweetest tones some portion of the Bible. Gradually the noise around her would cease, eager ears would be bent to drink the music of her voice, and at last attention and silence would reign around her. On one occasion, a young man was observed to listen attentively, although ordinarily one of the most turbulent and violent of the patients. He became subdued even to tears. When Mrs. Fry ceased reading, the poor maniac exclaimed to her: "*Hush, the angels have lent you their voices!*" Fancy and reason combined could not have offered a more beautiful compliment to goodness and benignity.

It was Mrs. Fry's regular practice to attend at Newgate on a particular morning of the week to read the Scriptures to the prisoners. The prison was open to any visitors whom she chose to ad mit, and her readings were attended both by our own countrymen and foreigners, among whom were many of rank and power. These were most affecting reunions, both to those who came as visitors, and they who claimed especially these services.

Mrs. Fry's attention was not wholly absorbed by Newgate. The female prisoners in other parts of the city were ministered to by her. In the prosecution of her plans of reformation, she was generously supported by the city authorities, and successive secretaries of state seconded her benevolent views. The British Ladies' Society for the reformation of female prisoners owes its origin to her exertions; and a similar system of reform, by means of associated committees, was begun in many prisons in Great Britain and Ireland.

Mrs. Fry's indefatigable zeal for good, induced her to press her views upon the governments and monarchs of the continental nations; and she and every lover of humanity had the inestimable satisfaction of seeing her plans adopted in France, Holland, Denmark, Russia, Switzerland, Prussia, several of the minor German States, and in Philadelphia, and other parts of the United States of America. Mrs. Fry materially promoted her objects by the publication of a pamphlet, in which she promulgated her views on the species of prison discipline necessary for females, and of the only sound principles of punishment. Death punishments, in her estimation, were completely inefficacious in stopping the progress of crime, and she disapproved of them also upon loftier grounds than that of expediency; she did not condemn the Draco-like proceedings of our judiciary from maudlin theory. She often visited the cells of condemned criminals on the day or night before their execution; she saw the agony of soul endured by some, the insolent bravado manifested by others, and she observed that death punishment generally produced an obduracy in its victims, which reacted on their criminal observers, or those who came to gaze on the last scene of all. Mrs. Fry and her associates had voluntarily conceded to them by government the care and superintendence of convict-ships for females about to be transported to New South Wales; and so important were their improvements, and judicious their regulations in this department, that the colonial authorities frequently transmitted them their grateful acknowledgments. All the poor convicts were supplied with several articles necessary for their comfort, and each was carefully provided with a copy of the Holy Scriptures.

Mrs. Fry's name is principally connected with her prison labors; but her humanity was boundless. She had sympathy for every species of distress, and a hand to aid in every object of human amelioration. By her influence—the influence of humble piety and active virtue—she stimulated many individuals possessing the power, to institute district societies for the effectual relief of the destitute and the houseless, and also for the educating of those neglected children whose only tuition had previously been that of crime. She chiefly assisted in the formation of libraries for the use of the coast-guard, in all their stations around the British isles.

In 1818, Mrs. Fry visited Scotland in company with her brother Joseph John Gurney, and her sister-in-law, Elizabeth Fry; and in 1827, she visited Ireland. Still the same benevolent spirit guided her. It may be emphatically said that she "went about doing good." In foreign lands, or in her own country, she meekly yet fearlessly interceded for the persecuted and oppressed, and to her is attributable much of that enlargement of the liberty of conscience, and the softening of the rigors of prison discipline, which has taken place in Europe of late years.

The king of Prussia courted the friendship of this great and good woman; and in 1842, when on a visit to Great Britain with his queen and family, he visited her at Upton. By his particular request she met him at the Mansion-house, between the hours of public worship on Sunday, 30th January, and they passed two hours in conversation together, at the close of which the king expressed a strong desire to meet her in Newgate, at her reading next day. She met him in company with her brother and sister, and the wife of the mayor, Lady Pirie. The king was attended by several noblemen, foreign and English. He led Mrs. Fry through the passages and apartments of the prison, until they reached the seats placed for them at the extremity of a line of tables, at which the prisoners, attentive and serious, were arranged. A solemn silence ensued. Mrs. Fry then read the 12th chapter of Romans, and a psalm. Stillness again reigned for a short space, and then she addressed all present, adverting to the perfect equality of all men in the sight of God, declaring that if, through the grace of our Lord Jesus Christ, we are brought to become his disciples, we are made *one* in him, even from the lowest and most degraded of the poor prisoners before her to the sovereign at her side. Mrs. Fry then knelt in prayer, the king kneeling down beside her, and in an extemporaneous effusion of great fervor and sweetness, she prayed in behalf of the prisoners, and also for his majesty's sanctification through the Holy Spirit. This solemn and affecting service being concluded, the king accompanied Mrs. Fry to her own residence.

In the summer of 1843, Mrs. Fry visited Paris for the last time, and concerted with several benevolent friends for the prosecution of works of goodness and charity. After her return home she became seriously indisposed, and the symptoms were such as to alarm her friends and family; yet she bore her trouble with Christian resignation, and recognized in all her pains the hand of God. As the spring of 1844 advanced, her health was so far restored as to permit her to ride out occasionally, and in the summer she joined her friends in public worship. On this occasion she was accompanied by several members of her family, and her son, William Storrs Fry, sat beside her and tenderly watched his feeble parent. Alas for the uncertainty of life and strength! He, with two of his children, were shortly afterward removed from the family circle, and his afflicted parent saw him pass away before her. She again attended the religious meeting of Friends at Plaistow, on the 13th of October, and addressed those assembled with great clearness and power. She gradually regained strength, and was enabled once more to resume her ministry of love. Near the close of the summer of 1845, she went with her husband to Ramsgate, an earnest hope being entertained that change of air and scene would benefit her. She attended a little meeting at Drapers, and repeatedly engaged in religious service among the few Friends there. She distributed a great many Bibles; and a ship crowded with German emigrants, bound for Texas, was provided with one for each of the passengers.

A few days before her death she applied to the committee of the British and Foreign Bible Society concerning the purchase of a supply of copies of the Scriptures. The committee, through their secretary, informed her that she should receive them gratis, and that they felt it a privilege to circulate them through her ministrations. They also sent her, as a token of esteem, a copy of their first translation of one of the gospels in the Chinese language. She was engaged in projects affecting the weal of mankind to the very hour in which she was seized with her fatal illness. On the evening of Saturday, the 11th of October, 1845, slight symptoms of paralysis were apparent. Early next morning, when very ill, she alluded to the conflict which nature then endured, adding, "*But I am safe.*" In a short time after she uttered a short prayer to God, and after this all consciousness appeared to forsake her. About four o'clock on the morning of the 12th, her pure spirit left its frail tenement of clay and ascended to Him who gave it.

The history of Mrs. Fry can hardly be said to end with her death. The deeds men do often die with them; not so with hers. Her spirit of active benevolence has been transmitted to many, and the works she promoted are carried on by others who have been impelled to engage in them by her example. We cannot leave our subject without assuring our readers that this eminently good woman was supported in her manifold labors by a constant faith in Christ, and an assurance of divine aid. May the humblest in life's lowly course be similarly strengthened, and, according to their means, may they profit by her example of love and charity! In closing this memoir, for the materials of which we have been mainly indebted to an eminent philanthropist and friend of Mrs. Fry, we extract the following truthful and beautiful tribute to her worth, written in 1816, by Francis Jeffrey: "We cannot *envy* the happiness which Mrs. Fry must enjoy from the consciousness of her own great achievements, but there is no happiness or honor of which we should be so proud to be partakers; and we seem to relieve our own hearts of their share of national gratitude in thus placing on her simple and modest brow that truly civic crown, which far outshines the laurels of conquest or the coronals of power, and can only be outshone itself by those wreaths of imperishable glory which awaits the champions of faith and charity in a higher state of existence."

THE JAIL MISSIONARY.

SARAH MARTIN,

WHO has won for herself the fame most desirable for a woman, that of Christian benevolence, a fame indeed unsurpassed in the annals of her sex, was born in 1791. Her father was a poor mechanic in Caister, a village three miles from Yarmouth. Sarah was the only child of her parents, who both died when she was very young: she had then to depend on her grandmother, a poor old widow, whose name was Bonnett, and who deserves to have it recorded for the kind care she took of her grand-daughter.

Sarah Martin's education was merely such as the village school afforded. At the age of fourteen she passed a year in learning the business of dress-making; and then gained her livelihood by going out and working at her trade by the day, among the families of the village. In the town of Yarmouth was the county prison, where criminals were confined: their condition was at that period most lamentable.

Their time was given to gaming, swearing, playing, fighting, and bad language; and their visitors were admitted from without with little restriction. There was no divine worship in the jail on Sundays, nor any respect paid to that holy day. There were underground cells (these continued even down to 1836), quite dark, and deficient in proper ventilation. The prisoners described their heat in summer as almost suffocating, but they preferred them for their warmth in winter; their situation was such as to defy inspection, and they were altogether unfit for the confinement of any human being.

No person in Yarmouth took thought for these poor, miserable prisoners; no human eye looked with pity on their dreadful condition; and had their reformation been proposed, it would, no doubt, have been scouted as an impossibility.

In August, 1819, a woman was committed to the jail for a most unnatural crime. She was a mother who had "forgotten her sucking child." She had not "had compassion upon the son of her womb," but had cruelly beaten and ill-used it. The consideration of her offence was calculated to produce a great effect upon a female mind; and there was one person in the neighborhood of Yarmouth who was deeply moved by it. Sarah Martin was a little woman, of gentle, quiet manners, possessing no beauty of person, nor, as it seemed, any peculiar endowment of mind. She was then just eight. and. twenty years of age, and had, for thirteen years past, earned her livelihood by going out to the houses of various families in the town as a day-laborer in her business of dress-making. From her residence at Caister, where she lived with her aged grandmother, she walked to Yarmouth and back again in the prosecution of her daily toil. This poor girl had long mourned over the condition of the inmates of the jail. Even as long back as in 1810, "whilst frequently passing the jail," she says, "I felt a strong desire to obtain admission to the prisoners to read the Scriptures to them; for I thought much of their condition, and of their sin before God; how they were shut out from society, whose rights they had violated, and how destitute they were of the scriptural instruction, which alone could meet their unhappy circumstances." The case of the unnatural mother stimulated her to make the attempt, but "I did not," she says, "make known my purpose of seeking admission to the jail until the object was attained, even to my beloved grandmother; so sensitive was my fear lest any obstacle should thereby arise in my way, and the project seem a visionary one. God led me, and I consulted none but Him." She ascertained the culprit's name, and went to the jail. She passed into the dark porch which overhung the entrance, fit emblem of the state of things within; and, no doubt with bounding heart, and in a timid, modest form of application, uttered with that clear and gentle voice, the sweet tones of which are yet well remembered, solicited permission to see the cruel parent. There was some difficulty—there is always a "lion in the way" of doing good—and she was not at first permitted to enter. To a wavering mind such a check would have appeared of evil omen; but Sarah Martin was too well assured of her own purposes and powers to hesitate. Upon a second application she was admitted.

The manner of her reception in the jail is told by herself with admirable simplicity. The unnatural mother stood before her. She "was surprised at the sight of a stranger." "When I told her," says Sarah Martin, "the motive of my visit, of her guilt, and of her need of God's mercy, she burst into tears and thanked me!"

Her reception at once proved the necessity for such a missionary, and her own personal fitness for the task; and her visit was repeated again and again, during such short intervals of leisure as she could spare from her daily labors. At first she contented herself with merely reading to the prisoners; but familiarity with their wants and with her own powers soon enlarged the sphere of her tuition, and she began to instruct them in reading and writing. This extension of her labor interfered with her ordinary occupations. It became necessary to sacrifice a portion of her time, and consequently of her means, to these new duties. She did not hesitate. "I thought it right," she says, "to give up a day in the week from dressmaking to serve the prisoners. This regularly given, with many an additional one, was not felt as a pecuniary loss, but was ever followed with abundant satisfaction, for the blessing of God was upon me."

In the year 1826, Sarah Martin's grandmother died, and she came into possession of an annual income of ten or twelve pounds, derived from the investment of "between two and three hundred pounds." She then removed from Caister to Yarmouth, where she occupied two rooms in a house situated in a row in an obscure part of the town; and, from that time devoted herself with increased energy to her philanthropic labors. A benevolent lady, resident in Yarmouth, had, for some years, with a view to securing her a little rest for her health's sake, given her one day in a week, by compensating her for that day in the same way as if she had been engaged in dressmaking. With that assistance, and with a few quarterly subscriptions, "chiefly 2*s*. 6*d*. each, for Bibles, Testaments, tracts, and other books for distribution," she went on devoting every available moment of her life to her great purpose. But dress-making, like other professions, is a jealous mistress; customers fell off, and, eventually, almost entirely disappeared. A question of anxious moment now presented itself, the determination of which is one of the most characteristic and memorable incidents of her life. Was she to pursue her benevolent labors, even although they led to utter poverty? Her little income was not more than enough to pay her lodging, and the expenses consequent upon the exercise of her charitable functions: and was actual destitution of ordinary necessaries to be submitted to? She never doubted; but her reasoning upon the subject presents so clear an illustration of the exalted character of her thoughts and purposes, and exhibits so eminent an example of Christian devotedness and heroism, that it would be an injustice to her memory not to quote it in her own words: "In the full occupation of dress-making, I had care with it, and anxiety for the future; but as that disappeared, care fled also. God, who had called me into the vineyard, had said, 'Whatsoever is right I will give you.' I had learned from the Scriptures of truth that I should be supported; God was my master, and would not forsake His servant; He was my father, and could not forget his child. I knew also that it sometimes seemed good in His sight to try the faith and patience of His servants, by bestowing upon them very limited means of support; as in the case of Naomi and Ruth; of the widow of Zarephath and Elijah; and my mind, in the contemplation of such trials, seemed exalted by more than human energy; for I had counted the cost, and my mind was made up. If, whilst imparting truth to others, I became exposed to temporal want, the privation so momentary to an individual would not admit of comparison with following the Lord, in thus administering to others."

Her next object was to secure the observance of

Sunday; and, after long urging and recommendation, she prevailed upon the prisoners "to form a Sunday service, by one reading to the rest; . . . . but aware," she continues, "of the instability of a practice in itself good, without any corresponding principle of preservation, and thinking that my presence might exert a beneficial tendency, I joined their Sunday-morning worship as a regular hearer."

After three years' perseverance in this "happy and quiet course," she made her next advance, which was to introduce employment, first for the women prisoners, and afterward for the men. In 1823, "one gentleman," she says, "presented me with ten shillings, and another, in the same week, with a pound, for prison charity. It then occurred to me that it would be well to expend it in material for baby-clothes; and having borrowed patterns, cut out the articles, fixed prices of payment for making them, and ascertained the cost of a set, that they might be disposed of at a certain price, the plan was carried into effect. The prisoners also made shirts, coats, etc. . . . . . . By means of this plan, many young women who were not able to sew, learned this art, and, in satisfactory instances, had a little money to take at the end of the term of imprisonment. . . . . . . The fund of one pound ten shillings for this purpose, as a foundation and perpetual stock (for whilst desiring its preservation, I did not require its increase), soon rose to seven guineas, and since its establishment, above four hundred and eight pounds' worth of various articles have been sold for charity."

The men were thus employed:

"They made straw hats, and, at a later period, bone spoons and seals; others made men's and boys' caps, cut in eight quarters—the material, old cloth or moreen, or whatever my friends could find to give me for them. In some instances, young men, and more frequently boys, have learned to sew gray cotton shirts, or even patch-work, with a view of shutting out idleness and making themselves useful. On one occasion I showed to the prisoners an etching of the chess-player, by Retzsch, which two men, one a shoemaker and the other a bricklayer, desired much to copy; they were allowed to do so, and being furnished with pencil, pen, paper, etc., they succeeded remarkably well. The chess-player presented a pointed and striking lesson, which could well be applied to any kind of gaming, and was, on this account, suitable to my pupils, who had generally descended from the love of marbles and pitch-half-penny in children, to cards, dice, etc., in men. The business of copying it had the advantage of requiring all thought and attention at the time. The attention of other prisoners was attracted to it, and for a year or two afterward many continued to copy it."

After another interval she proceeded to the formation of a fund which she applied to the furnishing of work for prisoners upon their discharge;

"affording me," she adds, "the advantage of observing their conduct at the same time."

She had thus, in the course of a few years—during which her mind had gradually expanded to the requirements of the subject before her—provided for all the most important objects of prison discipline: moral and intellectual tuition, occupation during imprisonment, and employment after discharge. Whilst great and good men, unknown to her, were inquiring and disputing as to the way and the order in which these very results were to be attained—inquiries and disputes which have not yet come to an end—here was a poor woman who was actually herself personally accomplishing them all! It matters not whether all her measures were the very wisest that could have been imagined. She had to contend with many difficulties that are now unknown; prison discipline was then in its infancy; every thing she did was conceived in the best spirit; and, considering the time, and the means at her command, could scarcely have been improved.

The full extent to which she was personally engaged in carrying out these objects, has yet to be explained. The Sunday service in the jail was adopted, as we have seen, upon her recommendation, and she joined the prisoners, as a fellow-worshipper, on Sunday morning. Their evening service, which was to be read in her absence, was soon abandoned; but finding that to be the case, she attended on that part of the day also, and the service was then resumed. "After several changes of readers, the office," she says, "devolved on me. That happy privilege thus graciously opened to me, and embraced from necessity, and in much fear, was acceptable to the prisoners, for God made it so; and also an unspeakable advantage and comfort to myself." These modest sentences convey but a very faint notion of the nature of these singular services. Fortunately, in a report of Captain Williams, one of the inspectors of prisons, we have a far more adequate account of the matter. It stands thus:

"Sunday, November 29, 1835.—Attended divine service in the morning at the prison. The male prisoners only were assembled; a female, resident in the town, officiated; her voice was exceedingly melodious, her delivery emphatic, and her enunciation extremely distinct. The service was the liturgy of the Church of England; two psalms were sung by the whole of the prisoners, and extremely well—much better than I have frequently heard in our best-appointed churches. A written discourse, of her own composition, was read by her; it was of a purely moral tendency, involving no doctrinal points, and admirably suited to the hearers. During the performance of the service, the prisoners paid the profoundest attention, and the most marked respect; and, as far as it is possible to judge, appeared to take a devout interest. Evening service was read by her afterward to the female prisoners."

We believe that there are gentlemen in the world who stand so stiffly upon the virtue of certain forms of ministerial ordination, as to set their faces against all lay, and especially against all female, religious teaching. We will not dispute as to what may, or may not, be the precise value of those forms. They ought to confer powers of inestimable worth, considering how stubbornly they are defended—and perhaps they do so; but every one amongst us knows and feels that the power of writing or preaching good sermons is not amongst the number. The cold, labored eloquence which boy-bachelors are authorized by custom and constituted authority to inflict upon us—the dry husks and chips of divinity which they bring forth from the dark recesses of the theology (as it is called) of the fathers, or of the middle ages, sink into utter worthlessness by the side of the jail addresses of this poor, uneducated seamstress. From her own registers of the prisoners who came under her notice, it is easy to describe the ordinary members of her congregation: pert London pickpockets, whom a cheap steamboat brought to reap a harvest at some country festival; boors, whom ignorance and distress led into theft; depraved boys, who picked up a precarious livelihood amongst the chances of a seaport town; sailors, who had committed assaults in the boisterous hilarity consequent upon a discharge with a paid-up arrear of wages; servants, of both sexes, seduced by bad company into the commission of crimes against their masters; profligate women, who had added assault or theft to the ordinary vices of a licentious life; smugglers; a few game-law criminals; and paupers transferred from a workhouse, where they had been initiated into crime, to a jail, where their knowledge was perfected. Such were some of the usual classes of persons who assembled around this singular teacher of righteousness.

Noble woman! A faith so firm, and so disinterested, might have removed mountains; a self-sacrifice founded upon such principles is amongst the most heroic of human achievements.

This appears to have been the busiest period of Sarah Martin's life. Her system, if we may so term it, of superintendence over the prisoners, was now complete. For six or seven hours daily she took her station amongst them; converting that which, without her, would have been, at best, a scene of dissolute idleness, into a hive of industry and order. We have already explained the nature of the employment which she provided for them; the manner of their instruction is described as follows: "Any one who could not read, I encouraged to learn, whilst others in my absence assisted them. They were taught to write also; whilst such as could write already, copied extracts from books lent to them. Prisoners who were able to read, committed verses from the Holy Scriptures to memory every day according to their ability or inclination. I, as an example, also committed a few verses to memory to repeat to them every day;

and the effect was remarkable; always silencing excuse when the pride of some prisoners would have prevented their doing it. Many said at first, 'It would be of no use;' and my reply was, 'It is of use to me, and why should it not be so to you? You have not tried it, but I have.' Tracts and children's books, and large books, four or five in number, of which they were very fond, were exchanged in every room daily, whilst any who could read more were supplied with larger books."

There does not appear to have been any instance of a prisoner long refusing to take advantage of this mode of instruction. Men entered the prison saucy, shallow, self-conceited, full of cavils and objections, which Sarah Martin was singularly clever in meeting; but in a few days the most stubborn, and those who had refused the most peremptorily, either to be employed or to be instructed, would beg to be allowed to take their part in the general course. Once within the circle of her influence, the effect was curious. Men old in years, as well as in crime, might be seen striving for the first time in their lives to hold a pen, or bending hoary heads over primers and spelling-books, or studying to commit to memory some precept taken from the Holy Scriptures. Young rascals, as impudent as they were ignorant, beginning with one verse, went on to long passages; and even the dullest were enabled by perseverance to furnish their minds and memories with "from two to five verses every day." All these operations, it must be borne in mind, were carried on under no authority save what was derived from the teacher's innate force of character. Aware of that circumstance, and that any rebellion would be fatal to her usefulness, she so contrived every exercise of her power as to "make a favor of it," knowing well that "to depart from this course, would only be followed by the prisoners doing less, and not doing it well." The ascendency she thus aquired was very singular. A general persuasion of the sincerity with which "she watched, and wept, and prayed, and felt for all," rendered her the general depositary of the little confidences, the tales of weakness, treachery, and sorrow, in the midst of which she stood; and thus she was enabled to fan the rising desire for emancipation, to succor the tempted, to encourage the timid, and put the erring in the way.

After the close of her labors at the jail, she proceeded, at one time of her life, to a large school which she superintended at the workhouse; and afterward, when that school was turned over to proper teachers, she devoted two nights in the week to a school for factory girls, which was held in the capacious chancel of the old church of St. Nicholas. There, or elsewhere, she was every thing. Other teachers would send their classes to stand by and listen while Sarah Martin, in her striking and effective way, imparted instruction to the forty or fifty young women who were fortunate enough to be more especially her pupils. Every countenance was upon her; and as the questions went round, she would explain them by a piece of poetry, or an anecdote, which she had always ready at command, and, more especially, by Scripture illustration. The Bible was, indeed, the great fountain of her knowledge and her power. For many years she read it through four times every year, and had formed a most exact reference book to its contents. Her intimate familiarity with its striking imagery and lofty diction, impressed a poetical character upon her own style, and filled her mind with exalted thoughts. After her class duties were over, there remained to be performed many offices of kindness, which with her were consequent upon the relation of teacher and pupil; there was personal communication with this scholar and with that; some inquiry here, some tale to listen to there; for she was never a mere schoolmistress, but always the friend and counselor, as well as the instructor.

The evenings on which there was no tuition were devoted by her to visiting the sick, either in the workhouse, or through the town generally; and occasionally an evening was passed with some of those worthy people in Yarmouth by whom her labors were regarded with interest. Her appearance in any of their houses was the signal for a busy evening. Her benevolent smile, and quick, active mannner communicated her own cheerfulness and energy to every one around her. She never failed to bring work with her, and, if young people were present, was sure to employ them all.

Something was to be made ready for the occupation of the prisoners, or for their instruction; patterns or copies were to be prepared, or old materials to be adjusted to some new use, in which last employment her ingenuity was pre-eminent. Odd pieces of woollen or cotton, scraps of paper, mere litters, things which other people threw away, it mattered not what, she always begged that such things might be kept for her, and was sure to turn them to some account. If, on such occasions, whilst everybody else was occupied, some one would read aloud, Sarah Martin's satisfaction was complete; and at intervals, if there were no strangers present, or if such communication were desired, she would dilate upon the sorrows and sufferings of her guilty flock, and her own hopes and disappointments in connection with them, in the language of simple, animated truth.

Her day was closed by no "return to a cheerful fireside prepared by the cares of another," but to her solitary apartments, which she had left locked up during her absence, and where "most of the domestic offices of life were performed by her own hands." There she kept a copious record of her proceedings in reference to the prisoners; notes of their circumstances and conduct during such time as they were under her observation, which generally extended long beyond the period of their imprisonment; with most exact accounts of the expenditure of the little subscriptions before mentioned, and also of a small annual payment from the British Ladies' Society, established by Mrs. Fry, and of all other money committed to her in aid of any branch of her charitable labors. These books of record and account have been very properly preserved, and have been presented to a public library in Yarmouth.

In scenes like these Sarah Martin passed her time, never appearing to think of herself; indeed her own scanty fare was hardly better than that of the poorest prisoner. Yet her soul was triumphant, and the joy of her heart found expression in sacred song. Nothing could restrain the energy of her mind. In the seclusion of a lonely chamber, "apart from all that could disturb, and in a universe of calm repose, and peace, and love;" when speaking of herself and her condition, she remarked, in words of singular beauty,

> ——"I seem to lie
> So near the heavenly portals bright,
> I catch the streaming rays that fly
> From eternity's own light."

Thus she cheered her solitary room with strains of Christian praise and gratitude, and entered the dark valley of the shadow of death with hymns of victory and triumph. She died on the 15th of October, 1843, aged fifty-two years.

Sarah Martin is one of the noblest of the Christian heroines the nineteenth century has produced. The two predominant qualities of her soul were love, or "the charity which hopeth all things," and moral courage; both eminently feminine endowments. She performed her wonderful works with true womanly discretion. She is, therefore, an example of excellence of whom her sex should be more than proud—they should be thankful for this light of moral loveliness enshrined in a female form. "Her gentle disposition," says one of her biographers, "never irritated by disappointment, nor her charity strai tened by ingratitude, present a combination of qualities which imagination sometimes portrays as the ideal of what is pure and beautiful, but which are rarely found embodied with humanity. She was no titular Sister of Charity, but was silently felt and acknowledged to be one, by the many outcast and destitute persons who received encouragement from her lips and relief from her hands, and by the few who were witnesses of her good works.

It is the business of literature to make such a life stand out from the masses of ordinary existences, with something of the distinctness with which a lofty building uprears itself in the confusion of a distant view. It should be made to attract all eyes, to excite the hearts of all persons who think the welfare of their fellow-mortals an object of interest or duty; it should be included in collections of biography, and chronicled in the high places of history; men should be taught to estimate it as that of one whose philanthropy has entitled her to renown, and children to associate the name of Sarah Martin with those of Howard, Buxton, Fry—the most benevolent of mankind.

THE WORKER OF CHARITY.

MARGARET MERCER,

WHO deserves a place among the most distinguished of her sex, for her noble philanthropy, and efforts in the cause of female education, was born at Annapolis, Maryland, United States, in 1791. The family of Mercer was descended from an ancient English stock, transplanted to America soon after its colonization, and the race has, in its new location, done honor to the source from whence it was derived. The father of Margaret was, at the time of her birth, governor of Maryland, a man of excellent education, refined taste, and large wealth. Retiring from public life, Governor Mercer withdrew to his estate at Cedar Fork, and devoted himself to agricultural pursuits, and the training of his children. Margaret was his only daughter, and her education was conducted under his immediate care, with little assistance from other teachers: she often remarked, that she had been "brought up at her father's feet." Margaret Mercer is another example of the beneficial influence which thorough mental training exercises on woman's character, by enabling her to make her moral power more respected and more effective. Scarcely an instance can be found where a father has aided and encouraged the mental improvement of his daughter, but that she has done honor to his care and kindness, and been one of the brightest jewels in his crown. Such was Margaret Mercer: proud as the family might well be of the name they bore, she added its holiest lustre. "Her character," says her biographer, Dr. Caspar Morris, in his excellent memoir of this noble woman, "comprised elements apparently very diverse, and yet all combined into a perfect whole, as the varied colors of a ray of light. Gentle, and full of affection for all, and ready to sympathize with sorrow wherever met with; feelings, the evidence of which will be found scattered everywhere around these traces of her path through life; she yet possessed an energy and firmness rarely found in this connection."

If we reflect further on the subject, remembering how few girls are trained as Margaret Mercer was —her mental powers developed, and directed to guide and strengthen rightly those delicate moral sensibilities and tender affections peculiar to her sex—one reason of her superiority becomes apparent.

After giving a sketch of her studies in botany, and love of gardening, etc., Dr. Morris says:

"But it was not upon these sportive fancies alone that her mind exerted its powers. Graver subjects occupied her attention, and performed their part in giving increased vigor to her reasoning faculties, whilst the others were adding to the already-abounding stores of her fertile imagination." She had access to a choice collection of works on history and general literature: these were her familiar companions, and her mind was thoroughly stored with their contents: whilst we find her at one time deep in mathematics, allowing herself but too little rest, that she might bring her mind under the wholesome discipline of this parent of careful thought; at another, theological discussions asserted strong empire over her mind, and in order to drink, as she supposed, more purely from the fountain itself, with less intervention of human teaching, she devoted herself with almost undivided attention to the study of Hebrew. A short time afterward, we find her carefully threading the intricate mysteries of medical science, that by the acquisition of a correct knowledge of the nature of diseases and their remedies, she might enlarge the sphere of her benevolent usefulness. The deep abstractions of metaphysics did not deter her from trying to fathom those abysses into which the mind plunges its line in vain, growing old in drawing up no certain token of reaching the solid foundation over which its deep waters roll so proudly. She remarks to a friend: "I do not come on very well with metaphysics; I dislike any thing so inconclusive, and should be tired of following an angel, if he talked so in a ring." A paper of "Thoughts on the Magnet" proves her to have given attention to natural philosophy, and at an early period to have wrestled with some of those mysterious truths which are now but dawning upon the horizon of human knowledge. But whilst on all these subjects she could express herself with ease and eloquence, there was a simplicity and delicacy about her character which separated her as widely as can be conceived from that class of "women of masculine understanding," whose assumption of claims to superiority over their own sex leads them to despise the refinements and delicacy which communicate an appropriate and attractive grace to the female character. These can never be laid aside without a violation of the laws of nature, and a consequent shock to that unity of action which constitutes the beauty of the works of Him who gave to each an appropriate part in the sublime hrrmony of that universe which attests His wisdom and power. Never was feminine grace more beautifully illustrated than in her whole career. She never forgot that it is the peculiar province of woman to minister to the comfort, and promote the happiness, first, of those most nearly allied to her, and then of those who, by the providence of God, are placed in a state of dependence upon her. To discharge these duties was her unceasing object, to the accomplishment of which she devoted herself with entire singleness of purpose. Thus she writes to a friend: "I, like every little mole toiling in his own dark passage, have been given to murmuring, and my great complaint for some time past has been, that I was cut off from every means of usefulness, and could not find any thing on earth to do that might not as well remain undone; and while I am fretting at having nothing to do, you find equal discomfort in having too much. Somebody, no matter who, has said the secret of happiness was, that the busy find leisure, and the idle find business, and it would seem so between us. And yet I doubt whether happiness is not a principle which belongs exclusively to God, and whether we can ever be satisfied till we wake up in His likeness. Whenever you can find that spot, sacred to religious peace and true friendship, send for me to your paradise; but remember this is the reward promised to those who *have gone through* the struggle of our great spiritual warfare."

At this time her pencil, her pen, and her needle, were all put in requisition in aid of the Greeks, in their struggle for liberty.

When Margaret Mercer was about two-and-twenty, she made a public profession of religion; in a letter to a friend, she thus commemorates this important event:

"I was confirmed, and had the pious blessing of our venerable old bishop, the day before I came from home. You cannot think how humble, how penitent, how happy I feel. It seems as though I still feel the pressure of his hand on my head. He has promised to come to see me next spring. . . . . I do not think I was ever made for a married woman; I feel as if I was not intended to take so great a share in worldly things. If I did, I should forget my God, perhaps; and may Providence load me with every human misery, and deprive me of every earthly good, rather than that."

And now that her fine talents had been cultivated by a liberal education and an extensive course of reading, and her naturally amiable disposition warmed and purified by true piety, she was ready for her work. Yet who that then looked upon her would have dreamed what that work was to be! Her biographer thus describes her at this period:

"In personal appearance, Miss Mercer was peculiarly attractive; her stature was originally tall, her carriage graceful, her eye beaming, with intelligence, and her whole countenance expressive of the loveliest traits of female character. Disease and care set their marks upon her face in after-life, and caused her form to lose its symmetry, but never quenched the beaming of the eye, nor darkened the radiance of her soul, which shone on every feature to the very last." There was a combination of attractive grace with the impressiveness of superior power, which is rarely met with; and while her manner was often sportive, and she could adorn the most common subjects of conversation by happy turns of thought and purity of language, there was frequently an elevation of thought, and force of expression, which carried those thrown into association with her into a higher sphere than that of common everyday existence. Even those who could not sympathize with, and appreciate her character, were still struck with this feature in it.

This is the true moral influence which woman, when her education is properly conducted, and her position rightly understood, will exercise over men, over society. That this moral power was held by woman, Miss Mercer felt to be true; and hence arose her distaste for the "chatter" of the vain, frivolous, *accomplished* young ladies, whom she met in society. Thus she writes of her visit at Washington:—

"I acknowledge that there are many persons around me vastly better than I am; but I am speaking of society, not people; and I confess that the 'unidea-ed chatter of females' is past my endurance; they are very capable of better things, but what of that? Is it not yet more annoying, that they will do nothing better? And besides all this, I have more painful feelings of embarrassment in company than I had at sixteen. I am *old*, too; and, when I go into gay scenes, the illusion is gone, and I fancy the illuminated hall to resemble the castle of enchantment, where Armida kept all who were capable of virtue bound in the lap of pleasure. I think how a M. Fellenberg has devoted a noble spirit to a grand system of education, and given them the model. All admire, all talk of it, and no one on the wide globe follows the example. Mrs. Fry opens the prison-gates—looses the bonds of the captive—carries healing into broken hearts, or plants virtue where vice was the only growth-what are all these chattering women about, that they cannot wear a simple garb, and follow her to jails and hospitals and poor-houses? No—if I cannot do good where there is so much to do, I never was and never will be a votary of folly."

She was now engaged in founding a Sunday-school. Writing to a friend, she says: "When my head turns to this subject, it seems to me I want forty heads, well-stored with strong sense; forty frames supported by vigorous strength and health; and a hundred hands as organs of execution for the plans and projects of my head."

Miss Mercer was to have a wider sphere for the office of teacher, which seemed her peculiar mission. Her mother died when Margaret was young. Her father's death, which took place at Philadelphia, whither she had accompanied him for his health, proved the crisis of her life. She had been accustomed to all the indulgences love and wealth can bestow. From this time, she was to prove what those endure who have their only faith in God and their own energies on which to rely. Much of her property consisted in slaves—these she liberated, provided for, and sent to Liberia. Thus Dr. Morris gives the summary:—

"This emancipation of her slaves was one of a chain of acts inseparably linked together, by which she reduced herself from *affluence* to absolute dependence on her own exertions for maintenance; and that not ignorantly and gradually, but instantly, and with full knowledge of the inevitable result.

She therefore apologizes to Mr. Gurley for doing so little for them, and remarks: 'Should any think I have not done my part by these poor creatures, I can but bear the blame *silently*. A formal remonstrance against my making such a disposition of my property has been addressed to me by —— and ——. But I have determined to abide the consequences.' These consequences were anxiety, toil, and poverty, endured without a murmur or regret, during twenty-five years of life enfeebled by disease."

And now she was to begin the world; she chose the arduous post of teacher in a school for young girls in Virginia; but her plans of charity were not given up. Thus she writes to a friend:—

"I have been desiring a day or two of repose that I might devote to you and your dearest mother. But, indeed, you have very little idea of the life I lead. Saturday is as laboriously spent in working for the Liberian Society, as any other day in the week; and on Sunday we have a Sunday-school, in which I have my part, and so make out to employ every day fully. Drawing keeps me on my feet for six hours every other day; and at first it was truly bewildering to teach twenty-three children who did not know how to make a straight line. You are anxious to know all about me, and you see I am free in my communication; there are many encouraging circumstances in the mode of life I have adopted; *for those very things that are most painful, prove how much there is to do;* and where there is much to do, steady laborious efforts to do good will doubtless be blessed, although we may in mercy be denied the luxury of seeing our work under the sun prosper. Mrs. G. is sometimes very much dispirited, at times without cause; for every little painful occurrence of misconduct in the children affords opportunity of more strenuously enforcing good principles. I never knew how to be thankful to my parents, above all to my God, for a good education, until I came to look into the state of young ladies generally."

The desire to be made instrumental in training souls for eternity was the ruling motive by which she was influenced; and, from the very first, her chief efforts were devoted to this great end, which was pursued without deviation throughout her whole career, though by no means to the neglect of those subsidiary acquirements which she esteemed as highly as any one could do, and labored most unremittingly to communicate to her pupils.

She continued in this, her chosen profession, for about twenty-five years; established a school of her own; and her example and influence have had a most salutary and wide-spread effect on the community where she resided. This admirable woman died in the autumn of 1846, aged fifty-five years. She prepared two works for her pupils, "Studies for Bible Classes," and a volume entitled "Ethics;" in the form of lectures to young ladies, which she employed as a text-book in teaching moral philosophy. It is admirably adapted to its purpose, conveying in chaste, yet glowing language, the feelings of a sanctified heart. Adopting the word of God as the only source of knowledge, as well as of the practical duties of life, she endeavors to explain and enforce the principles there laid down for the formation of character, and the government of life. It is a work well worthy of the study of every woman who desires to attain to a high degree of moral worth. We give one extract:—

CONVERSATION.

"If you are conscious that the sin of idle talking prevails among you; if you are sensible of so offending individually; or, if the sad effect of this low, disgraceful, and corrupting vice disturbs the peace and serenity of your little circle, let me entreat you as the most certain corrective of the evil, to form some common plan for promoting the perfection and happiness of your fellow-creatures. Imbue your hearts with the spirit of active charity, and the gossip of the worldly-minded will, indeed, sound on your ears like *idle words.* No conversation will then appear to you worthy of notice, but such as has some evident bearing upon the improvement or happiness of the human race. When this has once become the main object of your hopes, your fears, your labors, and your prayers, it will become the most interesting subject of your thoughts, and the favorite theme of your conversations. Imagine Mr. Howard, or Mrs. Fry, to return home at evening, with souls filled with images of the poor prisoners they had visited, handcuffed and chained, lying upon a pile of filthy straw, perishing with cold and hunger; or, worse, in the horrid bondage of sin, blaspheming, drinking, and fighting in their subterrene hole. Do you think they would be agreeably amused, if, when their efforts were directed to "stir up the pure minds fervently," of the young around them, to aid in their noble labors, they were called upon to join in the childish prattle of girls discussing the ribbands on their hair, or the rings on their fingers; or, in the equally contemptible jargon of young men of fashion, of their hat-rims, or coat-capes, or shoe-ties, or, still worse, the cruel, wicked custom usual with both sexes, of dissecting characters, and speaking evil of others, merely to excite some interest in their vapid conversation? *Conversation is to works what the flower is to the fruit.* A godly conversation shelters and cherishes the new-born spirit of virtue, as the flower does the fruit from the cold, chill atmosphere, of a heartless world; and the beauty of holiness expanding in conversation, gives rational anticipation of noble-minded principles ripening into the richest fruits of good works. You know the tree as well by the flower as the fruit, and never need you hope to see the fig follow the thistle flower, or grapes the wild bloom of the thorn-tree. Honor God, then, with your bodies and spirits, in your lives and conversations; show forth *holiness* out of a good conversation: for the king's daughter is *all glorious within*."

THE TEACHER IN THE WILDS.

SARAH BOARDMAN JUDSON.*

In the merchants' windows, at the corners of streets, and amongst the other multifarious announcements of our busy days, people may from time to time perceive little handbill intimations anent meetings, at which some devoted one is to be set apart to labor amongst the far-off heathens. These notices produce little or no effect upon the world generally; but to the Christian churches they are usually of the most lively interest. They illustrate the chivalry of the church, if we may so speak; they exhibit the Christian heroism of our age, and present a lovely moral and religious contrast to the destructive heroism of the world. It is easy to become a warrior; the poor neglected immortals, whose ferocity has alone been trained, have gained the reputation of dauntless heroism. The applause of the world is of itself sufficient to incite any man to rush into the deadly rift of battle, but the courage requisite for a missionary appears to us to be of the most sublime and noble kind. No world's applause could sustain a man or woman, full of heart-affection for friends and home, amidst the dreary desolate wastes of heathen lands during a life-time. Nothing but the religious sense of duty, and the applause of a pure conscience, could so elevate and sustain the soul amongst weary labors and pestilential airs. When we look at courage through the true medium, how immeasurably superior to the ferocious passions of a Cæsar or a Napoleon do the faithful souls of a Williams, Roberts, and Waddel, appear. The book of history is full of the fame of the former, and their monuments are on almost every chimney-piece; the latter are only known to the Christian world of Great Britain and America, the angels, and the heathen; but their place of remembrance shall be heaven.

The missionary field, however, is not exclusively reserved for the strong and faithful and forward man. As Christianity is woman's bond of equality with man, so is the vineyard of Christ equally her place of labor, and she also goes forth in the faith that maketh strong, to do the will of Him who sends her.

Perhaps it might appear invidious to sketch the life of any one of those amiable heroines of the cross, when the lives of all are so full of true courage and faith; but as, on the other hand, the life of one, save in its incidents, may be looked upon as a parallel to that of all others, it is both necessary and profitable to particularize.

Sarah Boardman Judson was born in 1803, at

Alstead, in the state of New Hampshire, and subsequently removed with her parents, Ralph and Abiah Hall, to Danvers, and then to Salem, in the state of Massachusetts. Sarah was the eldest of five children; and, as her parents were of the industrious class, she was constrained, like the majority of poor men's eldest daughters, to devote herself more to the care of her younger brothers and sisters than to the regular cultivation of her own mind. There are some minds that would never grow strong unless they had something to struggle against. The latent courage of the noblest souls is only aroused and developed by those opposing forces that seem any thing but blessings. Mysterious are the ways of Providence, however, and finite and partial the judgments of men. We know not how the circumstances of life may operate toward the soul—God knows. Deprived of the power of attending school, Sarah Hall was thrown upon herself. She had no teacher save experience, no guide in her lessons save her books, and to these she applied herself with heroic diligence. Care produced thus early in Sarah Hall that thoughtfulness and patience which, when matured, so beautifully adorn the Christian character, and her self-education was just the path to riper self-reliance. She early began to observe and think, and to write down her thoughts in a little day-book; and then in the form of poetry, when her ideas became more expanded and matured. At seventeen years of age, Sarah Hall had devoted herself to the business of instructing others, in order that she might obtain the means of educating herself. During the day she taught, and at night she devoted her mind to the acquisition of logic, geometry, and Latin, etc.—a course of severe procedure that none but those who have pursued it can properly estimate. The baptism of Sarah Hall seems to have awakened in her the whole force of her inward life; and her meditations and aspirations seem, shortly after this event, to have been toward the path of a missionary. "I am privileged to worship the true God," she would say, "but, alas! for the poor perishing heathen who has never known Him." There is something so admirable in the spirit of these musings and expressions that, apart from their religious character, they are sufficient to claim the respect of every generous heart. A sense of blessings and privileges, and a strong desire to impart them to others, despite of toil, and uncertainty, and distance, and disease, are the glorious principles which animate those who bear the cross to distant lands. How unlike the vain-glorious spirit of those who go forth to slay! As time wore onward Sarah Hall's name began to be heard in the literary world, and many looked upon her as a rising poetess, when she married the Rev. George Dana Boardman on the 4th of July, 1825, and the same month proceeded with him to join the American missionaries recently settled at Burmah, in the East Indies. It was here that the most interesting and eventful part of Sarah's life began. It was here that all her self-reliance and courage were called into requisition. Mr. Boardman and his wife settled at a station called Amherst, in order to become acquainted with the key to the heart of the heathen, which is his language. Dr. Judson and his family resided here, and assisted in the studies of the new comers, as well as in encouraging them in their labors.

Burmah was at this time in a most unfavorable condition for receiving from white men the religion of peace, for war and force were the first instruments which the whites had exercised toward the Burmese in visiting their country, and they had little confidence in any peaceful attempt that was made for their good. After studying for some time at Amherst, Mr. and Mrs. Boardman removed to Maulmain, to a lonely and dangerous mission-house. The spot where it stood was a mile beyond the cantonments, close beside the thick jungle, where, during the night, the wild beasts made dismal howlings. Behind the station rose a fine range of hills, whose solitary aspect was relieved by the gilded masonry of handsome pagodas, and before rolled the broad deep river, where rode an English sloop of war, and where danced the boats of the natives. Just across the river was the Burman province of Martaban, whose terrible freebooters issued from their fastnesses during the night, armed with knives, spears, and sometimes muskets, driving away or slaying the peaceful inhabitants, while they seized upon the produce of their toil. The English general suggested to Mr. Boardman the necessity of having an armed guard; but this would have totally deprived the missionary of gaining the confidence of the people, and it was declined. It was to study the language, habits, and charácter of the natives that he had gone thither, and not as a conqueror. About a month after her settlement at Maulmain, Mrs. Boardman wrote to a friend: "We are in excellent health, and as happy as it is possible for human beings to be upon earth. It is our earnest desire to live, and labor, and die, among this people." The life of a missionary is not one of ease and safety, as the following thrilling incident in the life of young Sarah Boardman will show. About the middle of June, as the meridian sun came down from its altitude, men in loose garments of gaily-plaided cloth, and with their long black hair wound about their heads, and confined by folds of muslin, looked curiously in at the door of the strange foreigner; and then encouraged by some kind word or glance, or the spreading of a mat, seated themselves in their own fashion, talked a little while with their host, though often, from misapprehension of each others meaning, at cross purposes, and went away, leaving him to his books and teacher. Women and children gathered more timidly, but with curiosity even less disguised, about the *Kalahma-pyoo* (white foreigners), wondering at her strange costume, the fairness of her skin, and the superiority displayed in her bearing;

and some of the bolder of them venturing to touch her hand, or to pass their tawny taper fingers from the covered instep to the toe of the neatly-formed slipper, so unlike their own clumsy sandals. But who, among all these came to inquire of Jesus Christ, or learn the way to heaven? Most emphatically could they say: "We have not so much as heard if there be a God." On the evening of the fourth day, as it deepened into night, the books of study were thrown aside, and the book of God taken in their stead; then the prayer was raised to heaven, and the little family went to rest. Feeble were the rays of the one pale lamp, close by the pillow of the young mother, scarce throwing its light upon the infant resting on her bosom, and penetrating into the remote darkness but by feeble flickerings. So sleep soon brooded over the shut eyelids, and silence folded its solemn wings about the little habitation. The infant stirred, and the mother opened her eyes. Why was she in darkness? and what objects were those scattered so strangely about her apartment, just distinguishable from the gray shadows? The lamp was soon relighted, and startling was the scene which it revealed. There lay in odd confusion, trunks, boxes, and chests of drawers, all rifled of their contents; and strewed carelessly about the floor, were such articles as the marauders had not considered worth their taking. While regarding in consternation, not appreciable by those who have access to the shops of an American city, this spoiling of their goods, Mrs. Boardman chanced to raise her eye to the curtain beneath which her husband had slept, and she thought of her lost goods no more. Two long gashes, one at the head and the other at the foot, had been cut in the muslin; and there had the desperate villains stood, glaring on the unconscious sleeper with their fierce, murderous eyes, while the booty was secured by their companions. The bared, swarthy arm was ready for the blow, and the sharp knife, or pointed spear, glittered in their hands. Had the sleeper opened his eyes, had he only stirred, had but a heavy, long-drawn breath startled the cowardice of guilt—ah, had it! But it did not. The rounded limbs of the little infant lay motionless as their marble counterfeit; for if their rosy lips had moved but to the slightest murmur, or the tiny hand crept closer to the loved bosom in her baby dreams, the chord in the mother's breast must have answered, and the death-stroke followed. But the mother held her treasure to her heart, and slept on. Murderers stood by the bedside, regarding with callous hearts the beautiful tableau; and the husband and father *slept.* But there was one eye open—the eye that never slumbers—a protecting wing was over them, and a soft invisible hand pressed down their sleeping lids. Nearly every article of value that could be taken away had disappeared from the house; and though strict search was made throughout the neighborhood, no trace of them was ever discovered.

It was at Tavoy, however, that the real labors of the Boardmans began, and here they had to struggle with the utmost difficulties. Both had suffered in their health, and both were called upon to exert themselves to the utmost in the acquirement of the dialect of the people, and in the pursuit of plans for their instruction. The missionaries had not only to contend with the climate, failing strength, and the other accidents of their position, but they had also to share the dangers and trials incidental to those states which forcibly base themselves upon the subjugation of their neighbors.

In August, 1827, at the dead of night, the natives of Tavoy revolted against the British, and drove the commandant of the whites and a hundred sepoys into a blockhouse on the quay. Here the Europeans maintained themselves until the arrival of Colonel Burney, when the revolt was suppressed; but the fatigue, agitation, and exposure, accelerated the decline of Mr. Boardman's already failing health, and hurried him on to that grave which he found on Burmah's distant shore. And now Mrs. Boardman was left alone with her only child, George. And now came the inquiry from Sarah's widowed heart, "What shall I do?" She wrote to America, to Maulmain, to Rangoon, and Amherst for advice, and prayed to be directed in the way that she should go. Her spirit inclined her, however, to remain in her appointed sphere, and she did remain. "When I first stood by the grave of my husband, I thought I must go home with

George. But these poor, inquiring, and Christian Karens, and the schoolboys, and the Burmese Christians, would then be left without any one to instruct them; and the poor, stupid Tavoyans would go on in the road to death, with no one to warn them of their danger. How then, oh, how can I go? We shall not be separated long. A few more years, and we shall all meet in yonder blissful world, whither those we love have gone before us. I feel thankful that I was allowed to come to this heathen land. Oh, it is a precious privilege to tell idolaters of the gospel; and when we see them disposed to love the Saviour, we forget all our privations and dangers. My beloved husband wore out his life in this glorious cause; and that remembrance makes me more than ever attached to the work, and the people for whose salvation he labored till death."

Mrs. Boardman now devoted herself with all the energy of her soul to the instruction of those so much cast upon her by the death of her husband, and moved about from place to place, encountering much danger and enduring much fatigue in her apostolic mission. She went into the jungle amongst the simple Karens, and established schools, with the supervision of which she taxed herself. These day-schools attracted the notice of the agents of the British government, and they were allowanced by the same, although differing somewhat in constitution from the formula prescribed in the East India Company's circular. She soon became a most excellent Burmese scholar, and was enabled to communicate in that language with great fluency. "Mrs. Boardman's tours in the Karen wilderness, with little George, borne in the arms of her followers, beside her—through wild mountain passes, over swollen streams and deceitful marshes, and among the craggy rocks and tangled shrubs of the jungle—if they could be spread out in detail, would doubtless present scenes of thrilling interest. But her singular modesty always made her silent on a subject which would present her in a light so enterprising and adventurous. Even her most intimate friends could seldom draw from her any thing on the subject; and they knew little more than that such tours were made, and that the progress of the gospel was not suspended among the Karens while her husband's successor was engaged in the study of the language. There is a note addressed to Mrs. Mason, from a zayat by the wayside, just before she reached the mountains; and this is the only scrap among her writings alluding in any way to these tours. It was sent back by a party of men who were to bring her provisions, and contains only directions about the things necessary to her journey. She says: 'Perhaps you had better send the chair, as it is convenient to be carried over the streams when they are deep. You will laugh when I tell you that I have forded all the smaller ones.' A single anecdote is related by Captain F——, a British officer, stationed at Tavoy; and he used to dwell with much unction on the lovely apparition which once greeted him among these wild, dreary mountains. He had left Tavoy, accompanied by a few followers, I think on a hunting expedition, and had strolled far into the jungle. The heavy rains which deluge this country in the summer had not yet commenced; but they were near at hand, and during the night had sent an earnest of their coming, which was any thing but agreeable. All along his path hung the dripping trailers, and beneath his feet were the roots of vegetables, half-bared, and half-imbedded in mud; while the dark clouds, with the rain almost incessantly pouring from them, and the crazy clusters of bamboo huts, which appeared here and there in the gloomy waste, and were honored by the name of village, made up a scene of desolation absolutely indescribable. A heavy shower coming up as he approached a zayat by the wayside, and far from even one of those primitive villages, he hastily took refuge beneath the roof. Here, in no very good humor with the world, especially Asiatic jungles and tropic rains, he sulkily 'whistled for want of thought,' and employed his eyes in watching the preparations for his breakfast. 'Uh! what wretched corners the world has, hidden beyond its oceans and behind its trees!' Just as he had made this sage mental reflection, he was startled by the vision of a fair, smiling face in front of the zayat, the property of a dripping figure, which seemed to his surprised imagination to have stepped that moment from the clouds.

But the party of wild Karen followers, which gathered around her, had a very human air; and the slight burthens they bore spoke of human wants and human cares. The lady seemed as much surprised as himself; but she curtsied with ready grace, as she made some pleasant remark in English, and then turned to retire. Here was a dilemma. He could not suffer the lady to go out into the rain, but—his miserable accommodations, and still more miserable breakfast! He hesitated and stammered; but her quick apprehension had taken it all at a glance, and she at once relieved him from his embarrassment. Mentioning her name and errand, she added, smiling, that the emergencies of the wilderness were not knew to her; and now she begged leave to put her own breakfast with his, and make up a pleasant morning party. Then beckoning to her Karens, she spoke a few unintelligible words, and disappeared under a low shed—a mouldering appendage of the zayat. She soon returned with the same sunny face, and in dry clothing; and very pleasant indeed was the interview between the pious officer and the lady-missionary. They were friends afterward; and the circumstances of their first meeting proved a very charming reminiscence."

After three years of widowhood, Mrs. Boardman was united to Dr. Judson, of the American mission, at Maulmain, whither she removed with her little son, where she devoted herself to the acquirement of a new language, called the Peguan, in which she made considerable advancement. She revised the standard tracts in Peguan, and the catechism and Gospel according to St. Luke; and, assisted by Ko-man-boke, a Peguan Christian, she translated the New Testament. The life at Maulmain was one of love, labor, and trial. Eight children were born to her here, and three of them withered away and died, while, to add to the depth of her trials, Dr. Judson was threatened with the fatal disease which had bereft her of her first husband. Here, too, had she parted from her oldest son, and endured all the pangs of a wife and loving mother. Her last child was born in December, 1844, when she was attacked with chronic diarrhœa, from which she had suffered much in the early part of her missionary life. It soon became evident, from the sinking of her physical powers, that death was in her cup, unless some remedy could be found to alleviate her sufferings: and a sea-voyage being the only thing that suggested itself to the physician, she departed with her husband and three eldest children for America. At first, the voyage seemed to produce the most beneficial results, and she even proposed to proceed alone from the Isle of France, but the disease returned once more with fatal virulence, and she died at sea on 1st September, 1845, and was buried at St. Helena. She sleeps amongst the distant mould of the sea-washed solitary isle, and over her ashes her husband has erected a monument, with the following inscription: "Sacred to the memory of Sarah B. Judson, member of the American Baptist Mission to Burmah, formerly wife of the Rev. George D. Boardman, of Tavoy, and lately wife of the Rev. Adoniram Judson, of Maulmain, who died in this port, September 1, 1845, on her passage to the United States, in the forty-second year of her age, and the twenty-first of her missionary life."

"Would that those who declare that there is no vitality in Christianity, could see and appreciate the courage and sacrifices which animate and are demanded from those who, like Mrs. Judson, go forth to tell the darkened savage of Christ!

THE NOBLE DAME.

RACHEL, LADY RUSSELL.

"She neither sought to shine in the world by the extent of her capacity, nor to display, by affected retirement, the elevation of her soul; and when circumstances obliged her to come forward on the stage of history, she showed herself in the appropriate character of a wife and a mother. *Hence we may believe, that the unobtrusive modesty of private life contains many a female capable of giving the same example to her sex, and to mankind.*"—LORD JOHN RUSSELL'S REMARKS ON THE CHARACTER OF RACHEL, LADY RUSSELL.

"A woman distinguished for ardent and tender affection; pious, reflecting, firm, and courageous; alike exemplary in prosperity and adversity, when observed by multitudes, or hidden in retirement."

RACHEL, LADY RUSSELL, second daughter of Thomas Wriothesley, Earl of Southampton, was born in 1636. She married first Lord Vaughan; and after his death she married, in 1669, William, Lord Russell, third son of William, first Duke of Bedford. One son and two daughters were the fruits of this union, which was a very happy one, though Lady Rachel was four or five years older than her husband. Lord Russell, being implicated in a conspiracy with the Duke of Monmouth, natural son of Charles II., Algernon Sidney, John Hampden, grandson to the celebrated patriot of that name, Essex, and Howard, to prevent the succession of the Duke of York to the throne, was arrested and sent to the Tower. Monmouth fled; Howard saved himself by revealing his accomplices; and Essex, Sidney, and Hampden, were apprehended on his evidence. They were also accused of conspiring against the life of Charles II., which was not true. The Protestant succession, and the prevention of encroachments on the liberties of the people, were their chief objects.

On the day of his trial Lord Russell asked leave of the court that notes of the evidence might be taken for his use. He was informed that he might have the assistance of one of his servants. "My wife is here, my lord, to do it," replied the noble prisoner. The spectators, seeing the daughter of the virtuous Southampton thus assisting her husband in his distress, melted into tears. Every application to save Lord Russell proved vain. The independent spirit, patriotism, popularity, courage, talents, and virtues of the prisoner, were his most dangerous offences, and became so many arguments against his escape.

Lady Russell threw herself at the feet of the king, and pleaded with tears the merits and loyalty of her father, as an atonement for her husband's offences. But Charles remained unmoved, and even rejected her petition for a respite of a few weeks. On finding every effort fruitless for saving the life of her husband, she collected her courage, and fortified her mind for the fatal stroke, confirming by her example the resolution of her husband. His courage never appeared to falter but when he spoke of his wife; his eyes would then fill with tears, and he appeared anxious to avoid the subject. When parting from Lady Russell, they mutually preserved a solemn silence; and when she left him, he said, "The bitterness of death was past." He then expressed his gratitude to Providence that had given him a wife who, to birth, fortune, talents, and virtue, united sensibility of heart; and whose conduct in this trying crisis, had even surpassed all her other virtues.

Lord Russell was executed July 21st, 1683. His widow proved the faithful guardian of his honor, a wise and active mother to his children, and a friend and patroness of his friends.

Her letters, written after her husband's death, give a touching picture of her conjugal affection and fidelity; but no expression of resentment or traces of a vindictive spirit mingle with the senti ment of grief by which they are pervaded.

Her only son, Wriothesley, Duke of Bedford, died in 1711, of the small-pox; and soon after her daughter, the Duchess of Rutland, died in childbed. Her other daughter, the Duchess of Devonshire, was also in childbed at the time of her sister's death; and Lady Russell again was called upon to give new proofs of her self-control. After beholding one daughter in her coffin, she went to the chamber of the other with a tranquil countenance. The Duchess of Devonshire earnestly inquir ing after her sister, Lady Russell calmly replied, "I have seen your sister out of bed to-day."

Some years after her husband's death, she was under apprehensions of an entire loss of sight; but this was prevented by an operation. Lady Russell died September 29th, 1723, aged eighty-seven. About fifty years afterward, her letters were collected and published, which established her fame in literature, as one of the most elegant writers of her time. In whatever light we consider her character, its moral excellence appears perfect. Such an example shows the power of female influence to promote good and resist evil. Even the noble Lord Russell was made better by his union with her. Amiable and prudent, as well as lovely, she was the means of reclaiming him from some youthful follies into which he had plunged at the time of the Restoration. With such a guardian angel by his side, no wonder he was strengthened to act his lofty part, and die a patriot martyr. His widow wore her weeds to the close of her life; their conjugal union of hearts was never broken, as the following extracts from her letters will show:—

TO DR. FITZWILLIAM—ON HER SORROW.

I am sure my heart is filled with the obligation, how ill soever my words may express it, for all those hours you have set apart (in a busy life) for my particular benefit, for the quieting of my distracted thoughts, and reducing them to a just measure of patience for all I have or can suffer. I trust I shall, with diligence, and some success, serve those ends they were designed to. They have very punctually, the time you intended them for, the last two sheets coming to my hands the 16th of this fatal month; it is the 21st completes my three years of true sorrow, which should be turned rather into joy; as you have laid it before me, with reasons strongly maintained, and rarely illustrated. Sure he is one of those has gained by a dismission from a longer attendance here; while he lived, his being pleased led me to be so too, and so it should do still; and then my soul should be full of joy; I should be easy and cheerful, but it is sad and heavy; so little we distinguish how, and why we love, to me it argues a prodigious fondness of one's self; I am impatient that is hid from me I took delight in, though he knows much greater than he did here. All I can say for myself, is, that while we are clothed with flesh, to the perfectest, some displeasure will attend a separation from things we love. This comfort I think I have in my affliction, that I can say, unless thy law had been my delight, I should have perished in my trouble. The rising from the dead is a glorious contemplation, doctor! nothing raises a drooping spirit like it; his Holy Spirit, in the mean time, speaking peace to our consciences, and through all the gloomy sadness of our condition, letting us discern that we belong to the election of grace, that our persons are accepted and justified. But still I will humble myself for my own sins, and those of our families, that brought such a day on us.

I have been under more than ordinary care for my eldest girl; she has been ill of St. Anthony's fire, as we call it, and is not yet free from it. I had a doctor down with her, but he found her so likely to do well he stayed only one day. I have sent you these Gazettes, and will send no more, for I reckon you will be in your progress of visits.

I wish with you Lord Campden would marry; but I want skill to prevail by what I can say. I hope I need employ none to persuade Dr. Fitzwilliam that I am very acknowledging, and very sincerely, etc.

TO THE SAME.

* * * * * * *

If I could contemplate the conducts of Providence with the uses you do, it would give ease indeed, and no disastrous events should much affect us. The new scenes of each day make me often conclude myself very void of temper and reason, that I still shed tears of sorrow and not of joy, that so good a man is landed safe on the happy shore of a blessed eternity; doubtless he is at rest, though I find none without him, so true a partner he was in all my joys and griefs; I trust the Almighty will pass by this my infirmity; I speak it in respect to the world, from whose enticing delights I can now be better weaned. I was too rich in possessions whilst I possessed him: all relish is now gone, I bless God for it, and pray, and ask of all good people (do it for me from such you know are so) also to pray that I may more and more turn the stream of my affections upward, and set my heart upon the ever-satisfying perfections of God; not starting at his darkest providences, but remembering continually either his glory, justice, or power is advanced by every one of them, and that mercy is over all his works, as we shall one day with ravishing delight see: in the mean time, I endeavor to suppress all wild imaginations a melancholy fancy is apt to let in; and say with the man in the gospel, "I believe, help thou my unbelief."

TO THE SAME.

Never shall I, good doctor, I hope, forget your work (as I may term it) of labor and love: so instructive and comfortable do I find it, that at any time when I have read any of your papers, I feel a heat within me to be repeating my thanks to you anew, which is all I can do toward the discharge of a debt you have engaged me in; and though nobody loves more than I do to stand free from engagements I cannot answer, yet I do not wish for it here; I would have it as it is; and although I have the present advantage, you will have the future reward; and if I can truly reap what I know you design me by it, a religious and quiet submission to all providences, I am assured you will esteem to have attained it here in some measure. Never could you more seasonably have fed me with such discourses, and left me with expectations of new repasts, in a more seasonable time, than these my miserable months, and in those this very week in which I have lived over again that fatal day that determined what fell out a week after, and that has given me so long and so bitter a time of sorrow. But God has a compass in his providences, that is out of our reach, and as he is all good and wise, that consideration should in reason slacken the fierce rages of grief. But sure, doctor, 'tis the nature of sorrow to lay hold on all things which give a new ferment to it, then how could I choose but feel it in a time of so much confusion as these last weeks have been, closing so tragically as they have done; and sure never any poor creature, for two whole years together, has had more awakers to quicken and revive the anguish of its soul than I have had; yet I hope I do most truly desire that nothing may be so bitter to me, as to think that I have in the least offended thee, O my God! and that nothing may be so marvellous in my eyes as the exceeding love of my Lord Jesus: that heaven being my aim, and the longing expectations of my soul, I may go through honor and dishonor, good report and bad report, prosperity and adversity, with some evenness of mind. The inspiring me with these desires is, I hope, a token of his never-failing love toward me, though an unthankful creature for all the good things I have enjoyed, and do still in the lives of hopeful children by so beloved a husband.

TO THE EARL OF GALWAY—ON FRIENDSHIP.

I have before me, my good lord, two of your letters, both partially and tenderly kind, and coming from a sincere heart and honest mind (the last a plain word, but, if I mistake not, very significant), are very comfortable to me, who, I hope, have no proud thoughts of myself as to any sort. The opinion of an esteemed friend, that one is not very wrong, assists to strengthen a weak and willing mind to do her duty toward that Almighty Being, who has, from infinite bounty and goodness, so chequered my days on this earth, as I can thankfully reflect I felt many, I may say many years of pure, and, I trust, innocent, pleasant content, and happy enjoyments as this world can afford, particularly that biggest blessing of loving and being loved by those I loved and respected; on earth no enjoyment certainly to be put in the balance with it. All other are like wine, intoxicates for a time, but the end is bitterness, at least not profitable. Mr. Waller (whose picture you look upon) has, I long remember, these words:

> "All we know they do above
> Is, that they sing, and that they love."

The best news I have heard is, you have two good companions with you, which, I trust, will contribute to divert you this sharp season, when, after so sore a fit as I apprehend you have felt, the air even of your improving pleasant garden cannot be enjoyed without hazard.

TO LADY SUNDERLAND—ON HEALTH, FRIENDSHIP, LOVE.

Your kind letter, madam, asks me to do much better for myself and mine, than to scribble so insignificantly as I do in a piece of paper; but for twenty several reasons you must have the advantage you offer me with obliging earnestness a thousand times greater than I deserve, or there can be cause for, but that you have taken a resolution to be all goodness and favor to me. And indeed what greater mark can you almost give than remembering me so often, and letting me receive the exceeding advantage of your doing so, by reading your letters, which are all so edifying? When I know you are continually engaged in so great and necessary employments as you are, and have but too imperfect health, which to any other in the world but Lady Sunderland would unfit for at least so great despatches as you are charged with. These are most visible tokens of Providence, that every one that aims to do their duty shall be enabled to do it.

I hope your natural strength is so great, that it will in some time, if you do your part, master what has been accidentally in the disorder of it. Health, if one strictly considers, is the first of earthly blessings; for even the conversation of friends, which as to spiritual profits, as you excellently observe, is the nearest approach we can make to heaven while we live in these tabernacles of clay; so it is in a temporal sense, also, the most pleasant and the most profitable improvement we can make of the time we are to spend on earth. But, as I was saying, if our bodies are out of tune, how ill do we enjoy what in itself is so precious? and how often must we choose, if we can attain it, a short slumber, that may take off our sense of pain, than to accept what we know in worth excels almost to infiniteness? No soul can speak more feelingly than my poor self on this subject; who can truly say, my friendships have made all the joys and troubles of my life; and yet who would live and not love? Those who have tried the insipidness of it would, I believe, never choose it. Mr. Waller says—"'Tis (with singing) all we know they do above." And it is enough; for if there is so charming a delight in the love, and suitableness in humors, to creatures, what must it be to our clarified spirits to love in the presence of God! Can there be a greater con-·mplation to provoke to diligence for our preparation to that great change, where we shall be perfected, and so continue for ever! I see I have scribbled a great deal of paper; I dare not read it, lest I should be sorry, Lady Sunderland should; and yet can now send her nothing if not this, for my eyes grow ill so fast, I resolve to do nothing of this sort by candle-light.

THE PATTERN OF DOMESTIC VIRTUE.

LUCY HUTCHINSON,

DAUGHTER of Sir Allan Apsley, was born in 1624. At the age of eighteen she was married to Colonel John Hutchinson, who distinguished himself as one of the most efficient among the Puritan leaders in the war between Charles I. and the Parliament. Their courtship was a very romantic one, as it is given by the lady in her "Memoir" of her husband. She says: "Never was there a passion more ardent and less idolatrous; he loved her better than his life; with inexpressible tenderness and kindness; had a most high, obliging esteem of her; yet still considered honor, religion, and duty, above her; nor ever suffered the intrusion of such a dotage as should blind him from marking her imperfections." That it was "not her face he loved," but "her honor and her virtue were his mistress," he abundantly proved; for, "on the day fixed for the marriage, when the friends of both parties were assembled, and all were waiting the appearance of the bride, she was suddenly seized with an illness, at that time often the most fatal to life and beauty.

She was taken ill of the small-pox; was for some time in imminent danger; and, at last, when her recovery was assured, the return of her personal attractions was considered more than doubtful." She says, indeed, herself, that her illness made her, for a long time after she had regained her health, "the most deformed person that could be seen." But Mr. Hutchinson's affection was as strong as his honor. He neither doubted nor delayed to prosecute his suit; but, thankful to God for her preservation, he claimed her hand as soon as she was able to quit her chamber, and when the clergyman who performed the service, and the friends who witnessed it, were afraid to look at the wreck of her beauty. He was rewarded; for her features were restored, unblemished as before; and her form, when he presented her as his wife, justified his taste as much as her more intrinsic qualities did his judgment. They were united to each other on the 3d of July, 1638.

Their union was an example of the happiness which marriage confers on those who fulfil its duties in holy truth and faithful love. In the perils of war, Mrs. Hutchinson was an attendant on her beloved husband; and when, after the restoration of Charles II., Colonel Hutchinson was imprisoned in the Tower, she followed him, and never ceased her exertions and importunities till she was permitted to visit him. When her husband was removed to Sandown Castle, in Kent, she, with some of her children, went also, and used every entreaty to be permitted to reside in the castle with him. This was refused; but she took lodgings in Deal, and walked every day to Sandown to see and cheer the prisoner. All that could be done to obtain his pardon or liberation she did; but as Colonel Hutchinson was a Puritan and a republican on principle, and would not disclaim his opinions, though he would promise to live in quiet, his enemies listened to no pleadings for mercy. What was to have been his ultimate punishment will never be known; the damp and miserable apartment in which he was confined brought on an illness which ended his life, September 11th, 1664, leaving his wife with eight children and an embarrassed estate, to mourn his irreparable loss. Mrs. Hutchinson was not with him at his death; she had gone to their home to obtain supplies, and bring away the children left there. His death-scene shows the estimation in which he held her. So long as he was able to sit up, he read much in the Bible; and on looking over some notes on the Epistle to the Romans, he said, "When my wife returns, I will no more observe their cross humors; but when her children are all near, I will have her in the chamber with me, and they shall not pluck her out of my arms. During the winter evenings she shall collect together the observations I have made on this Epistle since I have been in prison."

As he grew worse, the doctor feared delirium, and advised his brother and daughter not to defer any thing they wished to say to him. Being informed of his condition, he replied with much composure, "The will of the Lord be done; I am ready." He then gave directions concerning the disposal of his fortune, and left strict injunctions that his children should be guided in all things by their mother. "And tell her," said he, "that as she is above other women, so must she on this occasion show herself a good Christian, and above the pitch of ordinary minds."

Faithfully she fulfilled these injunctions; evincing her sorrow and her love, not by useless repinings, but by training up her children to be like their father, and employing her talents in constructing a monument to his fame. For this purpose she undertook her great work, "The Life of Colonel Hutchinson, by his widow Lucy." This has been republished lately, and the "Edinburgh Review" thus closes a notice of the work:

"Education is certainly far more generally diffused in our days, and accomplishments infinitely more common; but the perusal of this volume has taught us to doubt whether the better sort of women were not fashioned of old, by a purer and more exalted standard; and whether the most eminent female of the present day would not appear to disadvantage by the side of Mrs. Hutchinson. There is something in the domestic virtue and calm commanding mind of this English matron, that makes the Corinnes and Heloises appear very insignificant. We may safely venture to assert that a nation which produces many such wives and mothers as Mrs. Lucy Hutchinson, must be both great and happy."

We should do injustice to the worth of female genius if we omitted to give at least a brief extract from this work of Mrs. Hutchinson. An "Address to her Children" forms the introduction to the memoir. Thus she writes:

"I, who am under a command not to grieve at the common rate of desolate women, while I am studying which way to moderate my woe, and, if it were possible, to augment my love, can find out none more just to your dear father, or more consoling to myself, than the preservation of his memory; which I need not gild with such flattering commendations as the hired preachers equally give to the truly and the nominally honorable; an undrest narrative, speaking the simple truth of him, will deck him with more substantial glory than all the panegyrics the best pens could ever consecrate to the virtues of the best men. To number his virtues is to give the epitome of his life, which was nothing else but a progress from one degree of virtue to another. His example was more instructive than the best rules of the moralists; for his practice was of a more divine extraction, drawn from the word of God, and wrought up by the assistance of his spirit. He had a noble method of government, whether in civil, military, or domestic administrations; which forced love and reverence even from unwilling subjects, and greatly endeared him to the souls of those who rejoiced to be governed by him. He had a native majesty that struck awe into the hearts of men, and a sweet greatness that commanded love.

* * * * * * *

"His affection for his wife was such, that whoever would form rules of kindness, honor, and religion, to be practised in that state, need no more, but exactly draw out his example. Man never had a greater passion or a more honorable esteem for woman; yet he was not uxorious, and never remitted that just rule which it was her honor to obey; but he managed the reins of government with such prudence and affection, that she who would not delight in such honorable and advantageous subjection must have wanted a reasonable soul. He governed by persuasion, which he never employed but in things profitable to herself. He loved her soul better than her countenance; yet even for her person he had a constant affection, exceeding the common temporary passion of fond fools. If he esteemed her at a higher rate than she deserved, he was himself the author of the virtue he doated on; for she was but a faithful mirror, reflecting truly, but dimly, his own glories upon him. When she ceased to be young and lovely, he showed her the most tenderness. He loved her at such a kind and generous rate as words cannot express; yet even this, which was the highest love any man could have, was bounded by a superior feeling; he regarded her, not as his idol, but as his fellow creature in the Lord, and proved that such a feeling exceeds all the irregularities in the world."

Mrs. Hutchinson brought up her children and lived to see some of them married. The time of her decease is not known.

THE FRIEND OF COLUMBUS.

ISABEL THE CATHOLIC.

To judge aright of the merits of Isabel the Catholic as an administratrix of public affairs, in virtue of which, and of her queenly arts and endowments, she became so firmly fixed in the hearts and affections of her subjects, it will be necessary to take a glance at the high state of prosperity and political consequence enjoyed by the kingdom of Castile previous to the accession of the house of Trastamara, in 1368, and of the causes of the subsequent decline of its glory among the nations, and the condition to which it had been reduced by long years of misrule, at the commencement of her most auspicious reign.

So far back as the fifth century, the germs of constitutional liberty and of many free institutions had been introduced into the Peninsula by that branch of the Teutonic race by which it was then overrun. These, however, had been only partially unfolded when the great Saracen invasion of the eighth century, which seemed at first to threaten their extinction, proved, on the contrary, the means of their more rapid development. The enjoyment of long peace and prosperity had done its usual work in relaxing the morals of both the court and the clergy. Driven by the invader beyond the sterile mountains of the north, they must toil for the most scanty subsistence, or, descending from their fastnesses, snatch it, sword in hand, from the mighty foe who lay stretched on the plains beneath. At length priest and people girded themselves for the conflict of centuries, and when the Spaniards descended into the open plains of Castile and Leon, they were never secure from the predatory incursions of the Arabs, until they had driven them beyond some natural boundary—a river, or a chain of mountains—securing their conquests by strong fortifications. The Castilian towns being specially open to these incursions, every citizen was trained to arms, and the burgesses were the most effective part of the militia. Charters of communion were early granted, the most ancient extant bearing date 1020. By these, the citizens had the right of electing their own magistrates, who appointed judges of the law.

In 1169, at Burgos, occurred the earliest instance on record of popular representation, almost a century before the parliament of Leicester. So great was the power of the popular branch of the Castilian cortes, whose members were originally nominated by the householders, but afterward by the municipal bodies, that no tax could be imposed without their consent; they narrowly watched and restrained the public expenditure, venturing even to regulate the economy of the royal household; and no title to the crown was valid without their consent. The nobles and clergy might attend in cortes, but legislative acts were valid without their sanction. Both these orders were exempt from taxation, and the situation of Castile was no less favorable to the growth of their power. Embarked with their king in rescuing their country from the infidel, they hesitated not to divide with him the spoil. Immense domains were thus accumulated, and each noble was a petty sovereign. In the end of the fourteenth century, when Castile had reached its zenith, the constable Davalos could ride through his own estates from Seville to Compostella, nearly the two extremities of the kingdom. Eighty towns and castles were under the sway of the Lord of Biscay. A court favorite could muster twenty thousand vassals. It is scarcely a figure of speech to say that they were warriors from their cradle. Mendoza tells of a descendant of the famous Marquis of Cadiz carrying out with him to battle his son, only thirteen years old, adding, "an ancient usage in that noble house." And the only son of Alfonso VI. was slain when only eleven, fighting manfully in the ranks.

Ever since that memorable day on which St. James had been seen hovering in the air, mounted on a milk-white steed, leading on to victory, and bearing aloft the banner of the cross, when seventy thousand infidels fell on the field, the name of *St.*

Jago had been the war-cry of the Spaniards; and, in imitation of the military apostle, their patron saint, priests militant went forth with the crucifix in their hands, leading on the soldiers to battle. In an age holding wealth in contempt, these warlike prelates amassed enormous riches, for when a town was rescued from the infidel, some ancient religious establishment must be supported, or a new one founded. The Archbishop of Toledo, primate of Spain, and grand chancellor of Castile, besides his immense revenues, could muster a greater number of vassals than any other subject, and had jurisdiction over fifteen large and populous towns. One lady-abbess of Castile had jurisdiction over fourteen capital towns, and more than fifty smaller places, and ranked next to the queen in dignity. Amusing and almost incredible stories are told of the luxurious banquetings of the nobles and prelates, while the king had often neither money nor credit. One bond of union alone existed between prince and people. Hand to hand they joined against the infidel, but every man's hand was also against his neighbor; and when at length the Moors were repulsed within the kingdom of Granada, and nearly a century of long minorities, or now weak and now vicious rule, was the fate of Castile, bitterly came then to be felt the evil effects of such an unnatural division of interests. The sacred name of law became a by-word. Rapine, murder, and incendiarism spread terror and desolation through the land. The insolent nobles not only waged open war with each other, but converted their castles into dens of robbers, plundering the traveler, and publicly selling his property in the cities. One robber chieftain carried on an infamous traffic with the Moors, selling to them as slaves Christian prisoners of both sexes. Every farm (*dehesa*, meaning protected ground) was a fortress, and it was in nearly hopeless despondency that the agriculturist committed the seed to the earth. So shameless was the adulteration of the coin, that the most common article was enhanced four and even six fold in value. One sovereign tried oppressive acts, a return to arbitrary taxation, and interference with freedom of election; while another turned a deaf ear to the groans of his people by giving himself up to the chase. Such at the birth of Isabel was the wretched state of the fertile and beautiful Castile.

At Madrigal, a town of Old Castile, on the 22d of April, 1451, was born Isabel, daughter of Juan II., by his second consort, a Princess of Portugal. Her father dying when she was in her fourth year, she, and her brother, Alfonso, who was two years younger, lived in the strictest retirement with their mother, the widowed queen; and the state of seclusion and even privation in which she is said to have passed the first ten years of her life, may account for the firmness, as the rigid practices of devotion, from the example of her mother, for the zeal, springing up into bigotry and bitter persecution, by which she was afterward so distinguished.

When in her seventh year, it was agreed she should marry Prince Ferdinand of Aragon, who was one year younger, both of them the children of second marriages, and neither heir apparent to the two kingdoms. Many events intervened to interrupt this project, and France, Portugal, and England sought her alliance. She was also on the point of being sacrificed to an ambitious and dissolute subject, when relieved by his death. Her biographers extol the wisdom and prudence of her reply when only thirteen, to a proposal for marrying her to the King of Portugal, a widower, with heirs to his throne, that a princess of Castile could not be disposed of in marriage without the consent of the cortes. The weak rule of her brother Enrique, doubts as to the legitimacy of his daughter, the death of her brother, Alfonso, caused an offer of the crown to be made to her, which she rejected, declaring she would lay no claim to the title so long as its present possessor lived. Resolving, however, to be no longer thwarted in her desire of marrying Ferdinand, who had been long carrying on a romantic courtship, faithfully recorded in the decades of the ancient chronicler Palencia, she eluded the vigilance of the king's spies, and protected by a body of troops, under the escort of the Archbishop of Toledo, she fled to Valladolid, whence the prince lost no time in following her, traveling with only five attendants, and in strict disguise, sometimes acting as servant to his companions.

The first interview realized the expectations

formed on both sides. Isabel was then in her nineteenth year, and is described as inheriting from Catharine of Lancaster blue eyes, auburn hair, and a fair complexion; her face regular and pleasing, rather than indicating any very high order of intellect; while Ferdinand, though a year younger, was of manly form, his limbs strengthened by hardship and exercise, his features regular and handsomé, the dark-brown hair on his ample forehead somewhat thinned from the helmet he had worn from his infancy. The prince was greatly inferior in education to Isabel. A soldier from his childhood, his attainments were limited to reading and writing; and so great was his poverty, he had to borrow money for the expenses of the nuptials. Gutierre de Cárdenas, who, on the entrance of the prince, was the first to point him out to Isabel, exclaiming, "Ese es, ese es" (this is he), was permitted to bear on his shield the letters SS, being like to the sound of these words in Spanish.

The marriage was celebrated on the 19th of October, 1469, in the presence of Isabel's two principal adherents, the Archbishop of Toledo and the Admiral of Castile, who was also Ferdinand's grandfather, and an assemblage of more than 2,000 persons. The young pair being within the forbidden degrees of consanguinity, and the Pope in the interests of the king, a bull of dispensation was forged by the king of Aragon and the archbishop, the discovery of which was a shock to Isabel, to whose honest mind everything like artifice was abhorrent, and she could only console herself that it was in good faith she had acted. The princess had long before this been acknowledged by the king, her brother, as heir to the crown, and it was now agreed that she and Ferdinand should reign jointly, but all essential power was vested in her, the prince not even being allowed to quit the kingdom without her consent. As future queen of Aragon, a magnificent dower was settled on her. She lost no time in informing the king, her brother, in the most respectful terms, of the step she had taken, but his only reply was, that "he would lay the matter before his council."

The weak rule of Enrique lasted yet five years, during which public favor fluctuated between Isabel and his daughter, whom he before his death declared to be legitimate, although he had formerly acknowledged Isabel as his heir. But the cortes never having revoked the allegiance they had sworn to her, when the news reached her at Segovia of the king's death, she at once caused herself to be proclaimed queen, Ferdinand being then absent in Aragon. Mounted on a white jennet, she proceeded to the public square, where a throne had been erected on a platform, on ascending which, the royal standard was unfurled, and the herald cried, "Castile, Castile, for the King Don Fernando, and his consort the Queen Donna Isabel;" after which simple ceremony, she returned thanks in the principal church, and the people swore allegiance to her, but not to the absent Ferdinand;

nor does it appear that she demanded this, which so greatly displeased him, that he said to Palencia, "Alfonso, thy learning far exceeds mine; tell me didst ever read in thy histories of any woman acting as the queen has done? She writes to her husband to return at his leisure, and in his absence causes herself to be proclaimed with pomp and ceremony."

This step, which shows the decided and independent character of the queen, gave rise to a dispute of great warmth; but she was too wary not to see that her soundest policy was union, and with infinite tact she sought to allay his wrath, and to persuade him that the difference in their authority was only nominal.

The king of Portugal having espoused the cause of the princess, there now followed the war of the succession, lasting nearly four years and a half, during which only one serious battle was fought, when the Portuguese standard-bearer, after losing both his arms, held the banner between his teeth, till cut down by the enemy. The better to carry on the operations of the war, the consorts separated, and the queen, sometimes endangering her health, hastened from place to place, dictated dispatches, addressed the soldiers, showed great moderation in victory, redressed grievances, while maintaining with a high hand her own authority, and thus before long gained both the confidence and affections of her subjects. For the expenses of the war, the clergy forced on her a loan of half the church plate in the kingdom, and she afterward carefully repaid the debt. The distractions of war did not prevent Isabel from turning her attention to the lawless state of her kingdom. She instituted, or rather revived under a different form, the institution of the *Santa Hermandad*, or Holy Brotherhood, a kind of rural police, consisting of 4,000 members, the half of whom were horsemen, having power to arrest, try, and execute criminals, without respect of persons, or appeal to any other tribunal. Its proceedings were at first excessively severe, and no institution could be better adapted to curb the power of the aristocracy, and to consolidate that of the sovereign. Its powers were increased or modified as the state of the times demanded; but the end having been attained, it was in 1498 shorn of its powers, and dwindled down, with some slight changes, to the form in which it exists at the present day, as a body of gendarmerie. The queen, too, sat every Friday on a chair of state, covered with cloth of gold, to administer justice. She ordered restitution of stolen property, and delinquents were executed without distinction of rank, which caused so much consternation that more than 8,000 persons fled from Seville, rather than stand a trial. After a time, however, the clergy and magistrates being alarmed at the decrease of population, the queen, willing to temper justice with lenity, published a general amnesty, on condition of the restoration of illegally-acquired property. She deprived of their possessions and privileges all the nobles who had taken up arms against her; amongst others her former powerful adherent the archbishop of Toledo, whose defection nothing could induce her to pardon. She well knew how to choose and reward wise and faithful counselors; and her fame would indeed have been stainless, were it not for the dark and remorseless bigotry which caused her to establish the tribunal of the Inquisition, whose frightful sway in the space of eighteen years destroyed 8,800 of her subjects by fire, otherwise torturing and punishing more than 96,000. It is said that her confessor predicted she would be queen of Castile while yet her two brothers lived, and that she promised on its fulfilment to extirpate heresy from the land. Of the horrors of the Inquisition, no detail is needed here. To Isabel belongs the praise of restoring peace and order in her distracted kingdom. But no sooner had her subjects sheathed their swords, than she unsheathed against them one which treacherously pierced their sides. With one hand she raised and protected prostrate industry, whilst with the other she dealt against it a blow which paralyzed its energies, the effects of which are still felt in that fair and goodly, dark, and bigoted land.

It is a relief to turn from such a picture, and behold the queen the joyful mother of a son; which event took place at Seville, in June, 1478, after an interval of seven years from the birth of her only other child, a daughter. The child was christened Juan, and we would willingly tell of the three days' rejoicings, and how at the baptism the church of Santa Maria was hung with satin, and the chapel with brocade; how the royal babe was carried under a canopy of rich brocade; and how the godmother wore a tabard of crimson silk, lined with damask, which she afterward gave to the king's fool, and a rich brocaded kirtle, embroidered with seed and large pearls, with many other raree shows and wonders, but that space would fail us to recount them. Soon after this event, the king and queen made a progress through part of her dominions, Isabel showing her usual firmness and intrepidity; enforcing relaxed laws; appointing extraordinary judges; on one occasion, to punish an outrage, taking horse alone amidst torrents of rain, before the captains of her guard had time to follow her.

In Gallicia alone, where anarchy still ruled, fifty towering strongholds, from which robber chieftains descended like birds of prey to levy black mail on the hapless district beneath, were razed to the ground, and no less than fifteen hundred malefactors compelled to fly.

In January, 1479, died Juan, King of Aragon. And now proud Castile saw herself mistress of nearly the whole of Spain. Aragon, and indeed all Spain, and even Portugal, had at one time or other done homage to Castile for their dominions, and this, with the sense of owing their conquests to their personal bravery, had induced among the nobles a proud and inflexible bearing, scarcely to be curbed by the iron rule of the Austrian dynasty, and which drew from the Venetian ambassador in the time of Charles V. the remark, that "if their power were equal to their pride, the world would not be able to withstand them."

The Inquisition being now firmly established in Castile, Ferdinand introduced it into his own dominions, which so maddened the people, that they arose and slew the chief inquisitor on the very steps of the altar. But torrents of blood were made to flow for that which had been shed on consecrated ground, and the galling yoke only weighed the more heavily. Such had been the horrors exhibited in Castile, that the Pope himself sent to remonstrate, but in this, and in all matters ecclesiastical, Isabel chose to be her own pope, as has been said of our Henry VIII., herself nominating to every benefice, which when the Pope attempted to do, she forced him by the most vigorous resistance to submit to her will. She thus bound burthens on her subjects which she herself refused to touch with one of her fingers.

In 1479 was born the unfortunate Juana; about three years after, Maria; and, in 1485, the equally unfortunate Catherine, called Catherine of Aragon, wife of Henry VIII., and the youngest child of the sovereigns. In 1489, Isabel, the eldest and best-beloved daughter of the queen, was betrothed to the heir of the Portuguese sovereign, and with amazing magnificence, considering the expense of the war, to defray which the queen had once actually pawned her jewels. The *fêtes* continued for a fortnight, the queen and the betrothed bride appearing at them all, dressed in cloth of gold, attended by seventy noble ladies, attired in brocade and resplendent with jewels. One historian says: "The principal articles of the *trousseau* were four costly necklaces of gold, set with pearls and precious stones; rich tapestries, woven of silk and gold; twenty silk and brocade robes; four of drawn golden threads; and six of silk, embroidered with pearls and gold." The whole wardrobe estimated at two hundred and twenty thousand florins. In eight months this brilliant bride was a widow, and returned to Castile in a litter hung with black.

The care the queen bestowed on the education of her children—indeed, the whole tenor of domestic life—cannot be too highly lauded. What she did could only be achieved by boundless energy, and never-failing resources. While actively engaged in war, and sometimes sitting up all night long engaged in state affairs, she neglected none of her private duties. She carefully cultivated the intellects of her children, whose dispositions were mild and amiable, and sought to eradicate every germ of evil. Her daughters, like herself, were well versed in Latin, in the solid branches of education, as well as in all the elegant accomplishments. That the prince might have the spur of emulation, as well as the benefit of private tuition, she caused ten noble youths, five of them his own age, and five somewhat older, to be brought up with him, partaking of all his advantages, and sharing in all his pleasures. These youths, and all who were brought into contact with him, and even his pages, were so carefully selected, that almost all of them were, in after life, distinguished by some superior excellence, while the fond object of so many hopes lay buried in an early grave. At the age of eighteen, a separate establishment was formed for him, and a council, in imitation of the council of state, assembled round him, in which public affairs were discussed. The profound wisdom of all this needs no comment. The queen also sought to inspire the young nobility with a taste for learning, and invited to her court all, both native and foreign, famed for their scholarship. The following year, the prince was married to Margaret, daughter of Maximilian, Emperor of Germany, afterward the celebrated governess of the Netherlands, and at the same time her brother, the Archduke Philip, to the Princess Juana; but sadly the eye turns from the page which records the festivities celebrated on the occasion of these ill-fated unions, for dismal reverses are at hand. Indeed, from this time to its close, the life of the queen presents an almost constant succession of domestic distresses, only varied by a few brilliant triumphs; her many private virtues sullied, also, by more than one public fault. By her unwearied encouragement and protection of Christopher Columbus, she added a new world to her dominions. But she signed an edict for the expulsion of the Jews, which was carried out with merciless severity; the creatures of luxury dying by the wayside; the hand of the Christian restrained who would have extended a cup of cold water to the sufferer; mothers and their new-born infants perishing from the pangs of hunger. True, they were permitted to sell their property, but this mercy was in reality a mockery, for, the time being limited, we are told, "a house was given for an ass, and a vineyard for a piece of cloth." Her Christian subjects were forbidden, under severe penalties, from giving shelter or assistance to the Jews, who had made a last effort to avert the blow, by offering to the queen thirty thousand ducats for the expenses of the late war, and the sovereigns were hesitating whether to accept their tempting bribe, when the chief inquisitor, abruptly entering the apartment, drew a crucifix from his bosom, saying, "Judas Iscariot sold the Saviour for thirty pieces of silver; your Highnesses are now selling him for thirty thousand. Behold him here; take him and barter him as you will;" and the insane fanatic threw the symbol on the table, and withdrew. Who need tell that mercy fled away, and fanaticism obtained the victory?

From the commencement of their reign, Ferdinand and Isabel had shown an earnest solicitude for the encouragement of commerce and nautical science, as is evinced by a variety of regulations which, however imperfect, from the misconception of the true principles of trade in that day, are sufficiently indicative of the dispositions of the government. Under them, and indeed under their predecessors as far back as Henry the Third, a considerable traffic had been carried on with the western coast of Africa, from which gold dust and slaves were imported into the city of Seville. The annalist of that city notices the repeated interference of Isabel in behalf of these unfortunate beings, by ordinances tending to secure them a more equal protection of the laws, or opening such social indulgences as might mitigate the hardships of their condition. A misunderstanding gradually arose between the subjects of Castile and Portugal, in relation to their respective rights of discovery and commerce on the African coast, which promised a fruitful source of collision between the two crowns; but which was happily adjusted by an article in the treaty of 1479, that terminated the war of the succession. By this it was settled that the right of traffic and of discovery on the western coast of Africa should be exclusively reserved to the Portuguese, who in their turn should resign all claims on the Canaries to the crown of Castile. The Spaniards, thus excluded from further progress to the south, seemed to have no other opening left for naval adventure than the hitherto untraveled regions of the great western ocean. Fortunately, at this juncture, an individual appeared among them, in the person of Christopher Columbus, endowed with capacity for stimulating them to this heroic enterprise, and conducting it to a glorious issue.

Some of the most striking features cf that great enterprise we shall here bring out. Using for that purpose, in a somewhat condensed form, the graphic narrative of Mr. Prescott, the painstaking and impartial historian of this notable reign.

Columbus was a native of Genoa, of humble parentage, though perhaps honorable descent. He was instructed in his early youth at Pavia, where he acquired a strong relish for the mathematical sciences, in which he subsequently excelled. At the age of fourteen, he engaged in a seafaring life, which he followed with little intermission till 1470.

Filled with lofty anticipations of achieving a discovery which would settle a question of such moment, so long involved in obscurity, Columbus submitted the theory on which he had founded his belief in the existence of a western route, to King John the Second, of Portugal. Here he was doomed to encounter for the first time the embarrassments and mortifications which so often obstruct the conceptions of genius, too sublime for the age in which they are formed. After a long and fruitless negotiation, and a dishonorable attempt on the part of the Portuguese to avail themselves clandestinely, of his information, he quitted Lisbon in disgust, determined to submit his proposals to the Spanish sovereigns, relying on their reputed character for wisdom and enterprise.

The period of his arrival in Spain being the latter part of 1484, would seem to have been the most unpropitious possible to his design. The nation was then in the heat of the Moorish war, and the sovereigns were unintermittingly engaged, as we have seen, in prosecuting their campaigns, or in active preparation for them. The large expenditure incident to this, exhausted all their resources; and indeed the engrossing character of this domestic conquest left them little leisure for indulging in dreams of distant and doubtful discovery.

Ferdinand and Isabel, desirous of obtaining the opinion of the most competent judges on the merits of Columbus's theory, referred him to a council selected by Talavera, from the most eminent scholars of the kingdom, chiefly ecclesiastics, whose profession embodied most of the science of that day. Such was the apathy exhibited by this learned conclave, and so numerous the impediments suggested by dullness, prejudice, or skepticism, that years glided away before it came to a decision. During this time, Columbus appears to have remained in attendance on the court, bearing arms occasionally in the campaigns, and experiencing from the sovereigns an unusual degree of deference and personal attention; an evidence of which is afforded in the disbursements repeatedly made by the royal order for his private expenses, and in the instructions issued to the municipalities of the different towns in Andalusia, to supply him gratuitously with lodging and other personal accommodations.

At length, however, Columbus, wearied out by this painful procrastination, pressed the court for a definite answer to his propositions; when he was informed that the council of Salamanca pronounced his scheme to be "vain, impracticable, and resting on grounds too weak to merit the support of the government." Many in the council, however, were too enlightened to acquiesce in this sentence of the majority; and the authority of these individuals had undoubtedly great weight with the sovereigns, who softened the verdict of the junto by an assurance to Columbus, that, "although they were too much occupied at present to embark in his undertaking, yet, at the conclusion of the war, they should find both time and inclination to treat with him." Such was the ineffectual result of Columbus's long and painful solicitation; and, far from receiving the qualified assurance of the sovereigns in mitigation of their refusal, he seems to have considered it as peremptory and final. In great dejection of mind, therefore, but without further delay, he quitted the court, and bent his way to the south, with the apparently almost desperate intent of seeking out some other patron to his undertaking.

Without wasting time in further solicitation, Columbus prepared, with a heavy heart, to bid adieu to Spain (1491), and carry his proposals to the king of France, from whom he had received a letter of encouragement while detained in Andalusia.

His progress, however, was arrested at the convent of La Rabida, which he visited previous to his departure, by his friend the guardian, who prevailed on him to postpone his journey till another effort had been made to move the Spanish court in his favor. For this purpose the worthy ecclesiastic undertook an expedition in person to the newly-erected city of Santa Fé, where the sovereigns lay encamped before Granada. Juan Perez had formerly been confessor of Isabel, and was held in great consideration by her for his excellent qualities. On arriving at the camp he was readily admitted to an audience, when he pressed the suit of Columbus with all the earnestness and reasoning of which he was capable. The friar's eloquence was supported by that of several eminent persons whom Columbus, during his long residence in the country, had interested in his project, and who viewed with sincere regret the prospect of its abandonment. Their representations, combined with the opportune season of the application, occurring at the moment when the approaching termination of the Moorish war allowed room for interest in other objects, wrought so favorable a change in the dispositions of the sovereigns, that they consented to resume the negotiation with Columbus. An invitation was accordingly sent to him to repair to Santa Fe, and a considerable sum provided for his suitable equipment, and his expenses on the road.

Columbus, who lost no time in availing himself of this welcome intelligence, arrived at the camp in season to witness the surrender of Granada, when every heart, swelling with exultation at the triumphant termination of the war, was naturally disposed to enter with greater confidence on a new career of adventure. At his interview with the king and queen, he once more exhibited the arguments on which his hypothesis was founded. He then endeavored to stimulate the cupidity of his audience, by picturing the realms of Mangi and Cathay, which he confidently expected to reach by this western route, in all the barbaric splendors which had been shed over them by the lively fancy of Marco Polo and other travelers of the middle ages; and he concluded with appealing to a higher principle, by holding out the prospect of extending the empire of the Cross over nations of benighted heathen, while he proposed to devote the profits of his enterprise to the recovery of the Holy Sepulchre. This last ebullition, which might well have passed for fanaticism in a later day, and given a visionary tinge to his whole project, was not quite so preposterous in an age in which the spirit of the crusades might be said still to linger, and the romance of religion had not yet been dispelled by sober reason. The more temperate suggestion of the diffusion of the gospel was well suited to affect Isabel, in whose heart the principle of devotion was deeply seated, and who, in all her undertakings, seems to have been far less sensible to the vulgar impulses of avarice or ambition, than to any argument connected, however remotely, with the interests of religion.

Amidst all these propitious demonstrations toward Columbus, an obstacle unexpectedly arose in the nature of his demands, which stipulated for himself and heirs the title and authority of admiral and viceroy over all lands discovered by him, with one-tenth of the profits. This was deemed wholly inadmissible. Ferdinand, who had looked with cold distrust on the expedition from the first, was supported by the remonstrances of Talavera, the new archbishop of Granada, who declared that "such demands savored of the highest degree of arrogance, and would be unbecoming in their Highnesses to grant to a needy foreign adventurer." Columbus, however, steadily resisted every attempt to induce him to modify his propositions. On this ground the conferences were abruptly broken off, and he once more turned his back upon the Spanish court, resolved rather to forego his splendid anticipations of discovery at the very moment when the career so long sought was thrown open to him, than surrender one of the honorable distinctions due to his services. This last act is, perhaps, the most remarkable exhibition in his whole life, of that proud, unyielding spirit which sustained him through so many years of trial, and enabled him at length to achieve his great enterprise, in the face of every obstacle which man and nature had opposed to it.

The misunderstanding was not suffered to be of long duration. Columbus's friends, and especially Louis de St. Angel, remonstrated with the queen on these proceedings in the most earnest manner.

He frankly told her that Columbus's demands, if high, were at least contingent on success, when they would be well deserved; that, if he failed, he required nothing. He expatiated on his qualifications for the undertaking, so signal as to insure in all probability the patronage of some other monarch, who would reap the fruits of his discoveries: and he ventured to remind the queen that her present policy was not in accordance with the magnanimous spirit which had hitherto made her the ready patron of great and heroic enterprise. Far from being displeased, Isabel was moved by his honest eloquence. She contemplated the proposals of Columbus in their true light; and, refusing to hearken any longer to the suggestions of cold and timid counselors, she gave way to the natural impulses of her own noble and generous heart. "I will assume the undertaking," said she, "for my crown of Castile, and am ready to pawn my jewels to defray the expenses of it, if the funds in the treasury shall be found inadequate." The treasury had been reduced to the lowest ebb by the late war; but the receiver, St. Angel, advanced the sums required from the Aragonese revenues deposited in his hands. Aragon, however, was not considered as adventuring in the expedition, the charges and emoluments of which were reserved exclusively for Castile.

Columbus, who was overtaken by the royal messenger at a few leagues' distance only from Granada, experienced the most courteous reception on his return to Santa Fé, where a definitive arrangement was concluded with the Spanish sovereigns, April 17th, 1492.

No sooner were the arrangements completed, than Isabel prepared with her characteristic promptness to forward the expedition by the most efficient measures; and on the morning of the 3d of August, 1492, the intrepid navigator, bidding adieu to the Old World, launched forth on that unfathomed waste of waters where no sail had ever been spread before.

While on a review of the circumstances, we are led more and more to admire the constancy and unconquerable spirit which carried Columbus victorious through all the difficulties of his undertaking, we must remember, in justice to Isabel, that, although tardily, she did in fact furnish the resources essential to its execution; that she undertook the enterprise when it had been explicitly declined by other powers, and when, probably, none other of that age would have been found to countenance it; and that, after once plighting her faith to Columbus, she became his steady friend, shielding him against the calumnies of his enemies, reposing in him the most generous confidence, and serving him in the most acceptable manner, by supplying ample resources for the prosecution of his glorious discoveries.

Passing over the well-known incidents of this memorable voyage, we may remark in passing, the singular fact, that Columbus sailed from Spain on a

Friday, discovered land on a Friday, and re-entered the port of Palos on a Friday. These curious coincidences should have sufficed, one might think, to dispel, especially with American mariners, the superstitious dread, still so prevalent, of commencing a voyage on that ominous day. Let us glance at the scene of the discoverer's return.

Great was the agitation in the little community of Palos, as they beheld the well-known vessel of the admiral re-entering their harbor. Their desponding imaginations had long since consigned him to a watery grave; for, in addition to the preternatural horrors which hung over the voyage, they had experienced the most stormy and disastrous winter within the recollection of the oldest mariners. Most of them had relatives or friends on board. They thronged immediately to the shore, to assure themselves with their own eyes of the truth of their return. When they beheld their faces once more, and saw them accompanied by the numerous evidences which they brought back of the success of the expedition, they burst forth in acclamations of joy and gratulation. They awaited the landing of Columbus, when the whole population of the place accompanied him and his crew to the principal church, where solemn thanksgivings were offered up for their return; while every bell in the village sent forth a joyous peal in honor of the glorious event. The admiral was too desirous of presenting himself before the sovereigns, to protract his stay long at Palos. He took with him on his journey specimens of the multifarious products of the newly-discovered regions. He was accompanied by several of the native islanders, arrayed in their simple barbaric costume, and decorated, as he passed through the principal cities, with collars, bracelets, and other ornaments of gold, rudely fashioned; he exhibited also considerable quantities of the same metal in dust, or in crude masses, numerous vegetable exotics possessed of aromatic or medicinal virtue, and several kinds of quadrupeds unknown in Europe, and birds whose varieties of gaudy plumage gave a brilliant effect to the pageant. The admiral's progress through the country was everywhere impeded by the multitudes thronging forth to gaze at the extraordinary spectacle, and the more extraordinary man, who, in the emphatic language of that time, which has now lost its force from its familiarity, first revealed the existence of a "New World." As he passed through the busy, populous city of Seville, every window, balcony, and housetop, which could afford a glimpse of him, is described to have been crowded with spectators. It was the middle of April before Columbus reached Barcelona. The nobility and cavaliers in attendance on the court, together with the authorities of the city, came to the gates to receive him, and escorted him to the royal presence. Ferdinand and Isabel were seated, with their son, Prince John, under a superb canopy of state, awaiting his arrival. On his approach they rose from their seats, and, extending their hands to him to salute, caused him to be seated before them. These were unprecedented marks of condescension to a person of Columbus's rank, in the haughty and ceremonious court of Castile. It was, indeed, the proudest moment in the life of Columbus. He had fully established the truth of his long-contested theory, in the face of argument, sophistry, sneer, skepticism, and contempt. He had achieved this, not by chance, but by calculation, supported through the most adverse circumstances by consummate conduct. The honors paid him, which had hitherto been reserved only for rank, or fortune, or military success, purchased by the blood and tears of thousands, were, in his case, an homage to intellectual power, successfully exerted in behalf of the noblest interest of humanity.

After a brief interval, the sovereigns requested from Columbus a recital of his adventures. His manner was sedate and dignified, but warmed by the glow of natural enthusiasm. He enumerated the several islands which he had visited, expatiated on the temperate character of the climate, and the capacity of the soil for every variety of agricultural production, appealing to the samples imported by him as evidence of their natural fruitfulness. He dwelt more at large on the precious metals to be found in these islands; which he inferred less from the specimens actually obtained, than from the uniform testimony of the natives to their abundance in the unexplored regions of the interior. Lastly, he pointed out the wide scope afforded to Christian zeal in the illumination of a race of men, whose minds, far from being wedded to any system of idolatry, were prepared, by their extreme simplicity, for the reception of pure and uncorrupted doctrine. The last consideration touched Isabel's heart most sensibly; and the whole audience, kindled with various emotions by the speaker's eloquence, filled up the perspective with the gorgeous coloring of their own fancies, as ambition, or avarice, or devotional feeling predominated in their bosoms. When Columbus ceased, the king and queen, together with all present, prostrated themselves on their knees in grateful thanksgivings, while the solemn strains of the Te Deum were poured forth by the choir of the royal chapel, as in commemoration of some glorious victory.

It would be beside our present purpose here to enlarge upon the progress of discovery; the trials of the enthusiastic sailor on his second, third, and fourth voyages; the misconduct of the colonists; the complaints against Columbus; and the ignominious treatment which he received at the hands of the royal commissioner Bobadilla, before that vain and foolish man could be withdrawn from an office which he had disgraced. Suffice it to say, that amidst all his trials and misfortunes the illustrious discoverer was always comforted by the sympathy of his royal mistress. He relied, and not in vain, on the good faith and kindness of Isabel; for, as an ancient Castilian writer remarks: "She had ever favored him beyond the king her husband, protecting his interests, and showing him especial kindness and goodwill."

In connection with the grand episode in the world's history, let it not be forgotten that Isabel's other measures generally were characterized by that practical good sense, without which the most brilliant parts may work more to the woe than to the weal of mankind. Though engaged all her life in reforms, she had none of the failings so common in reformers. Her plans, though vast, were never visionary. The best proof of this is, that she lived to see the most of them realized.

She was quick to discern objects of real utility. She saw the importance of the new discovery of printing, and liberally patronized it from the first moment it appeared. She had none of the exclusive local prejudices too common with her countrymen. She drew talent from the most remote quarters to her dominions by munificent rewards. She imported foreign artisans for her manufactures; foreign engineers and officers for the discipline of her army; and foreign scholars to imbue her martial subjects with more cultivated tastes. She consulted the useful in all her subordinate regulations; in her sumptuary laws, for instance, directed against the fashionable extravagances of dress, and the ruinous ostentation so much affected by the Castilians in their weddings and funerals. Lastly, she showed the same perspicacity in the selection of her agents; well knowing that the best measures become bad in incompetent hands.

In the beginning of 1495, Isabel lost her chief counsellor and great favorite, the Cardinal Mendoza, whom she visited on his death-bed, undertaking the office of his executrix, and at whose suggestion she named as his successor Francisco Ximenes—afterward so famous—a humble friar of the order of St. Francis, who had been for some time the queen's confessor; to whom we are indebted for the great monastic reforms introduced into Spain, the queen herself aiding in the work by entering the different cloisters, and, while employed with her needle and distaff, by the force of her example and her exhortations proving to the idle and dissipated nuns the beneficial effects of a well-spent life. Cardinal Ximenes was a man of pure and ascetic life, a stern, unbending disposition, unbounded fanaticism and perseverance, unscrupulous in the use of means, but untinged by worldly considerations. It was under Isabel's sanction that this man undid in a few months the beneficent work that seven years of peace and a rule of matchless wisdom and integrity had effected in the conquered kingdom of Granada, himself directing that terrible engine, the Inquisition, and forcing on an insurrection which was not put down till, at least in name, not a Moor was to be found in the kingdom. But Christian blood also flowed in torrents; amongst others fell the brave Aguilar, the fifth lord of his illustrious race who had met death in the field fighting against the Moors.

We must say a single word as to the beneficent

sway of the two eminent men whose labors were thus overthrown. The Count of Tendilla, the military commander, was the very soul of honor; Talavera, the archbishop, was conspicuous for his Christian virtues. They went hand in hand in every good work. Talavera's maxim was, that the Moors were yet but babes, and must be fed on milk. Though already an old man, he studied Arabic, and translated portions of the Scriptures, to facilitate his work with the infidels, but was very wary in baptizing converts. He spent nearly his entire revenues in public works and alms. In times of scarcity, he several times sold his furniture, and his plate was twice bought back by the Count Tendilla, the aged man declaring he would sell it a hundred times to relieve the wants of the people. At another time, he gave away his only mule, saying, "He could not afford to keep her while the poor were hungering." Two hundred and fifty persons fed daily at his table. But we quit the subject, having given only a tithe of the glories and benefits which were now, alas! brought to naught. He saw the destruction of the people whom he loved as his own soul, but dare not stretch forth a hand to succor them. Soon, however, he was not, for God took him. Isabel, soon after these events, published a decree for the expulsion of all the adult Moors from Castile and Leon, and parents were thus torn from their children, unless when in despair they embraced the alternative of baptism. It was for such services as these that the Pope bestowed on Isabel the title of Catholic!

We have now little else to record than a long, sad list of domestic losses and trials. Six months after his marriage, and before the *fêtes* were concluded, Prince Juan, who had never been strong, was cut down by fever, in a few days' illness. In her anguish the queen found strength to say, "The Lord hath given and the Lord hath taken away; blessed be his name!" The whole nation mourned the loss, and the court wore sackcloth as mourning, instead of the white serge formerly used. The prince's favorite hound, Brutus, followed the corpse to the tomb, and there lay down and died. Hopes were entertained of an heir, but these, too, were blasted by the birth of a still-born child. The succession now devolved on the queen's eldest daughter, Isabel, who had at this time married the King of Portugal, cousin and successor of her first husband; but in eighteen months she died in giving birth to a son, a frail little being, who in his second year sank into the grave, as if unable to sustain the triple diadem which hung suspended over his head. From the shock of these successive blows, the queen never thoroughly recovered. For some time, indeed, after the death of her idolized Isabel, she had remained seriously ill. It was with sadness she now saw that her fair inheritance must descend to her daughter Juana, who already showed symptoms of that weakness of intellect, which ended in the total loss of reason. In 1500 this unfortunate princess had given birth to a son, afterward the renowned Emperor Charles V., and in the following year Philip and Juana arrived in Spain, and were sworn heirs to the kingdom. Whatever comfort the queen might have had in the society of her daughter, was embittered by her daily-increasing alienation of mind, and by the sight of Philip's open indifference and disrespect toward his wife, who doated on him. Deaf to all arguments, he soon left her, and returned to the Netherlands, and we do not remember reading of any thing more affecting than the inconsolable condition of the unhappy Juana, whose whole soul was centred in her cold, careless husband. She spent her weary days mute and motionless, her eyes fixed on the ground, and not even the birth of her second son, Ferdinand, afterward emperor, had the power of rousing her or assuaging her grief. At length, having received an invitation from her husband, she, in the dreary month of November, and in the queen's absence, went forth on foot, without making the slightest preparation, evidently with the vague intention of joining her husband. Remonstrance being vain, her attendants closed the castle gates, which so infuriated the princess, that, vowing vengeance, she refused to return to her apartments, and remained uncovered all night at the gates. This went on for some days, all she would concede being to take refuge during the night in a wretched outbuilding used as a kitchen, but there she was again at the gates from the dawn of day to its close; and when the queen returned, as fast as her own growing weakness would permit, it needed all her influence to persuade the wretched princess to re-enter the castle. Behold, revolve, and learn, ere you turn away from the sight of this daughter of a hundred kings, the heir of two mighty kingdoms, standing at the closed portal, a poor, shivering maniac, bereft of all, and strong in nothing save love, that undying love, at once woman's greatest glory and her deepest misfortune.

Isabel, now seeing how vain was all opposition, soon suffered her daughter to depart: but grief and fatigue told fatally on her own broken health, and the news of a disgraceful scene that had occurred between Philip and Juana, in which, in a fit of jealousy, she personally assaulted the fair object of it, and caused the beautiful locks which had excited his admiration to be shorn, threw the unhappy queen into a violent fever, which she never entirely threw off. The deepest gloom overspread the kingdom. Prayers, processions, and pilgrimages were made for their queen, while an earthquake and tremendous hurricane were to the superstitious portents of coming evil. There she lay, at Medina del Campo, "her whole system pervaded by a consuming fever," while to every Spaniard it seemed as if the nation itself were about to pass away with her who was its greatest glory. Amidst pain, mental and physical, Isabel retained her dauntless energy, and from her couch directed the affairs of her kingdom, which had lately been threatened with a French invasion. She received and conversed with distinguished foreigners, amongst others the celebrated Prospero Colonna, who said, "he had come to see the woman who, from her couch, governed the world." Isabel died November 26, 1504, in the fifty-fourth year of her age. Her last moments were uncheered by the presence of any of her family. In her will were many wise provisions, and much tender mention of Ferdinand, who seems, by his many infidelities and selfish coldness, to have ill requited her constant regard. She desired to be buried with the utmost simplicity, and in her favorite city of Granada. The funeral procession was assailed by such storms, that three weeks elapsed ere it reached its destination. The swollen mountain torrents tore up the roads; bridges were carried away, and plains submerged. Horses and mules, and more than one of their riders perished. During the whole time, the sad cavalcade saw neither sun nor stars. At length dust to dust, and, in the monastery of St. Isabel, within the glorious Alhambra, lay side by side the conqueror and the conquered. Her remains were afterward removed, and placed beside those of Ferdinand, who survived her twelve years, in the mausoleum of the cathedral church of Granada.

In the downward progress of things in Spain, some of the most ill-advised measures of her administration have found favor, and been perpetuated, while the more salutary have been forgotten.

This may lead to a misconception of her real merits. In order to estimate these, we must listen to the voice of her contemporaries, the eye-witnesses of the condition in which she found the state, and in which she left it. We shall then see but one judgment formed of her, whether by foreigners or natives. The French and Italian writers equally join in celebrating the triumphant glories of her reign, and her magnanimity, wisdom, and purity of character. Her own subjects extol her as "the most brilliant exemplar of every virtue," and mourn over the day of her death as "the last of the prosperity and happiness of their country." While those who had nearer access to her person are unbounded in their admiration of those amiable qualities, whose full power is revealed only in the unrestrained intimacies of domestic life. The judgment of posterity has ratified the sentence of her own age. The most enlightened Spaniards of the present day, by no means insensible to the errors of her government, but more capable of appreciating its merits than those of a less-instructed age, bear honorable testimony to her deserts; and, while they pass over the bloated magnificence of succeeding monarchs, who arrest the popular eye, dwell with enthusiasm on Isabel's character, as the most truly great in their line of princes.

THE EARNEST CHRISTIAN.

MRS. ELIZABETH ROWE.

The tyrannic measures which Charles II. was induced to adopt against the nonconformists, consigned to the jail of Ilchester, in Somersetshire, Walter Singer, a gentleman of good family, and a dissenting minister, but neither a native nor an inhabitant of the place where he was imprisoned. Mrs. Elizabeth Portness, a pious lady of Ilchester, visited those persons who suffered for conscience sake; an acquaintance thus began, which ended in marriage when Mr. Singer was released. They had three daughters, two of whom died young. After the death of his wife, Mr. Singer removed from Ilchester to Frome, in the same county, where he had an estate.

Mr. Singer was firm in his own principles, but tolerant to those of others. He was on terms of friendship with Lord Weymouth, and was frequently visited by Bishop Kenn. He brought up his children in his own spirit of charity, and the whole life of his daughter Elizabeth revealed the pure and gentle influence of such teaching. She was the eldest of his three children, and the only one who lived to an advanced age: of her two sisters, she lost one in childhood; the other, who had a passion for study, and especially for medicine, in which she made considerable proficiency, reached her twentieth year, and died.

Elizabeth was born in 1674. She early displayed a great fondness for books, and a taste for poetry and painting, remarkable in one of her years. She was scarcely twelve when she began to write verses; at a still earlier age, she made attempts in drawing, and squeezed out the juices of herbs to serve her instead of colors. Mr. Singer procured her a master; and though she never attained any extraordinary proficiency in this delightful art, it was to her a source of constant pleasure during the whole of her long life.

Poetry was, however, the favorite amusement of Elizabeth Singer; for she does not appear to have ever considered it in any other light. She wrote verses with great facility, but seldom corrected her compositions; to which she attached little value. Poetry was to her an elegant and harmonious expression of thought and feeling; but she did not seek, and she certainly did not reach, that ideal beauty which is at once the delight and despair of art. Her temper was, however, essentially artistic, warm, and overflowing with life. Her conversation is represented as extremely captivating; she made many friends, and kept them all.

At the time when her poetic efforts were confined to the circle of home, some verses which she wrote drew the attention of the Weymouth family. She was not then twenty; but this incident was the origin of a long and pleasant friendship. The Honorable Mr. Thynne, son of Lord Weymouth, undertook to teach her the Italian language, in which she made rapid progress. In 1696, being then twenty-two, she published, at the request of her friends, various poems, to which she prefixed the poetical name of Philomela. A paraphrase of the thirty-eighth chapter of Job, written at the suggestion of Bishop Kenn, procured her some reputation.

Literary success changed nothing in her calm and domestic life; the friendship of the polite and the great, found and left her in her quiet home. The happiness which she thus enjoyed was deep, though peaceful. She loved her father with all the tenderness and reverence due to his virtues; an extract from a letter shows her feelings: "I have ease and plenty to the extent of my wishes, and can form desires of nothing but what my father's indulgence would procure; and I ask nothing of heaven but the good old man's life. The perfect sanctity of his life, and the benevolence of his temper make him a refuge to all in distress, to the widow and fatherless; the people load him with blessings and prayers when he goes abroad, which he never does but to reconcile his neighbors, or to right the injured and oppressed; the rest of his hours are entirely devoted to his private devotions, and to books, which are his perpetual entertainment." This excellent man, to whose example his daughter was, no doubt, deeply indebted, died in 1719, in sentiments of great piety. A friend, who witnessed his last hours, observed that he settled his affairs, and took leave of the world, with as much freedom and composure as if he had been setting out on a journey. His great care was to see that the widows and orphans with whose concerns he had been intrusted, might not be injured after his death. His cheerfulness and sweetness of temper never forsook him; but he sometimes felt his pulse, complained that it was still so regular, and smiled with a Christian's triumph at every sign and symptom of approaching death.

His only surviving daughter was already a widow when this event took place. Her charming countenance, agreeable conversation, and gentle temper, had early secured her a sufficient number of admirers; amongst the rest, Prior, the poet, who answered one of her pastorals in a very tender strain, and wished, it is said, to marry her; but she would not go beyond friendship with him. The young and learned Thomas Rowe was the preferred suitor. They were married in 1710; Elizabeth Singer being then thirty-six, her husband but twenty-three. Time, which had not taken from her the simplicity and purity of youth, had left her its freshness and comely aspect; without being a perfect beauty, she was extremely attractive. She had hair of a fine auburn hue; eyes of a deep grey, inclining to blue, and full of fire; her complexion was exquisitely pure; her voice soft and harmonious. The passion which her husband felt for her was both ardent and sincere; her gentleness, her compliance with his wishes, the many virtues which he daily witnessed in her life, endeared her to him; and marriage only increased his affection. They had been united about five years, when a fatal consumption, partly brought on by intense study, carried him off, in the twenty-eighth year of his age. He died, as he had wished to die, in the arms of his wife. She had attended on him during his illness with devoted affection; and though she survived him many years, she could not, a short time before her own death, hear his name mentioned without shedding fresh tears at the loss it recalled.

It was only to please her husband that Mrs. Rowe had ever lived, even for a time, in London. After his death she indulged her passion for solitude, by residing almost entirely at Frome; where, like her father, she devoted her days to piety, good deeds, and books. She gave little time to dress, none to play or pleasure; her leisure was devoted to literary works of a moral character, and to labors of charity. She was constantly engaged in making garments for the poor; she did so not only for the natives of the lower Palatinate, when the war drove them from their country, but also for whosoever around her needed such aid. She visited the sick, and instructed poor children; or caused them to be instructed at her expense. She never went out without being provided with coins of different value, to give away to objects of charity. The first sum of money which she received from a publisher was bestowed on a family in distress, and she once sold a piece of plate for a similar purpose.

She carried her indifference in money matters to an excess; there was no life she hated so much as the sordid and ungenerous love of gold, and none of which she was less guilty. She let her estates beneath their real value, and would not even allow unwilling tenants to be threatened with the seizure of their goods. But another trait of her character seems to us to paint her in a still more amiable light. Mrs. Rowe did not confine her charity to the miserable; she thought that "it was one of the greatest benefits that could be done to mankind, to free them from the cares and anxieties that attend a narrow fortune;" and she accordingly made large presents to persons who were not in the extremity of want. There are few, we believe, who are unable to feel the pleasure which attends the relief of great misery; but only the most delicate minds, and the most generous hearts, can experience the peculiar gratification which Mrs. Rowe found in relieving, not mere physical distress, but also those many painful cares which are the torment of poverty, as distinguished from want.

The solitude in which Mrs. Rowe lived did not separate her from many valued friends. Her name occurs frequently in the pleasant letters addressed by the Countess of Hartford to Dr. Isaac Watts;

and when this eminent man edited her "Devout Exercises of the Heart," it was to the countess that he dedicated them. All the poetical ardor which characterized Mrs. Rowe's turn of mind appears in this work; once widely popular, and still read by those who are not tempted to smile at the mysticism of a pure and pious heart. Tenderness and enthusiasm are essential to the religion of woman: that of man is more properly belief; hers is love. We will make no extracts from the Devout Exercises, but we will transcribe from Mrs. Rowe's secret effusions a page which needs no comment.

"I consecrate half of my yearly income to charitable uses; and though by this, according to human appearances, I have reduced myself to some necessity, I cast all my care on that gracious God to whom I am devoted, and to whose truth I subscribe with my hand. I attest his faithfulness, and bring in my testimony to the veracity of his word; I set to my seal that God is true; and O, by the God of truth, I swear to perform this, and beyond this . . . . . All that I have, beyond the bare convenience and necessity of life, shall surely be the Lord's; and O grant me sufficiency, that I may abound in every good work! O let me be the messenger of consolation to the poor! Here I am, Lord; send me. Let me have the honor to administer to the necessities of my brethren. I am, indeed, unworthy to wipe the feet of the least of the servants of my Lord, much more unworthy of this glorious commission; and yet, O send me, for thy goodness is free. Send whom thou wilt on embassies to kings and rulers of the earth, but let me be a servant to the servants of my Lord. Let me administer to the afflicted members of my exalted and glorious Redeemer. Let this be my lot, and I give the glories of the world to the wind."

This solemn vow, which, as Mrs. Rowe herself expressed it, in another part of her manuscripts, "was not made in an hour of fear and distress, but in the joy and gratitude of her soul," was religiously fulfilled, even when it exposed her to much personal inconvenience. To the end of her life, the poor shared with her in those blessings which she held from the bounty of God.

In 1736, her health began to fail. She prepared herself for death in that cheerful spirit with which she had lived. There seemed, however, no immediate cause for fear. After spending an evening in friendly conversation, she went up to her room; where, shortly afterward, her servant found her in the agonies of death. She was, according to her request, quietly buried by the side of her father, in their place of worship at Frome. Like him, she was lamented by all those who had known her, and by none more than the poor. Amongst her papers were found several letters addressed to valued friends. They express, in ardent and confident language, the belief that, like the spirit, the affections are immortal. To the end, the religion of Elizabeth Rowe remained a religion of love. To love God and his creatures had been her delight on earth, and she hoped to do both in heaven. As she fervently expresses it, "That benignity, that divine charity, which just warms the soul in these cold regions, will shine with new lustre, and burn with an eternal ardor in the happy seats of peace and love."

THE STAR OF AUSTRIA.

MARIA THERESA,

ARCHDUCHESS of Austria, Queen of Hungary and Bohemia, and Empress of Germany, born in 1717, was the eldest daughter of Charles VI. of Austria, Emperor of Germany. In 1724, Charles, by his will, known as the Pragmatic Sanction, regulated the order of succession in the house of Austria, declaring that in default of male issue, his eldest daughter should be heiress of all the Austrian dominions, and her children after her. The Pragmatic Sanction was guaranteed by the diet of the empire, and by all the German princes, and by several powers of Europe, but not by the Bourbons. In 1736, Maria Theresa married Francis of Lorraine, who, in 1737, became Grand-duke of Tuscany; and in 1739, Francis, with his consort, repaired to Florence.

Upon the death of Charles VI., in 1740, the ruling powers of Prussia, Bavaria, Saxony, France, Spain, and Sardinia, agreed to dismember the Austrian monarchy, to portions of which each laid claim. Maria Theresa, however, went immediately to Vienna, and took possession of Austria, Bohemia, and her other German states; she then repaired to Presburg, took the oaths to the constitution of Hungary, and was solemnly proclaimed queen of that kingdom in 1741. Frederic of Prussia offered the young queen his friendship on condition of her giving up to him Silesia, which she resolutely refused, and he then invaded that province. The Elector of Bavaria, assisted by the French, also invaded Austria, and pushed his troops as far as Vienna. Maria Theresa took refuge in Presburg, where she convoked the Hungarian diet; and appearing in the midst of them with her infant son in her arms, she made a heart-stirring appeal to their loyalty. The Hungarian nobles, drawing their swords, unanimously exclaimed, "Moriamur pro Rege nostro, Maria Theresa!" "We will die for our queen, Maria Theresa." They raised an army and drove the French and Bavarians out of the hereditary states. What would have been their reflections could those brave loyal Hungarians have foreseen that, in little more than a century, a descendant of this idolized queen would trample on their rights, overthrow their constitution, massacre the nobles and patriots, and ravage and lay waste their beautiful land! Well would it be for men to keep always in mind the warning of the royal Psalmist, "Put not your trust in princes."

In the mean time, Charles Albert, Elector of Bavaria, was chosen Emperor of Germany, by the diet assembled at Frankfort, under the name of Charles VII.

Frederic of Prussia soon made peace with Maria Theresa, who was obliged to surrender Silesia to him. In 1745, Charles VII. died, and Francis, Maria Theresa's husband, was elected emperor. In 1748, the peace of Aix-la-Chapelle terminated the war of the Austrian succession, and Maria Theresa was left in possession of all her hereditary dominions, except Silesia. In 1756, began the Seven Years' war between France, Austria, and Russia, on one side, and Prussia on the other. It ended in 1763, leaving Austria and Prussia with the same boundaries as before. In 1765, Maria Theresa lost her husband, for whom she wore mourning till her death. Her son Joseph was elected emperor. She however retained the administration of the government.

The only act of her political life with which she can be reproached is her participation in the first partition of Poland; and this she did very unwillingly, only when she was told that Russia and Prussia would not regard her disapproval, and that her refusal would endanger her own dominions.

The improvements Maria Theresa made in her dominions were many and important. She abolished torture, also the rural and personal services the peasants of Bohemia owed to their feudal superiors. She founded or enlarged in different parts of her extensive dominions several academies for the improvement of the arts and sciences; instituted numerous seminaries for the education of all ranks of the people; reformed the public schools, and ordered prizes to be distributed among the students who made the greatest progress in learning, or were distinguished for propriety of behavior, or purity of morals. She established prizes for those who excelled in different branches of manufacture, in geometry, mining, smelting metals, and even spinning. She particularly turned her attention to agriculture, which, on a medal struck by her order, was entitled the "Art which nourishes all other arts;" and founded a society of agriculture at Milan, with bounties to the peasants who obtained the best crops. She took away the pernicious rights which the convents and churches enjoyed of affording sanctuary to all criminals without distinction, and in many other ways evinced her regard for the welfare of the people. Although she was a pious and sincere Roman Catholic, not a blind devotee, but could discriminate between the temporal and spiritual jurisdiction. She put a check on the power of the Inquisition, which was finally abolished during the reign of her sons. She possessed the strong affection of her Belgian subjects; and never was Lombardy so prosperous or tranquil as under her reign. The population increased from 900,000 to 1,130,000. During her forty years' reign she showed an undeviating love of justice, truth, and clemency; and her whole conduct was characterized by a regard for propriety and self-respect.

Maria Theresa was, in her youth, exceedingly beautiful; and she retained the majesty, grace, and elegance of queenly attractiveness to the close of her life. She was sincere in her affection for her husband, and never marred the power of her loveliness by artifice or coquetry. She used her gifts and graces not for the gratification of her own vanity, to win lovers, but as a wise sovereign to gain over refractory subjects; and she succeeded: thus showing how potent is the moral strength with which woman is endowed. This queen has been censured for what was styled "neglect of her children."

Maria Theresa was the mother of sixteen children, all born within twenty years. There is every reason to suppose that her naturally warm affection, and her strong sense, would have rendered her, in a private station, an admirable, an exemplary parent; and it was not her fault, but rather her misfortune, that she was placed in a situation where the most sacred duties and feelings of her sex became in some measure secondary. While her numerous family were in their infancy, the empress was constantly and exclusively occupied in the public duties and cares of her high station; the affairs of government demanded almost every moment of her time. The court physician, Von Swietar, waited on her each morning at her *levee*, and brought her a minute report of the health of the princes and princesses. If one of them was indisposed, the mother, laying aside all other cares, immediately hastened to their apartment. They all spoke and wrote Italian with elegance and facility. Her children were brought up with extreme simplicity. They were not allowed to indulge in personal pride or caprice; their benevolent feelings were cultivated both by precept and example. They were sedulously instructed in the "Lives of the Saints," and all the tedious forms of unmeaning devotion, in which, according to the sincere conviction of their mother, all true piety consisted. A high sense of family pride, an unbounded devotion to the house of Austria, and to their mother, the empress, as the head of that house, was early impressed upon their minds, and became a ruling passion, as well as a principle of conduct with all of them.

We have only to glance back upon the history of the last fifty years to see the result of this mode of education. We find that the children of Maria Theresa, transplanted into different countries of Europe, carried with them their national and family prejudices; that some of them, in later years, supplied the defects of their early education, and became remarkable for talent and for virtue; that all of them, even those who were least distinguished and estimable, displayed occasionally both goodness of heart and elevation of character; and that their filial devotion to their mother, and what they considered *her* interests, was carried to an excess, which in one or two instances proved fatal to themselves. Thus it is apparent that her maternal duties were not neglected: had this been the case, she could never have acquired such unbounded influence over her children.

Maria Theresa had long been accustomed to look death in the face; and when the hour of trial came, her resignation, her fortitude, and her humble trust in heaven, never failed her. Her agonies during the last ten days of her life were terrible, but never drew from her a single expression of complaint or impatience. She was only apprehensive that her reason and her physical strength might fail her together. She was once heard to say, "God grant that these sufferings may soon terminate, for otherwise, I know not if I can much longer endure them."

After receiving the last sacraments, she summoned all her family to her presence, and solemnly recommended them to the care of the Emperor Joseph, her eldest son. "My son," said she, "as you are the heir to all my worldly possessions, I cannot dispose of them; but my children are still, as they have ever been, my *own*. I bequeath them to you; be to them a father. I shall die contented if you promise to take that office upon you." She then turned to her son Maximilian and her daughters, blessed them individually, in the tenderest terms, and exhorted them to obey and honor their elder brother as their father and sovereign. After repeated fits of agony and suffocation, endured, to the last, with the same invariable serenity and patience, death at length released her, and she expired on the 29th of November, 1780, in her sixty-fourth year. She was undoubtedly the greatest and best ruler who ever swayed the imperial sceptre of Austria; while, as a woman, she was one of the most amiable and exemplary of those in high station who lived in the eighteenth century.

THE PASTOR'S HELPMATE.

MADELEINE SALOME OBERLIN,

DISTINGUISHED for her intelligence, piety, and the perfect unison of soul which she enjoyed with her husband, the good and great John Frederic Oberlin, was born at Strasburg, in France. Her father, M. Witter, a man of property, who had married a relative of the Oberlin family, gave his daughter an excellent education. John James Oberlin was the pastor of Waldbach, a small village in the Ban de la Roche, or Valley of Stones, a lonely, sterile place, in the north-eastern part of France. Here he devoted himself to the duties of his holy office, doing good to all around him. Under his care and instruction, the poor, ignorant peasantry became pious, industrious, and happy. In all his actions he followed what he believed to be a divine influence, or the leadings of Providence; and his courtship and marriage were guided by his religious feelings. Oberlin's sister resided with him at Waldbach, and managed his house. Madeleine Witter came to visit Sophia Oberlin. Miss Witter was amiable, and her mind had been highly cultivated; but she was fond of fashion and display. Twice had Frederic Oberlin declined to marry young ladies who had been commended to him, because he had felt an inward admonition that neither of these was for him. But now when Madeleine came before him, the impression was different. Two days prior to her intended departure, a voice seemed to whisper distinctly, "Take her for thy partner!" "It is impossible," thought he; "our dispositions do not agree." Still the secret voice whispered, "Take her for thy partner!" He slept little that night, and in his morning prayer, he earnestly entreated God to give him a sign whether this event was in accordance with the divine will; solemnly declaring that if Madeleine acceded to the proposition with great readiness, he should consider the voice he had heard as a leading of Providence.

He found his cousin in the garden, and immediately began the conversation by saying, "You are about to leave us, my dear friend. I have received an intimation that you are destined to be the partner of my life. Before you go will you give me your candid opinion whether you can resolve upon this step?"

With blushing frankness, Madeleine placed her hand within his; and then he knew that she would be his wife.

They were married on the 6th of July, 1768. Miss Witter had been accustomed to protest that she would not marry a clergyman; but she was devotedly attached to her excellent husband, and cordially assisted in all his plans. No dissatisfaction at her humble lot, no complaints of the arduous duties belonging to their peculiar situation, marred their mutual happiness. They were far removed from the vain excitements and tinsel splendor of the world; they were surrounded by the rude, illiterate peasantry; and every step in improvement was contested by ignorance and prejudice; but they were near each other, and both were near to God.

The following prayer, written soon after their union, shows what spirit pervaded their peaceful dwelling:—

PRAYER OF OBERLIN AND HIS WIFE FOR THE BLESSING AND GRACE OF GOD.

"Holy Spirit! descend into our hearts; assist us to pray with fervor from our inmost souls. Permit thy children, O gracious Father, to present themselves before thee, in order to ask of thee what is necessary for them. May we love each other only in thee, and in our Saviour Jesus Christ, as being members of his body. Enable us at all times to look solely to thee, to walk before thee, and to be united together in thee; that thus we may grow daily in the spiritual life.

"Grant that we may be faithful in the exercise of our duties, that we may stimulate each other therein, warning each other of our faults, and seeking together for pardon in the blood of Jesus Christ. When we pray together (and may we pray much and frequently), be thou, O Lord Jesus, with us; kindle our fervor, O Heavenly Father, and grant us, for the sake of Jesus Christ, whatever thy Holy Spirit shall teach us to ask.

"Seeing that in this life thou hast placed the members of our household under our authority, give us wisdom and strength to guide them in a manner conformable to thy will. May we always set them a good example, following that of Abraham, who commanded his children and his household after him, to keep the way of the Lord, in doing what is right. If thou givest us children, and preservest them to us, O grant us grace to bring them up to thy service, to teach them early to know, to fear, and to love thee, and to pray to that God who has made a covenant with them, that, conformably to the engagement which will be undertaken for them at their baptism, they may remain faithful from the cradle to the grave. O Heavenly Father, may we inculcate thy word, according to thy will, all our lives, with gentleness, love and patience, both at their rising up and lying down, at home and abroad, and under all circumstances; and do thou render it meet for the children to whom thou hast given life only as a means of coming to thee.

"And when we go together to the Holy Supper, O ever give us renewed grace, renewed strength, and renewed courage, for continuing to walk in the path to heaven; and, as we can only approach thy table four times in the year, grant that in faith we may much more frequently be there, yes, every day and every hour; that we may always keep death in view, and always be prepared for it; and if we may be permitted to solicit it of thee, O grant that we may not long be separated from each other, but that the death of the one may be speedily, and very speedily, followed by that of the other.

"Hear, O gracious Father, in the name of Jesus Christ, thy well-beloved son. And, O merciful Redeemer, may we both love thee with ardent devotion, always walking and holding communion with thee, not placing our confidence in our own righteousness and in our own works, but only in thy blood, and in thy merits. Be with us; preserve us faithful; and grant, Lord Jesus, that we may soon see thee. Holy Spirit, dwell always in our hearts; teach us to lift our thoughts continually to our gracious Father; impart to us thy strength, or thy consolation, as our wants may be. And to thee, to the Father, and to the Son, be praise, honor, and glory, for ever and ever. Amen."

For sixteen years Mrs. Oberlin was a beloved friend and useful assistant to her husband. In their tastes and pursuits, in their opinions and feelings, they became entirely one. She managed his household discreetly, educated their children judiciously, and entered into all his benevolent plans with earnestness and prudence.

She died suddenly, in January, 1784, a few weeks after the birth of her ninth and last child. Her death was deeply mourned in the Ban de la Roche, for her assistance and sympathy had always been freely offered to the poor and the afflicted.

Oberlin survived his wife forty-two years; but never separated himself from her memory. He devoted several hours every day to thoughts of her; and held, as he thought, communion with her soul. Thus holy and eternal may be the true love of husband and wife.

THE CHILDREN'S FAVORITE.

ANNA LETITIA BARBAULD.

To WHOM the cause of rational education is much indebted, was the eldest child, and only daughter, of the Rev. John Aiken, D.D. She was born on the 20th of June, 1743, at Kibworth Harcourt, in Leicestershire, England, where her father was at that time master of a boys' school. From her childhood she manifested great quickness of intellect, and her education was conducted with much care by her parents. In 1773, she was induced to publish a volume of her poems, and within the year four editions of the work were called for. In the same year she published, in conjunction with her brother, Dr. Aiken, a volume called "Miscellaneous Pieces in Prose." In 1774, Miss Aiken married the Rev. Rochemont Barbauld, a dissenting minister, descended from a family of French Protestants. He had charge, at that time, of a congregation at Palgrave, in Suffolk, where he also opened a boarding-school for boys, the success of which is, in a great measure, to be attributed to Mrs. Barbauld's exertions. She also took several very young boys as her own entire charge, among whom were Lord Denman, afterward Chief Justice of England, and Sir William Gell. It was for these boys that she composed her "Hymns in Prose for Children." In 1775, she published a volume entitled, "Devotional Pieces, compiled from the Psalms of David," with "Thoughts on the Devotional Taste, and on Sects and Establishments;" and also her "Early Lessons," which still stands unrivaled among children's books.

In 1786, after a tour on the continent, Mr. and Mrs. Barbauld established themselves at Hampstead, and there several tracts proceeded from the pen of our authoress on the topics of the day, in all which she espoused the principles of the Whigs. She also assisted her father in preparing a series of tales for children, entitled "Evenings at Home," and she wrote critical essays on Akenside and Collins, prefixed to editions of their works. In 1802, Mr. Barbauld became pastor of the congregation (formerly Dr. Price's) at Newington Green, also in the vicinity of London; and, quitting Hampstead, they took up their abode in the village of Stoke Newington. In 1803, Mrs. Barbauld compiled a selection of essays from the "Spectator," "Tatler," and "Guardian," to which she prefixed a preliminary essay; and, in the following year, she edited the correspondence of Richardson, and wrote an interesting and elegant life of the novelist. Her husband died in 1808, and Mrs. Barbauld has recorded her feelings on this melancholy event in a poetical dirge to his memory, and also in her poem of "Eighteen Hundred and Eleven." Seeking relief in literary occupation, she also edited a collection of the British novelists, published in 1810, with an introductory essay, and biographical and critical notices. After a gradual decay, this accomplished and excellent woman died on the 9th of March, 1825. Some of the lyrical pieces of Mrs. Barbauld are flowing and harmonious, and her "Ode to Spring" is a happy imitation of Collins. She wrote also several poems in blank verse, characterized by a serious tenderness and elevation of thought. "Her earliest pieces," says her niece, Miss Lucy Aiken, "as well as her more recent ones, exhibit, in their imagery and allusions, the fruits of extensive and varied reading. In youth, the power of her imagination was counterbalanced by the activity of her intellect, which exercised itself in rapid but not unprofitable excursions over almost every field of knowledge. In age, when this activity abated, imagination appeared to exert over her an undiminished sway." Charles James Fox is said to have been a great admirer of Mrs. Barbauld's songs; but they are by no means the best of her compositions, being generally artificial, and unimpassioned in their character.

Her works show great powers of mind, an ardent love of civil and religious liberty, and that genuine and practical piety which ever distinguished her character.

In many a bosom has Mrs. Barbauld, "by deep,

strong, and permanent association, laid a foundation for practical devotion" in after life. In her highly-poetical language, only inferior to that of Holy Writ, when "the winter is over and gone, and buds come out on the trees, and the crimson blossoms of the peach and the nectarine are seen, and the green leaves sprout," what heart can be so insensible as not to join in the grand chorus of nature, and "on every hill, and in every green field, to offer the sacrifice of thanksgiving and the incense of praise!"

With each revolving year, the simple lessons of infancy are recalled to our minds, when we watch the beautiful succession of nature, and think, "How doth every plant know its season to put forth? They are marshaled in order; each one knoweth his place, and standeth up in his own rank."

"The snowdrop and the primrose make haste to lift their heads above the ground. When the spring cometh they say, here we are! The carnation waiteth for the full strength of the year; and the hardy laurustinus cheereth the winter months."

Who can observe all this, and not exclaim with her, "Every field is like an open book; every painted flower hath a lesson written on its leaves.

"Every murmuring brook hath a tongue; a voice is in every whispering wind.

"They all speak of him who made them; they all tell us he is very good."

Such sentiments, instilled into the hearts of children, have power, with the blessing of God, to preserve the moral feelings pure and holy; and also to keep the love of nature and the memories of early life among the sweetest pleasures of mature life.

In a memoir written by Miss Lucy Aiken, the niece of Mrs. Barbauld, and kindred in genius as well as in blood, we find this beautiful and just description of the subject of our sketch:

"To claim for Mrs. Barbauld the praise of purity and elevation of mind may well appear superfluous. Her education and connections, the course of her life, the whole tenor of her writings, bear abundant testimony to this part of her character. It is a higher, or at least a rarer commendation to add, that no one ever better loved 'a sister's praise,' even that of such sisters as might have been peculiarly regarded in the light of rivals. She was acquainted with almost all the principal female writers of her time; and there was not one of the number whom she failed frequently to mention in terms of admiration, esteem, or affection, whether in conversation, in letters to her friends, or in print. To humbler aspirants in the career of letters, who often applied to her for advice or assistance, she was invariably courteous, and in many instances essentially serviceable. The sight of youth and beauty was peculiarly gratifying to her fancy and her feelings; and children and young persons, especially females, were accordingly large sharers in her benevolence: she loved their society, and would often invite them to pass weeks or months in her house, when she spared no pains to amuse and instruct them; and she seldom failed, after they had quitted her, to recall herself from time to time to their recollection, by affectionate and playful letters, or welcome presents.

"In the conjugal relation her conduct was guided by the highest principles of love and duty. As a sister, the uninterrupted flow of her affection, manifested by numberless tokens of love—not alone to her brother, but to every member of his family—will ever be recalled by them with emotions of tenderness, respect, and gratitude. She passed through a long life without having dropped, it is said, a single friend."

Since the decease of Mrs. Barbauld, her productions have been collected, published in three volumes, and circulated widely both in England and the United States. Some of the prose articles are of extraordinary merit: the one which we here insert has rarely been excelled for originality of thought and vigor of expression. Its sentiments will never become obsolete, nor its truths lose their value.

ON EDUCATION.

The other day I paid a visit to a gentleman with whom, though greatly my superior in fortune, I have long been in habits of an easy intimacy. He rose in the world by honorable industry, and married rather late in life, a lady to whom he had been long attached, and in whom centered the wealth of several expiring families. Their earnest wish for children was not immediately gratified. At length they were made happy by a son, who, from the moment he was born, engrossed all their care and attention. My friend received me in his library, where I found him busied in turning over books of education, of which he had collected all that were worthy of notice, from Xenophon to Locke, and from Locke to Catharine Macauley. As he knows I have been engaged in the business of instruction, he did me the honor to consult me on the subject of his researches, hoping, he said, that, out of all the systems before him, we should be able to form a plan equally complete and comprehensive; it being the determination of both himself and his lady to choose the best that could be had, and to spare neither pains nor expense in making their child all that was great and good. I gave him my thoughts with the utmost freedom, and after I returned home, threw upon paper the observations which had occurred to me.

The first thing to be considered, with respect to education, is the object of it. This appears to me to have been generally misunderstood. Education, in its largest sense, is a thing of great scope and extent. It includes the whole process by which a human being is formed to be what he is, in habits, principles, and cultivation of every kind. But of this, a very small part is in the power even of the parent himself; a smaller still can be directed by purchased tuition of any kind. You engage for your child masters and tutors at large salaries; and you do well, for they are competent to instruct him; they will give him the means, at least, of acquiring science and accomplishments; but in the business of education, properly so called, they can do little for you. Do you ask, then, what will educate your son? Your example will educate him; your conversation with your friends; the business he sees you transact; the likings and dislikings you express; these will educate him;—the society you live in will educate him; your domestics will educate him; above all, your rank and situation in life, your house, your table, your pleasure-grounds, your hounds and your stables will educate him. It is not in your power to withdraw him from the continual influence of these things, except you were to withdraw yourself from them also. You speak of *beginning* the education of your son. The moment he was able to form an idea his education was already begun; the education of circumstances—insensible education—which, like insensible perspiration, is of more constant and powerful effect, and of infinitely more consequence to the habit, than that which is more direct and apparent. This education goes on at every instant of time; it goes on like time; you can neither stop it nor turn its course. What these have a tendency to make your child, that he will be. Maxims and documents are good precisely till they are tried, and no longer; they will teach him to talk, and nothing more. The *circumstances* in which your son is placed will be even more prevalent than your example; and you have no right to expect him to become what you yourself are, but by the same means. You, that have toiled during youth, to set your son upon higher ground, and to enable him to begin where you left off, do not expect that son to be what you were—diligent, modest, active, simple in his tastes, fertile in resources. You have put him under quite a different master. Poverty educated you; wealth will educate him. You cannot suppose the result will be the same. You must not even expect that he will be what you now are; for though relaxed perhaps from the severity of your frugal habits, you still derive advantage from having formed them; and, in your heart, you like plain dinners, and early hours, and old friends, whenever your fortune will permit you to enjoy them. But it will not be so with your son: his tastes will be formed by your present situation, and in no degree by your former one. But I take great care, you will say, to counteract these tendencies, and to bring him up in hardy and simple manners; I know their value, and am resolved that he shall acquire no other. Yes, you make him hardy; that is to say, you take a counting-house in a good air, and make him run, well clothed and carefully attended, for, it may be, an hour in a clear frosty winter's day upon your graveled terrace; or perhaps you take the puny shivering infant from his warm bed, and dip him in an icy-cold bath, and you think you have done great matters.

And so you have; you have done all you can. But you were suffered to run abroad half the day on a bleak heath, in weather fit and unfit, wading barefoot through dirty ponds, sometimes losing your way benighted, scrambling over hedges, climbing trees, in perils every hour both of life and limb. Your life was of very little consequence to any one; even your parents, encumbered with a numerous family, had little time to indulge the softnesses of affection, or the solicitude of anxiety; and to every one else it was of no consequence at all. It is not possible for you, it would not even be right for you, in your present situation, to pay no more attention to your child than was paid to you. In these mimic experiments of education, there is always something which distinguishes them from reality; some weak part left unfortified, for the arrows of misfortune to find their way into. Achilles was a young nobleman, *dios Achilleus*, and therefore, though he had Chiron for his tutor, there was one foot left undipped. You may throw by Rousseau; your parents practised without having read it; you may read, but imperious circumstances forbid you the practice of it.

You are sensible of the advantages of simplicity of diet; and you make a point of restricting that of your child to the plainest food, for you are resolved that he shall not be nice. But this plain food is of the choicest quality, prepared by your own cook; his fruit is ripened from your walls; his cloth, his glasses, all the accompaniments of the table, are such as are only met with in families of opulence; the very servants who attend him are neat, well dressed, and have a certain air of fashion. You may call this simplicity; but I say he will be nice—for it is a kind of simplicity which only wealth can attain to, and which will subject him to be disgusted at all common tables. Besides, he will from time to time partake of those delicacies which your table abounds with; you yourself will give him of them occasionally; you would be unkind if you did not: your servants, if good natured, will do the same. Do you think you can keep the full stream of luxury running by his lips, and he not taste of it? Vain imagination!

I would not be understood to inveigh against wealth, or against the enjoyments of it; they are real enjoyments, and allied to many elegances in manners and in taste; I only wish to prevent unprofitable pains and inconsistent expectations.

You are sensible of the benefit of early rising; and you may, if you please, make it a point that your daughter shall retire with her governess, and your son with his tutor, at the hour when you are preparing to see company. But their sleep, in the first place, will not be so sweet and undisturbed amidst the rattle of carriages, and the glare of tapers glancing through the rooms, as that of the village child in his quiet cottage, protected by silence and darkness; and moreover, you may depend upon it, that as the coercive power of education is laid aside, they will in a few months slide into the habitudes of the rest of the family, whose hours are determined by their company and situation in life. You have, however, done good, as far as it goes; it is something gained, to defer pernicious habits, if we cannot prevent them.

There is nothing which has so little share in education as direct precept. To be convinced of this, we need only reflect that there is no one point we labor more to establish with children, than that of their speaking truth; and there is not any in which we succeed worse. And why? Because children readily see we have an interest in it. Their speaking truth is used by us as an engine of government—"Tell me, my dear child, when you have broken any thing, and I will not be angry with you." "Thank you for nothing," says the child; "if I prevent you from finding it out, I am sure you will not be angry:" and nine times out of ten he can prevent it. He knows that, in the common intercourses of life, you tell a thousand falsehoods. But these are necessary lies on important occasions.

Your child is the best judge how much occasion he has to tell a lie: he may have as great occasion for it as you have to conceal a bad piece of news from a sick friend, or to hide your vexation from an unwelcome visitor. That authority which extends its claims over every action, and even every thought, which insists upon an answer to every interrogation, however indiscreet or oppressive to the feelings, will, in young or old, produce falsehood;

or, if in some few instances the deeply-imbibed fear of future and unknown punishment should restrain from direct falsehood, it will produce a habit of dissimulation, which is still worse. The child, the slave, or the subject, who, on proper occasions, may not say, "I do not choose to tell," will certainly, by the circumstances in which you place him, be driven to have recourse to deceit, even should he not be countenanced by your example.

I do not mean to assert that sentiments inculcated in education have no influence;—they have much, though not the most: but it is the sentiments we let drop occasionally, the conversation they overhear when playing unnoticed in a corner of the room, which has an effect upon children; and not what is addressed directly to them in the tone of exhortation. If you would know precisely the effect these set discourses have upon your child, be pleased to reflect upon that which a discourse from the pulpit, which you have reason to think merely professional, has upon you. Children have almost an intuitive discernment between the maxims you bring forward for their use, and those by which you direct your own conduct. Be as cunning as you will, they are always more cunning than you. Every child knows whom his father and mother love and see with pleasure, and whom they dislike; for whom they think themselves obliged to set out their best plate and china; whom they think it an honor to visit, and upon whom they confer honor by admitting them to their company. "Respect nothing so much as virtue," says Eugenio to his son; "virtue and talents are the only grounds of distinction." The child presently has occasion to inquire why his father pulls off his hat to some people and not to others; he is told, that outward respect must be proportioned to different stations in life. This is a little difficult of comprehension: however, by dint of explanation, he gets over it tolerably well. But he sees his father's house in the bustle and hurry of preparation; common business laid aside, everybody in movement, an unusual anxiety to please and to shine. Nobody is at leisure to receive his caresses or attend to his questions; his lessons are interrupted, his hours deranged. At length a guest arrives: it is my Lord ——, whom he has heard you speak of twenty times as one of the most worthless characters upon earth. Your child, Eugenio, has received a lesson of education. Resume, if you will, your systems of morality on the morrow, you will in vain attempt to eradicate it. "You expect company, mamma: must I be dressed to-day?" "No, it is only good Mrs. Such-a-one." Your child has received a lesson of education, one which he well understands, and will long remember. You have sent your child to a public school; but to secure his morals against the vice which you too justly apprehend abounds there, you have given him a private tutor, a man of strict morals and religion. He may help him to prepare his tasks; but do you imagine it will be in his power to form his mind? His school-fellows, the allowance you give him, the manners of the age and of the place, will do that; and not the lectures which he is obliged to hear. If these are different from what you yourself experienced, you must not be surprised to see him gradually recede from the principles, civil and religious, which you hold, and break off from your connections, and adopt manners different from your own. This is remarkably exemplified amongst those of the Dissenters who have risen to wealth and consequence. I believe it would be difficult to find an instance of families, who for three generations have kept their carriage and continued Dissenters.

Education, it is often observed, is an expensive thing. It is so; but the paying for lessons is the smallest part of the cost. If you would go to the price of having your son a worthy man, you must be so yourself; your friends, your servants, your company must be all of that stamp. Suppose this to be the case, much is done: but there will remain circumstances which perhaps you cannot alter, that will still have their effect. Do you wish him to love simplicity? Would you be content to lay down your coach, to drop your title? Where is the parent who would do this to educate his son? You carry him to the workshops of artisans, and show him different machines and fabrics, to awaken his ingenuity. The necessity of getting his bread would awaken it much more effectually. The single circumstance of having a fortune to get, or a fortune to spend, will probably operate more strongly upon his mind, not only than your precepts, but even than your example. You wish your child to be modest and unassuming; you are so, perhaps, yourself—and you pay liberally a preceptor for giving him lessons of humility. You do not perceive, that the very circumstance of having a man of letters and accomplishments retained about his person, for his sole advantage, tends more forcibly to inspire him with an idea of self-consequence than all the lessons he can give him to repress it. "Why do not you look sad, you rascal?" says the undertaker to his man in the play of 'The Funeral;' "I give you I know not how much money for looking sad, and the more I give you, the gladder I think you are." So will it be with the wealthy heir. The lectures that are given him on condescension and affability, only prove to him upon how much higher ground he stands than those about him; and the very pains that are taken with his moral character will make him proud, by showing him how much he is the object of attention. You cannot help these things. Your servants, out of respect to you, will bear with his petulance; your company, out of respect to you, will forbear to check his impatience. And you yourself, if he is clever, will repeat his observations.

In the exploded doctrine of sympathies, you are directed, if you have cut your finger, to let that alone, and put your plaster upon the knife. This is very bad doctrine, I must confess, in philosophy;

but very good in morals. Is a man luxurious, self-indulgent? do not apply your *physic of the soul* to him, but cure his fortune. Is he haughty? cure his rank, his title. Is he vulgar? cure his company. Is he diffident or mean-spirited? cure his poverty, give him consequence—but these prescriptions go far beyond the family recipes of education.

What then is the result? In the first place, that we should contract our ideas of education, and expect no more from it than it is able to perform. It can give instruction. There will always be an essential difference between a human being cultivated and uncultivated. Education can provide proper instructors in the various arts and sciences, and portion out to the best advantage those precious hours of youth which never will return. It can likewise give, in a great degree, personal habits; and even if these should afterward give way under the influence of contrary circumstances, your child will feel the good effects of them, for the later and the less will he go into what is wrong. Let us also be assured that the business of education, properly so called, is not transferable. You may engage masters to instruct your child in this or the other accomplishment, but you must educate him yourself. You not only ought to do it, but you must do it, whether you intend it or no. As education is a thing necessary for all; for the poor and for the rich, for the illiterate as well as for the learned; Providence has not made it dependent upon systems uncertain, operose, and difficult of investigation. It is not necessary, with Rousseau or Madame Genlis, to devote to the education of one child the talents and the time of a number of grown men; to surround him with an artificial world; and to counteract, by maxims, the natural tendencies of the situation he is placed in in society. Every one has time to educate his child: the poor man educates him while working in his cottage—the man of business, while employed in his counting-house.

Do we see a father who is diligent in his profession, domestic in his habits, whose house is the resort of well-informed intelligent people—a mother whose time is usefully filled, whose attention to her duties secures esteem, and whose amiable manners attract affection? Do not be solicitous, respectable couple, about the moral education of your offspring; do not be uneasy because you cannot surround them with the apparatus of books and systems; or fancy that you must retire from the world to devote yourselves to their improvement. In your world they are brought up much better than they could be under any plan of factitious education which you could provide for them; they will imbibe affection from your caresses; taste from your conversation; urbanity from the commerce of your society; and mutual love from your example. Do not regret that you are not rich enough to provide tutors and governors to watch his steps with sedulous and servile anxiety, and furnish him with maxnns it is morally impossible he should act upon when grown up. Do not you see how seldom this over-culture produces its effect, and how many shining and excellent characters start up every day from the bosom of obscurity with scarcely any care at all?

Are children then to be neglected? Surely not; but having given them the instruction and accomplishments which their situation in life requires, let us reject superfluous solicitude, and trust that their characters will form themselves from the spontaneous influence of good examples, and circumstances which impel them to useful action.

But the education of your house, important as it is, is only a part of a more comprehensive system. Providence takes your child where you leave him. Providence continues his education upon a larger scale, and by a process which includes means far more efficacious. Has your son entered the world at eighteen, opinionated, haughty, rash, inclined to dissipation? Do not despair; he may yet be cured of these faults, if it please Heaven. There are remedies which you could not persuade yourself to use, if they were in your power, and which are specific in cases of this kind. How often do we see the presumptuous, giddy youth changed into the wise counselor, the considerate, steady friend! how often the thoughtless, gay girl into the sober wife, the affectionate mother! Faded beauty, humbled self-consequence, disappointed ambition, loss of fortune—this is the rough physic provided by

Providence to meliorate the temper, to correct the offensive petulances of youth, and bring out all the energies of the finished character. Afflictions soften the proud; difficulties push forward the ingenious; successful industry gives consequence and credit, and develops a thousand latent good qualities. There is no malady of the mind so inveterate, which this education of events is not calculated to cure if life were long enough; and shall we not hope that He, in whose hand are all the remedial processes of nature, will renew the discipline in another state, and finish the imperfect man?

States are educated as individuals—by circumstances; the prophet may cry aloud, and spare not; the philosopher may descant on morals; eloquence may exhaust itself in invective against the vices of the age; these vices will certainly follow certain states of poverty or riches, ignorance or high civilization. But what these gentle alternatives fail of doing may be accomplished by an unsuccessful war, a loss of trade, or any of those great calamities by which it pleases Providence to speak to a nation in such language as *will* be heard. If, as a nation, we would be cured of pride, it must be by mortification; if of luxury, by a national bankruptcy, perhaps; if of injustice, or the spirit of domination, by a loss of national consequence. In comparison of these strong remedies, a fast, or a sermon, are prescriptions of very little efficacy.

A short extract from another excellent Essay we

will here introduce, for its good sense, and striking application to the present times:—

ON INCONSISTENCY IN OUR EXPECTATIONS.

"But is it not some reproach upon the economy of Providence that such a one, who is a mean, dirty fellow, should have amassed wealth enough to buy half a nation?" Not in the least. He made himself a mean dirty fellow for that very end. He has paid his health, his conscience, his liberty for it; and will you envy him his bargain? Will you hang your head and blush in his presence, because he outshines you in equipage and show? Lift up your brow with a noble confidence, and say to yourself, I have not these things, it is true; but it is because I have not sought, because I have not desired them; it is because I possess something better. I have chosen my lot. I am content and satisfied.

You are a modest man—you love quiet and independence, and have a delicacy and reserve in your temper which renders it impossible for you to elbow your way in the world, and be the herald of your own merits. Be content then with a modest retirement, with the esteem of your intimate friends, with the praises of a blameless heart, and a delicate, ingenuous spirit; but resign the splendid distinctions of the world to those who can better scramble for them.

The man whose tender sensibility of conscience

and strict regard to the rules of morality make him scrupulous and fearful of offending, is often heard to complain of the disadvantages he lies under in every path of honor and profit. "Could I but get over some nice points, and conform to the practice and opinion of those about me, I might stand as fair a chance as others for dignities and preferment." And why can you not? What hinders you from discarding this troublesome scrupulosity of yours, which stands so grievously in your way? If it be a small thing to enjoy a healthful mind, sound at the very core, that does not shrink from the keenest inspection; inward freedom from remorse and perturbation; unsullied whiteness and simplicity of manners; a genuine integrity—

> "Pure in the last recesses of the mind;"

if you think these advantages an inadequate recompense for what you resign, dismiss your scruples this instant, and be a slave-merchant, a parasite, or —what you please—

> "If these be motives weak, break off betimes;"

and as you have not spirit to assert the dignity of virtue, be wise enough not to forego the emoluments of vice.

I much admire the spirit of the ancient philosophers, in that they never attempted, as our moralists often do, to lower the tone of philosophy, and make it consistent with all the indulgences of indolence and sensuality. They never thought of having the bulk of mankind for their disciples; but kept themselves as distinct as possible from a worldly life. They plainly told men what sacrifices were required, and what advantages they were which might be expected:—

> "Si virtus hoc una potest dare, fortis omisses
> Hoc age deliciis . . . ."

If you would be a philosopher, these are the terms. You must do thus and thus; there is no other way. If not, go and be one of the vulgar.

There is no one quality gives so much dignity to a character as consistency of conduct. Even if a man's pursuits be wrong and unjustifiable, yet if they are prosecuted with steadiness and vigor, we cannot withhold our admiration. The most characteristic mark of a great mind is to choose some one important object, and pursue it through life. It was this made Cæsar a great man. His object was ambition; he pursued it steadily, and was always ready to sacrifice to it every interfering passion or inclination.

* * * * *

There is a different air and complexion in characters as well as in faces, though perhaps equally beautiful; and the excellences of one cannot be transferred to the other. Thus, if one man possesses a stoical apathy of soul, acts independent of the opinion of the world, and fulfils every duty with mathematical exactness, you must not expect that man to be greatly influenced by the weakness of pity, or the partialities of friendship; you must not be offended that he does not fly to meet you after a short absence; or require from him the convivial spirit and honest effusions of a warm, open, susceptible heart. If another is remarkable for a lively active zeal, inflexible integrity, a strong indignation against vice, and freedom in reproving it, he will probably have some little bluntness in his address not altogether suitable to polished life; he will want the winning arts of conversation; he will disgust by a kind of haughtiness and negligence in his manner, and often hurt the delicacy of his acquaintance with harsh and disagreeable truths.

We do not consider the poetry of Mrs. Barbauld equal to her prose writings; but there is a benignity, mingled with vivacity, in some of her poetical productions which make them always pleasant, as the face of a cheerful friend.

WASHING-DAY.

THE Muses are turn'd gossips; they have lost
The buskin'd step, and clear high-sounding phrase,
Language of gods. Come then, domestic Muse,
In slipshod measure loosely prattling on
Of farm or orchard, pleasant curds and cream,
Or drowning flies, or shoe lost in the mire
By little whimpering boy, with rueful face;
Come, Muse, and sing the dreaded Washing-Day.
Ye who beneath the yoke of wedlock bend,
With bowed soul, full well ye ken the day
Which week, smooth sliding after week, brings on

Too soon;—for to that day nor peace belongs
Nor comfort;—ere the first gray streak of dawn,
The red-armed washers come and chase repose.
Nor pleasant smile, nor quaint device of mirth,
E'er visited that day; the very cat,
From the wet kitchen scared and reeking hearth,
Visits the parlor—an unwonted guest.
The silent breakfast-meal is soon dispatch'd;
Uninterrupted, save by anxious looks
Cast at the lowering sky, if sky should lower.
From that last evil, O preserve us, heavens!
For should the skies pour down, adieu to all
Remains of quiet; then expect to hear
Of sad disasters—dirt and gravel stains
Hard to efface, and loaded lines at once
Snapped short—and linen-horse by dog thrown down,
And all the petty miseries of life.
Saints have been calm while stretched upon the rack,
And Guatimozin smiled on burning coals;
But never yet did housewife notable
Greet with a smile a rainy washing-day.
—But grant the welkin fair, require not thou
Who call'st thyself perchance the master there,
Or study swept or nicely dusted coat,
Or usual 'tendance;—ask not, indiscreet,
Thy stockings mended, though the yawning rents
Gape wide as Erebus; nor hope to find
Some snug recess impervious; shouldst thou try
The 'customed garden walks, thine eye shall rue
The budding fragrance of thy tender shrubs,
Myrtle or rose, all crushed beneath the weight
Of coarse check'd apron—with impatient hand
Twitched off when showers impend; or crossing lines
Shall mar thy musings, as the wet cold sheet
Flaps in thy face abrupt. Woe to the friend
Whose evil stars have urged him forth to claim
On such a day the hospitable rites!
Looks, blank at best, and stinted courtesy
Shall he receive. Vainly he feeds his hopes
With dinner of roast chicken, savory pie,

Or tart, or pudding;—pudding he nor tart
That day shall eat; nor, though the husband try,
Mending what can't be helped, to kindle mirth
From cheer deficient, shall his consort's brow
Clear up propitious;—the unlucky guest
In silence dines, and early slinks away.
I well remember, when a child, the awe
This day struck into me; for then the maids,
I scarce knew why; look'd cross, and drove me from them.
Nor soft caress could I obtain, nor hope
Usual indulgences; jelly or creams,
Relic of costly suppers, and set by
For me their petted one; or butter'd toast,
When butter was forbid; or thrilling tale
Of ghost, or witch, or murder—so I went
And shelter'd me beside the parlor fire;
There my dear grandmother, eldest of forms,
Tended the little ones, and watched from harm,
Anxiously fond, though oft her spectacles
With elfin cunning hid, and oft the pins
Drawn from her ravell'd stocking, might have sour'd
One less indulgent.—
At intervals my mother's voice was heard,
Urging dispatch; briskly the work went on,
All hands employ'd to wash, to rinse, to ring,
To fold, and starch, and clap, and iron, and plait.
Then would I sit me down, and ponder much
Why washings were. Sometimes through hollow bowl
Of pipe amused we blew, and sent aloft
The floatting bubbles; little dreaming then
To see, Mongolfier, thy silken ball
Ride buoyant through the clouds—so near approach
The sports of children and the toils of men.
Earth, air, and sky, and ocean, hath its bubbles,
And verse is one of them—this most of all.

* * * * * * * *

PAINTED FLOWERS.

Flowers to the fair; to you these flowers I bring,
And strive to greet you with an earlier spring,
Flowers, sweet and gay, and delicate like you,
Emblems of innocence and beauty too.
With flowers the Graces bind their yellow hair,
And flowery wreaths consenting lovers wear.
Flowers, the sole luxury which Nature knew,
In Eden's pure and guiltless garden grew.
To loftier forms are rougher tasks assign'd;
The sheltering oak resists the stormy wind,
The tougher yew repels invading foes,
And the tall pine for future navies grows;
But this soft family, to cares unknown,
Were born for pleasure and delight alone:
Gay without toil, and lovely without art,
They spring to cheer the sense, and glad the heart,
Nor blush, my fair, to own you copy these,
Your best, your sweetest empire is—to please.

THE DEVOTED PATRIOT.

REBECCA MOTTE,

DAUGHTER of Robert Brewton, an English gentleman, who had emigrated to South Carolina, was born in 1738, in Charleston. When about twenty, she married Mr. Jacob Motte, who died soon after the commencement of the revolutionary war. Captain McPherson, of the British army, who was in command of the garrison at Fort Motte, had taken possession of the large new house of Mrs. Motte, and fortified it, so that it was almost impregnable. Mrs. Motte herself had been obliged to remove to an old farm-house in the vicinity. In order to dislodge the garrison before succors could arrive, Generals Marion and Lee, who were commanding the American forces there, could devise no means but burning the mansion. This they were very reluctant to do, but Mrs. Motte willingly assented to the proposal, and presented, herself, a bow and its apparatus, which had been imported from India, and was prepared to carry combustible matter. We will conclude this scene from the eloquent description of Mrs. Ellet, to whose admirable work* we are indebted for the interesting materials for this sketch.

"Every thing was now prepared for the concluding scene. The lines were manned, and an additional force stationed at the battery, to meet a desperate assault, if such should be made. The American entrenchments being within arrow-shot, McPherson was once more summoned, and again more confidently—for help was at hand—asserted his determination to resist to the last.

"The scorching rays of the noon-day sun had prepared the shingle roof for the conflagration. The return of the flag was immediately followed by the shooting of the arrows, to which balls of blazing rosin and brimstone were attached. Simms tells us the bow was put into the hands of Nathan Savage, a private in Marion's brigade. The first struck, and set fire; also the second and third, in different quarters of the roof. McPherson immediately ordered men to repair to the loft of the house, and check the flames by knocking off the shingles; but they were soon driven down by the fire of the six-pounder; and no other effort to stop the burning being practicable, the commandant hung out the white flag, and surrendered the garrison at discretion.

"If ever a situation in real life afforded a fit subject for poetry, by filling the mind with a sense of

* "Women of the American Revolution."

moral grandeur, it was that of Mrs. Motte contemplating the spectacle of her home in flames, and rejoicing in the triumph secured to her countrymen —the benefit to her native land, by her surrender of her own interest to the public service. I have stood upon the spot, and felt that it was indeed classic ground, and consecrated by memories which should thrill the heart of every American. But the beauty of such memories would be marred by the least attempt at ornament; and the simple narrative of that memorable occurrence has more effect to stir the feelings than could a tale artistically framed and glowing with the richest hues of imagination.

"After the captors had taken possession, McPherson and his officers accompanied them to Mrs. Motte's dwelling, where they sat down together to a sumptuous dinner. Again, in the softened picture, our heroine is the principal figure. She showed herself prepared, not only to give up her splendid mansion to ensure victory to the American arms, but to do her part toward soothing the agitation of the conflict just ended. Her dignified, courteous, and affable deportment adorned the hospitality of her table; she did the honors with that unaffected politeness which wins esteem as well as admiration; and by her conversation, marked with ease, vivacity, and good sense, and the engaging kindness of her manners, endeavored to obliterate the recollection of the loss she had been called upon to sustain, and at the same time to remove from the minds of the prisoners the sense of their misfortunes."

Another portion of her history is important, as illustrating her high sense of honor, her energy, and patient, self-denying perseverance. Her husband, in consequence of the difficulties and distresses growing out of our war for independence, became embarrassed in his business; and after his death, and termination of the war, it was found impossible to satisfy these claims.

"The widow, however, considered the honor of her deceased husband involved in the responsibilities he had assumed. She determined to devote the remainder of her life to the honorable task of paying the debts. Her friends and connections, whose acquaintance with her affairs gave weight to their judgment, warned her of the apparent hopelessness of such an effort. But, steadfast in the principles that governed all her conduct, she persevered. Living in an humble dwelling, and relinquishing many of her habitual comforts, she devoted herself with such zeal, untiring industry, and indomitable resolution, to the attainment of her object, that her success triumphed over every difficulty, and exceeded the expectations of all who had discouraged her. She not only paid her husband's debts to the full, but secured for her children and descendants a handsome and unencumbered estate. Such an example of perseverance under adverse circumstances, for the accomplishment of a high and noble purpose, exhibits in yet brighter colors the heroism that shone in her country's days of peril!"

Mrs. Motte died in 1815, at her plantation on the Santee.

THE ESTIMABLE GOVERNESS.

SUZANNE CURCHOD, MADAME NECKER,

WAS descended, on the maternal side, from an ancient family in Provence, who had taken refuge in Switzerland on the revocation of the Edict of Nantes. She was born at Grassy, her father, M. Curchod, being the evangelical minister in that little village. He was a very learned man, and trained his daughter with great care, even giving her the severe and classical education usually bestowed only on men. The young Suzanne Curchod was renowned throughout the whole province for her wit, beauty, and intellectual attainments.

Gibbon, the future historian, but then an unknown youth studying in Lausanne, met Mademoiselle Curchod, fell in love with her, and succeeded in rendering his attachment acceptable to both the object of his affections and her parents. When he returned, however, to England, his father indignantly refused to hear of the proposed marriage between him and the Swiss minister's portionless daughter. Gibbon yielded to parental authority, and philosophically forgot his learned mistress.

After her father's death, which left her wholly unprovided for, Suzanne Curchod retired with her mother to Geneva. She there earned a precarious subsistence by teaching persons of her own sex. When her mother died, a lady named Madame de Vermenoux induced Mademoiselle Curchod to come to Paris, in order to teach Latin to her son. It was in this lady's house that she met Necker. He was then in the employment of Théllusson, the banker, and occasionally visited Madame de Vermenoux. Struck with the noble character and grave beauty of the young governess, Necker cultivated her acquaintance, and ultimately made her his wife. Mutual poverty had delayed their marriage for several years; but it was not long ere Necker rose from his obscurity. Madame Necker had an ardent love of honorable distinction, which she imparted to her husband, and which greatly served to quicken his efforts: his high talents in financial matters were at length recognized: he became a wealthy and respected man. Shortly after her marriage, Madame Necker expressed the desire of devoting herself to literature. Her husband, however, delicately hinted to her that he should regret seeing her adopt such a course. This sufficed to induce her to relinquish her intention: she loved him so entirely, that, without effort or repining, she could make his least wish her law.

As Necker rose in the world, Madame Necker's influence increased; but it never was an individual power, like that of Madame du Deffand, or of the

Maréchale de Luxembourg. Over her husband she always possessed great influence. Her virtues and noble character had inspired him with a feeling akin to veneration. He was not wholly guided by her counsels, but he respected her opinions as those of a high-minded being, whom all the surrounding folly and corruption could not draw down from her sphere of holy purity. If Madame Necker was loved and esteemed by her husband, she may be said to have almost idolized him; and her passionate attachment probably increased the feelings of vanity and self-importance of which Necker has often been accused. This exclusive devotedness caused some wonder amongst the friends of the minister and his wife; for seldom had these skeptical philosophers witnessed a conjugal union so strict and uncompromising, and yet so touching in its very severity.

When Necker became, in 1776, Director-General of the Finances, his wife resolved that the influence her husband's official position gave her should not be employed in procuring unmerited favors for flatterers or parasites. She placed before herself the far more noble object of alleviating misfortune, and pointing out to her reforming husband some of the innumerable abuses which then existed in every department of the state. One of her first attempts was to overthrow the lottery. She pressed the point on Necker's attention; but though he shared her convictions, he had not the power of destroying this great evil: he did, however, all he could to moderate its excesses. The prisons and hospitals of Paris greatly occupied the attention of Madame Necker during the five years of her husband's power. Her devotedness to the cause of humanity was admirable, and shone with double lustre amidst the heartless selfishness of the surrounding world. She once happened to learn that a certain Count of Lautrec had been imprisoned in a dungeon of the fortress of Ham for twenty-eight years! and that the unhappy captive now scarcely seemed to belong to human kind. A feeling of deep compassion seized her heart. To liberate a state prisoner was more than her influence could command, but she resolved to lighten, if possible, his load of misery. She set out for Ham, and succeeded in obtaining a sight of M. de Lautrec. She found a miserable-looking man, lying listlessly on the straw of his dungeon, scarcely clothed with a few tattered rags, and surrounded by rats and reptiles. Madame Necker soothed his fixed and sullen despair with promises of speedy relief; nor did she depart until she had kept her word, and seen M. de Lautrec removed to an abode where, if still a prisoner, he might at least spend in peace the few days left him by the tyranny of his oppressors.

Acts of individual benevolence were not, however, the only object of the minister's wife. Notwithstanding the munificence of her private charities, she aimed none the less to effect general good. Considerable ameliorations were introduced by her in the condition of the hospitals of Paris.

She entered, with unwearied patience, into the most minute details of their actual administration, and with admirable ingenuity, rectified errors or suggested improvements. Her aim was to effect a greater amount of good with the same capital, which she now saw grossly squandered and misapplied. The reforms which she thus introduced were both important and severe. She sacrificed almost the whole of her time to this praiseworthy task, and ultimately devoted a considerable sum to found the hospital which still bears her name. Beyond this, Madame Necker sought to exercise no power over her husband, or through his means. She loved him far too truly and too well to aim at an influence which might have degraded him in the eyes of the world. Necker was, however, proud of his noble-hearted wife, and never hesitated to confess how much he was indebted to her advice. When he retired from office, in 1781, and published his famous "Compte Rendu," he seized this opportunity of paying a high and heartfelt homage to the virtues of his wife. "Whilst retracing," he observes at the conclusion of his work, "a portion of the charitable tasks prescribed by your majesty, let me be permitted, sire, to allude, without naming her, to a person gifted with singular virtues, and who has materially assisted me in accomplishing the designs of your majesty. Although her name was never uttered to you, in all the vanities of high office, it is right, sire, that you should be aware that it is known and frequently invoked in the most obscure asylums of suffering humanity. It is no doubt most fortunate for a minister of finances to find, in the companion of his life, the assistance he needs for so many details of beneficence and charity, which might otherwise prove too much for the strength and attention. Carried away by the tumults of general affairs—often obliged to sacrifice the feelings of the private man to the duties of the citizen—he may well esteem himself happy, when the complaints of poverty and misery can be confided to an enlightened person who shares the sentiment of his duties."

If Madame Necker has not left so remarkable a name as many women of her time; if her contemporaries, justly, perhaps, found her too cold and formal; yet she shines at least in that dark age, a noble example of woman's virtues—devoted love, truth, and purity. She died in 1794, calm and resigned throughout the most acute sufferings; her piety sustained her. The literary works she left are chiefly connected with her charities, or were called forth by the events around her. Among these works are the following:—"Hasty Interments," "Memorial on the Establishment of Hospitals," "Reflections on divorce," and her "Miscellanies." Her only child was the celebrated Madame de Staël.

THE PATIENT ASTRONOMER.

CAROLINE LUCRETIA HERSCHEL,

SISTER, and for a long time assistant, of the celebrated astronomer, Sir William Herschel, was born at Hanover on the 16th of March, 1750. She is herself distinguished for her astronomical researches, and particularly for the construction of a selenographical globe, giving in relief the surface of the moon. But it was for her brother, Sir William Herschel, that the activity of her mind was awakened. From the first commencement of his astronomical pursuits, her attendance on both his daily labors and nightly watches was put in requisition; and was found so useful, that on his removal to Datchet, and subsequently to Slough—he being then occupied with his reviews of the heavens and other researches—she performed the whole of the arduous and important duties of his astronomical assistant, not only reading the clocks, and noting down all the observations from dictation as an amanuensis, but subsequently executing the whole of the extensive and laborious numerical calculations necessary to render them available to science, as well as a multitude of others relative to the various objects of theoretical and experimental inquiry in which, during his long and active career, he at any time engaged. For the performance of these duties, his majesty, King George III., was pleased to place her in the receipt of a salary sufficient for her singularly moderate wants and retired habits.

Arduous, however, as these occupations must appear, especially when it is considered that her brother's observations were always carried on (circumstances permitting) till daybreak, without regard to season, and indeed chiefly in the winter, they proved insufficient to exhaust her activity. In their intervals she found time for both actual astronomical observations of her own, and for the execution of more than one work of great extent and utility.

The observations here alluded to were made with a small Newtonian sweeper, constructed for her by her brother; with which, whenever his occasional absence, or any interruption to the regular course of his observations permitted, she searched the heavens for comets, and that so effectively as on no less than eight several occasions to be rewarded by their discovery. On five of these occasions (recorded in the pages of the "Philosophical Transactions" of London) her claim to the *first* discovery is admitted. These sweeps, moreover, proved productive of the detection of several remarkable nebulæ and clusters of stars previously unobserved, among which may be specially mentioned the superb Nebula, No. 1, Class V., of Sir William Herschel's catalogues—an object bearing much resemblance to the celebrated nebula in Andromeda, discovered by Simeon Inarius.

The astronomical works which she found leisure to complete were 1st. "A Catalogue of 561 Stars observed by Flamsteed," but which having escaped the notice of those who framed the "British Catalogue" from that astronomer's observations, are not therein inserted. 2. "A General Index of Reference to every Observation of every Star inserted in the British Catalogue." These works were published together in one volume by the Royal Society; and to their utility in subsequent researches Mr. Baily, in his "Life of Flamsteed," bears ample testimony. She further completed the reduction and arrangement as a "Zone Catalogue" of all the nebulæ and clusters of stars observed by her brother in his sweeps; a work for which she was honored with the Gold Medal of the Astronomical Society of London, in 1828; which society also conferred on her the unusual distinction of electing her an honorary member.

On her brother's death, in 1822, she returned to Hanover, which she never again quitted, passing the last twenty-six years of her life in repose—enjoying the society and cherished by the regard of her remaining relatives and friends—gratified by the occasional visits of eminent astronomers—and honored with many marks of favor and distinction on the part of the King of Hanover, the crown prince, and his amiable and illustrious consort.

Until within a very short period of her death, her health continued uninterrupted, her faculties perfect, and her memory (especially of the scenes and circumstances of former days) remarkably clear and distinct. Her end was tranquil and free from suffering—a simple cessation of life.

The writer of this very interesting memoir has, however, omitted to state, that besides being an Honorary Member of the Royal Astronomical Society, Miss Herschel was also similarly honored by the Royal Irish Academy.

The following just and eloquent tribute to the merits of Miss Herschel is from Dr. Nichol's "Views of the Architecture of the Heavens:"

"The astronomer (Sir William Herschel), during these engrossing nights, was constantly assisted in his labors by a devoted maiden sister, who braved with him the inclemency of the weather—who heroically shared his privations that she might participate in his delights—whose pen, we are told, committed to paper his notes of observations as they issued from his lips. 'She it was,' says the best of authorities, 'who, having passed the nights near the telescope, took the rough manuscripts to her cottage at the dawn of day, and produced a fair copy of the night's work on the ensuing morning; she it was who planned the labor of each succeeding night, who reduced every observation, made every calculation, and kept everything in systematic order,' she it was—Miss Caroline Herschel—who helped our astronomer to gather an imperishable name. This venerable lady has in one respect been more fortunate than her brother; she has lived to reap the full harvest of their joint glory. Some years ago, the gold medal of our Astronomical Society was transmitted to her to her native Hanover, whither she removed after Sir William's death; and the same learned society has recently inscribed her name upon its roll; but she has been rewarded by yet more, by what she will value beyond all earthly pleasures; she has lived to see her favorite nephew, him who grew up under her eye unto an astronomer, gather around him the highest hopes of scientific Europe, and prove himself fully equal to tread in the footsteps of his father."

In 1847, she celebrated the ninety-seventh anniversary of her birth, when the King of Hanover sent to compliment her, the Prince and Princess Royal visited her; and the latter presented her with a magnificent arm-chair embroidered by herself; and the King of Prussia sent her the gold medal awarded for the Extension of the Sciences.

Miss Herschel died at the opening of the following year, January 9th, 1848, crowned with the glory which woman's genius may gain, working in the way Divine Providence appointed her—as the helper of man.

THE QUIET REFORMER.

HANNAH MORE.

In estimating the merits of distinguished individuals, our opinion must obviously be modified by a knowledge of the external influences to which they were subjected. According as the tendency of these is to counteract or to forward their aims, a greater or less tenacity of purpose is demanded. And looking at the whole of a life, this is a quality that has more to do with greatness than may at first strike us; for greatness depends not so much upon the possession of brilliant talents, as upon steadiness and perseverance in pursuing a laudable object. A most obstinate struggle with circumstances has to be kept up by such as would rise to eminence from the humbler walks of life; but a contest on a more extended scale has to be encountered by whosoever aspires to be a reformer, as in this case the obstacles result from the condition of a nation or of society. They are also of a complex nature; the reformer has first to disentangle his own mind from the shackles of custom and prejudice, and next undertake the same task for others.

Hannah More was a reformer; we conceive one who did so much, by example, and purse, and pen, toward purifying the morality and advancing the cause of religion in England, to be well worthy of such a title, and all the greatness it implies. It is true she had the primary advantage of a sound and religious education, and was thus placed so as to have a Pisgah-like view of existing defects; but next to the difficulty of divesting our minds of the warpings of habit and popular opinion, is that of preventing ourselves from being caught in their meshes.

Of the state of religious knowledge, even amongst the higher classes, in the days of Hannah More, we may have a pretty accurate idea, from the anecdote related in connection with Sir Joshua Reynolds' "Samuel." When this celebrated painting was finished, numerous visitors flocked to his studio to see it, and amongst them were several who proposed the intelligent question, "Who was Samuel?" The manners and morality of the period were quite in agreement with this; and though it is by no means denied that there were many fine exceptions, it was then the *fashion* to be irreligious and immoral. Hannah More, when little above twenty years of age, was taken from the comparatively quiet coteries of Bristol, and plunged into the whirl of the gay world of London; the caresses and blandishments of the witty, the great, and the learned, were heaped upon her, but her keen, instinctive sense of right was in no degree blunted, and the endeavors of the world to win her to its side only served to draw forth the more unequivocal declaration of her principles. These principles, like the course of every great mind, deepened and widened with progressing years. We find her whose first essay was penned with the design of fostering a purer morality, gradually increasing her efforts for the same praiseworthy end, and by and by retiring from the vortex of fashionable life, to devote herself to the study of the Scriptures, and the composition of works bearing more immediately on the subject of religion.

Besides her literary reputation, Mrs. Hannah More was eminent for her piety and philanthropy; so much so, that, although she had not obtained celebrity by her writings, her memory would have been deservedly cherished as a Christian and philanthropist. She was ever prompt to originate or help forward philanthropic movements; she wrote for them—books for the drawing-rooms of the great, and tracts and ballads that insinuated themselves into the workshops of the town, and the cottages of the country; and she established schools for bestowing the blessings of education and a knowledge of the truths of the gospel on the poor. She was considerate and liberal to that class during her lifetime, and at her death, the sums bequeathed by her to religious and charitable institutions were on the most munificent scale. But perhaps the truest and most touching proof of her generosity and kindness to the poor, was that given on the day of her funeral, when each, with some semblance of mourning, they came crowding from village and hamlet to pay a last tribute to their benefactress, and give "all they had to give—a tear."

In reading the life of this celebrated person, we cannot fail to be struck with the large amount of good that she effected; and yet she was but a "lone woman;" and, in addition to the disadvantages pertaining to her sex, Mrs. Hannah More was at all times delicate in health, and subject to very frequent illness. In consequence of this, she was deeply impressed with the evil of procrastination, and has recorded in her diary how necessary she felt it to be to prosecute her work assiduously during her intervals of freedom from sickness. This goes to prove that greatness, in general, as well as success, arises less from the possession of great talents, or from favorable circumstances, than the selection of a proper aim, and the resolution to follow it unswervingly. There are multitudes of examples in the world, of a stern and successful resistance of circumstances more overwhelming than any we are likely to encounter, that may serve for encouraging and inciting us to emulation. We are disposed to lay too much stress on the force of circumstances, forgetting that we are to some extent the originators of them. Then we consider this a capital excuse for our indolence; it is this that is keeping us inactive; we are waiting for an opening, instead of making an opening. As for a favorable opportunity, it is vain for us to plead the want of them; we must not be too scrupulous, but seize the best that happens to come within our reach.

Hannah More was the youngest of five sisters, and was born at Stapleton, in Gloucestershire, in the year 1745. Her father having lost his money by the unfavorable termination of a lawsuit, lived here in a secluded manner. He was the son of the former master of an endowed school in the neighborhood, who, not being encumbered with a superabundance of pupils, had plenty of leisure to "rear the tender thought" of his son. He, in his turn, "kept the ball moving," as Franklin says of kindness, and devoted his time to the education of his daughters; and as he brought a highly creditable amount of talents and learning to the task, and had good materials to work upon, it is not surprising that he was very successful. This was particularly the case with Hannah, who was a somewhat precocious child, and her aptness in the acquisition of the first principles of geometry, and the rudiments of Latin, must have delighted the old man, and transformed the labor of instruction into a pleasant relaxation. The bias of her tastes very early displayed itself: one of her childish amusements was riding on a chair, accompanied by the announcement that "she was going to London to see booksellers and bishops." It was a darling object of her ambition to attain to the possession of a whole quire of paper, and when some friend gratified her wish, it was speedily filled with letters to imaginary personages.

The talents of the whole family were so much above the average that they soon attracted attention, and under the auspices of Dr. Stonehouse and others, the Misses More established a day-school in Bristol: this shortly after gave place to a boarding-school, which long maintained the character of being one of the best and most flourishing in that part of England. To this school Hannah was removed when twelve years of age, and eagerly availed herself of the means of extending her knowledge now placed within her reach. She acquired a perfect and idiomatical knowledge of the French. and afterward of the Italian and Spanish languages.

Even at this early period her conversational powers were so fascinating that Dr. Woodward, an eminent scholar, when attending her in his medical capacity, under their influence on one occasion so far forgot the object of his visit, that he was proceeding down stairs, when, suddenly recollecting himself, he returned to the room, exclaiming, "Bless me! I forgot to ask the girl how she is."

In the year 1762, she gave her first literary composition to the world, in the shape of a pastoral drama, entitled, "The Search after Happiness." Having met with the approval of Garrick, Dr. Stonehouse, and other persons of literary taste, it was issued from the Bristol press, and its popularity was so great, that in a few months it passed through three editions. The poem, as the authoress informs us, had for its object "an earnest wish to furnish a substitute for the very improper custom, which then prevailed, of allowing plays, and these not always of the purest kind, to be acted by young ladies in boarding-schools."

About this time a proposal of marriage was made to her by a landed proprietor in the neighborhood; and though Mr. Turner was many years her senior, his offer was accepted, and she resigned her share in the management of the boarding-school. Owing to various circumstances, however, the engagement was broken off, and although the gentleman soon after sought to renew it, the lady would not give her consent. Her feelings had undeniably been trifled with, and she made a resolution to eschew all such overtures in future. It is but due to Mr. Turner to state that he settled an annuity on her, and bequeathed her at his death the sum of one thousand pounds. Perhaps, if we knew it, the lives of many of the tea-bibbing, scandal-mongering class, denominated "old maids," contain a little episode of such a vexation, and such a determination; and perhaps the secret of their railing at the world in general is that "there is a cross in their hearts."

When in her twenty-second year, Hannah More paid her visit to London, and returned the following year, to reside for a short time with the Garricks, at their beautiful retreat at Hampton. Here she became acquainted with Johnson, Burke, Reynolds, and others of the *élite* of the literary world.

The great moralist in particular had a most affectionate regard for her, terming her "Child," "Little Fool," "Love," and "Dearest." One of her sisters, in writing home, gives the following interesting account of a conversation between herself and Johnson. "After much critical discourse, he turns round to me, and with one of his most amiable looks, which must be seen to form the least idea of it, he says, 'I have heard that you are engaged in the useful and honorable employment of teaching young ladies;' upon which, with all the same ease, familiarity, and confidence as we should have done, had only our own Dr. Stonehouse been present, we entered upon the history of our birth, parentage, and education, showing how we were born with more desires than guineas, and how, as years increased, our appetites increased also, the cupboard at home being too small to gratify them; and how, with a bottle of water, a bed, and a blanket, we set out to seek our fortunes; and how we found a great house with nothing in it; and how it was like to remain so, till looking into our knowledge-box, we happened to find a little *larning*, a good thing when land is gone, or rather when there is none; and so, at last, by giving a little of this little *larning* to those who had less, we got a good store of gold in return, but how! alas! we wanted the wit to keep it. 'I love you both,' cried the inamorato; 'I love you all five. I never was at Bristol—I will come on purpose to see you. What! five women live happily together!

I will come and see you. I have spent a happy evening—I am glad I came. God for ever bless you; you live to shame duchesses.' He took his leave with so much warmth and tenderness, we were quite affected at his manner." In what an amiable light does the great moralist appear in such an anecdote as this; and Madame D'Arblay, another of his pets, has many similar in her gossiping diary; and with all his faults, can we help loving him still?

In the midst of the adulation which was now lavished on the youthful authoress, it is most gratifying to find her writing thus to one of her sisters: "For my own part, the more I see of the honored, famed, and great, the more I see of the littleness, the unsatisfactoriness of all created good, and that no earthly pleasure can fill up the wants of the immortal principle within." After her return to Bristol, she produced two short poems—"The Bleeding Rock," and "Sir Eldred of the Bower;" the latter a moral tale in two parts, in the ballad style. A handsome sum was paid for these pieces by Mr. Caddell, and their success was so great, that a thousand copies were sold in a fortnight. She now plumed her wing for a higher flight, and the direction which it took was no doubt influenced by her intimacy with the Garricks, as well as the success of her pastoral drama. "The Inflexible Captive," a regular piece in five acts, appeared in 1774, and on its performance in the theatre at Bath was favorably received. It is founded on the well-known classical story of Regulus, the Roman ambassador to Carthage, and displays considerable power. There are many fine passages, and the interest is sustained throughout.

Within the three following years, the two tragedies of "Percy" and the "Fatal Falsehood" were produced; the former was deservedly the most popular of Miss More's dramatic works. It greatly exceeds "The Inflexible Captive" in point of dramatic interest; the various characters are brought out with much clearness and precision; and that of Elwina is a particularly fine sketch.

In the year 1780, Miss Hannah More paid another visit to London, during which she resided at the house of the amiable and accomplished widow of Dean Delany, and had the privilege of enlarging the number of her literary acquaintances, which, in addition to many distinguished prelates, now included the names of Walpole, Jenyns, Pepys, Mrs. Boscawen, Mrs. Chapone, and Mrs. Carter. About this time she published a small volume in prose, entitled "Essays for Young Ladies," now very scarce, and a volume of "Sacred Dramas." These dramas were greatly esteemed, and a specimen of a translation of one of them into the Cingalese language, was presented to the authoress, written on a Palmyra leaf, and enclosed in a beautifully-painted wooden case. Nor was this the only instance of her works being read in countries where one would little expect them to have found their way, for a Russian princess, who had procured some of her short tracts, translated them into Russ, and wrote a complimentary letter to the authoress.

We have hitherto traced the career of Hannah More merely as a popular authoress, who was gradually gaining favor in the eyes of the public; but the time was now come when the results of her careful education in the truths of the Christian religion, and the influence which those principles possess over every well-constituted mind, were to be more broadly manifested. The death of her friend Garrick severed the strongest link between her and the dramatic world, and the sense of the hollowness of worldly enjoyments pressed upon her mind with ever-increasing force. She had all along retained her native simplicity of character, and the adulation that was lavished on her had left as little trace as water on the plumage of a bird: she had never suffered herself to be intoxicated by the pleasures of the world; and what a testimony it is to their unsatisfactoriness, that they palled upon the taste of one who had enjoyed those of the most refined description, and always with a due regard to moderation. The cast of her mind was eminently practical; this was evidenced as early as the time that her juvenile pastoral, "The Search after Happiness," was produced, for, as we have stated, it sprang from a nobler wish than a youthful love of notoriety. Even the three most ambitious effusions of her dramatic muse were not written as mere passports to fame. Her own reading, and the society in which she mingled at that period, gave her thoughts a strong bent toward the stage; but she viewed it not only as an entertainment, but as a powerful lever of the heart, and one which she hoped to enlist on the side of virtue. Her plays were written under that impression, though in after years she abandoned the hope of metamorphosing the theatre into a school of virtue, and became convinced that "this utopian good could not be produced, until not only the stage itself had undergone a complete purification, but until the audience was purified also."

In conformity with her desire of withdrawing more from the world, Hannah More, in 1786, purchased a neat cottage in the neighborhood of Bristol, called Cowslip Green. Naught of ascetism, however, entered into her ideas of retirement; she who had tasted wisely and temperately of the pleasures of society, partook in equal moderation of the sweets of seclusion. Her annual visits to her friend, Mrs. Garrick, in London, were still continued, and from time to time she indulged in intercourse with the most eminent literary characters of the day.

Theology had even in early life been one of her favorite studies, and she gladly embraced the opportunity now afforded her of prosecuting it with greater vigor. Two years after her retreat to Cowslip Green, she published a small tract, entitled, "Thoughts on the Manners of the Great," followed in the same year by a poem on "Slavery."

About ten miles distant from the residence of

Miss Hannah More and her sisters, lay the village of Chedder. It is picturesquely situated at the mouth of a narrow ravine in the Mendip Hills: close to the town, fantastically-shaped cliffs of lime-stone shoot abruptly upward, to the height of several hundreds of feet; and those who penetrate into the gorge, which extends for nearly three miles, are rewarded by a display of the grandest rocky scenery in all "merry England." The country around is rich pasture-land; and the dairies have long been celebrated for their cheese, which in the days of Camden was so good and so great, that it required more than one man to hoist a cheese on to the table. But it was not the garden-like fertility of the country, nor the romantic beauty of the village, that drew toward it the notice of Hannah More. The rural population of this fine district were in a state of terrible demoralization, which will be best described by the following extract from a letter of Miss More to her friend Wilberforce: "We found more than two thousand people in the parish, almost all very poor; no gentry; a dozen wealthy farmers, hard, brutal, and ignorant. We saw but one Bible in all the parish, and that was used to prop a flower-pot. No clergyman had resided in it for forty years. One rode over, three miles from Wells, to preach once on a Sunday, but no weekly duty was done, or sick persons visited; and children were often buried without any funeral service. Eight persons in the morning, and twenty in the afternoon, was a good congregation." But,

> "For man's neglect, *she* loved it more."

A wide field was extended on which to exert her energies, and nobly she and her two sisters labored in the performance of their self-appointed work.

The influence which the French Revolution exercised on the lower classes in this country induced her to publish a tract, entitled "Village Politics, in a Dialogue between two Mechanics." The sale and circulation of this little work were astonishing, and led her, in 1795, to commence a regular series, which was issued monthly from Bath, under the name of the "Cheap Repository Tracts." During the same year, which was one of horror and commotion abroad, and anxiety and scarcity at home, her purse and hand were no less readily opened to relieve the one, than her pen had been used to counteract the influence of the other. At her hospitable door the poor were supplied with soup and food, and every means in her power were taken to assist them, and mitigate their sufferings. Nor was her liberality restricted to her own countrymen, for the sum of £240, the proceeds of a publication, "Remarks on a Production of M. Dupont, a French Atheist," was devoted to the relief of the French emigrant clergy, who flocked in considerable numbers to our shores.

In the year 1799, Hannah More (who now assumed the title of Mrs.) wrote her "Strictures on the Modern System of Female Education." From some of the opinions advanced in this work, and from the opposition to her schools reviving in a quarter where it might least have been expected, Mrs. More was subjected to a series of calumniations and persecutions that would have been trying to a person of ordinary sensibility, and must have been severely so to a woman who was desirous of living as much in retirement as was compatible with the schemes of usefulness she sought to carry out.

Mrs. More, in 1802, changed her residence from Cowslip Green to Barley Wood—beautiful Barley Wood—familiar to every one as a household name. To this charming retreat, where she dwelt for more than twenty years, crowds of the wisest, greatest, and best congregated to visit her. It was proposed at this period to commit to her the superintendence of the education of the Princess Charlotte of Wales. This scheme was not carried into effect, but it probably led to the publication, in 1805, of two volumes, "Hints towards Forming the Character of a Young Princess." This work, which was anonymous, procured the author the flattering compliment of several letters from the heads of the church, beginning and ending with "Sir." It was dedicated to Dr. John Fisher, bishop of Exeter, then tutor to her Royal Highness, and he brought it under the notice of her Majesty, who signified her gracious approval of it. A few years afterward, the novel of "Cœlebs in Search of a Wife" came out, in two volumes, and, like its predecessor, without the author's name. "The discerning public," however, were not slow in attributing it to its proper source. This novel achieved a wide popularity.

We have already mentioned that theology and scriptural subjects possessed great attractions in the estimation of Mrs. More, and she now gave to the world some of the fruits of her studies. She printed, in 1811, a very excellent treatise, entitled, "Practical Piety; or, the Influence of the Religion of the Heart on the Conduct of Life;" and the succeeding year, a work on "Christian Morals." In the preface to the last, she tendered her thanks to the public for their long-continued patronage, apologized for another appearance as an authoress, and bade them adieu in that capacity. We know not what Joshua Geddes, or those of his sect, would have said to the "taking back her word," which followed thereupon; but the public in general had reason to esteem it a fortunate circumstance, and surely such sensible people as the Society of Friends would be of the same opinion. It was indeed one of her grandest literary performances that she gave to the world in 1815, under the title of "An Essay on the Character and Writings of St. Paul." The design of this work was to delineate the alluring features of the Christian life, as they were displayed in the conduct of the apostle, "for a pattern to them which should hereafter believe." In the year 1819, she printed another work, "Moral

Sketches of Prevailing Opinions and Manners, Foreign and Domestic, with Reflections on Prayer," forming a sequel to her "Practical Piety," and "Christian Morals." The sale of this publication also was extensive and speedy, though it was for the most part merely a collection of sketches from real life, which had formerly made their appearance in the pages of the "Christian Observer."

We cannot resist the temptation of transcribing here a portion of a letter which gives a most graphic picture of the occupant of Barley Wood at this period of her life:—

"I was much struck by the air of affectionate kindness with which the old lady welcomed me to Barley Wood; there was something of courtliness about it, at the same time the courtliness of the *vieille cour* which one reads of, but so seldom meets. Her dress was of light green Venetian silk; a yellow, richly embroidered crape shawl enveloped her shoulders; and a pretty net cap, tied under her chin with white satin ribbon, completed the costume. Her figure is singularly *petite;* but to have any idea of the expression of her countenance, you must imagine the small withered face of a woman in her eighty-seventh year; and imagine also (shaded, but not obscured, by long and perfectly white eyelashes) eyes dark, brilliant, flashing, and penetrating; sparkling from object to object with all the fire and energy of youth, and smiling welcome on all around.

"When I first entered the room, Lady S——

and her family were there; they soon prepared to depart; but the youngest boy, a fine little fellow of six, looked anxiously in Mrs. More's face after she had kissed him, and his mamma said, 'You will not forget Mrs. Hannah, my dear?' He shook his head. 'Do not forget me, my dear child,' said the kind old lady, assuming a playful manner; 'but they say your sex is naturally capricious. There, I will give you another kiss; keep it for my sake, and when you are a man, remember Hannah More.'—'I will,' he replied, 'remember that you loved children.' It was a beautiful compliment."

Mrs. More was now doomed to experience the sorrowful compensation that must be paid for a life prolonged to the verge of fourscore and ten years. Of the five talented Mores—the five women who, to Dr. Johnson's amazement, lived happily together—Hannah was the sole representative; her sister Sarah having died in 1817, and her favorite Patty, two years later. And beside those members of her own family, there were many losses to be bewailed of those friends with whom, in other years, she had "taken sweet counsel together." As she herself remarked to a visitor, "Johnson, Burke, Garrick, Reynolds, Porteous—all—all the associates of my youth are gone."

"Yet when as one by one sweet sounds
And wandering lights departed,
She wore no less a loving face,
Although so broken hearted."

Her own health was decidedly failing, but, though she had become so infirm as to be unable to leave her room, her mind had lost none of its accustomed vigor, and, in 1822, she occupied her self during an illness with preparing for the press a small volume on Prayer. With this work she laid aside for ever the powerful pen that had been wielded so well to "defend the right;" but there still lingered for a season, the eloquence of the lips and of the life. And eloquent indeed those must have been to all who heard and saw her, standing as she was "in the shadow of coming death;" and inconceivably "sublime and sublimating" must have been the shadow that coming events cast before it, over her who had left behind a long vista of years spent in glorifying God, and doing good to man.

In consequence of the disgraceful conduct of her servants, which was accidentally discovered by a visitor, Mrs. More considered it advisable to leave her much-loved haunt of Barley Wood, and take up her abode at Clifton, whither she removed in 1825. Mrs. Hannah More lived in Clifton for several years after this event, honored, respected, and beloved by all about her; as how could they choose but love one who was "cheerful as the day," and had such depths of tenderness in her dark eyes, or else her portrait sadly belies her? But her long and useful life was drawing to a close. She became more and more subject to catarrhal attacks, and, during the winter months of 1832, had occasional paroxysms of delirium. The account of her last illness is thus given by an eye-witness:—"During this illness of ten months, the time was passed in a series of alternations between restlessness and composure, long sleeps and long wakefulness, with occasional great excitements, elevated and sunken spirits. At length nature seemed to shrink from further conflict, and the time of her deliverance drew near. On Friday, the 6th of September, 1833, we offered up the morning family devotion by her bedside; she was silent, and apparently attentive, with her hands devoutly lifted up. From eight in the evening of this day till nearly nine, I sat watching her. Her face was smooth and glowing; there was an unusual brightness in its expression. At about ten, the symptoms of speedy departure could not be doubted. She fell into a dozing sleep, and slight convulsions succeeded, which seemed to be attended with no pain. Contrary to expectation, she survived the night. She continued till ten minutes after one, when I saw the last gentle breath escape, and one more was added 'to that multitude which no man can number, who sing the praises of God and of the Lamb for ever and ever.'"

Her remains were interred on the 13th of September, beside those of her sisters, in the churchyard of Wrington, not far from the grave of Locke. It was her own wish that her funeral should be private, and that, instead of money being expended in useless show, suits of mourning should be given to fifteen old men, whom she nominated. The bells of all the churches were tolled as the cortége passed through Bristol, and a short distance from Wrington the whole of the gentlemen of the neighbourhood joined the procession. But perhaps the most affecting part of all the pageant was the lines of weeping villagers formed on each side of the road, every one in the nearest approximation to mourning that poverty would allow.

THE SCULPTOR'S ASSISTANT.

ANN FLAXMAN,

WIFE of John Flaxman, the celebrated sculptor, deserves a place among distinguished women, for the admirable manner in which she devoted herself to sustain her husband's genius, and aid him in his arduous career.

Her maiden name was Denman: she married John Flaxman when he was about twenty-seven years old, and she twenty-two. They had been for some time mutually attached to each other; but he was poor in purse, and though on the road to fame, had no one but this chosen partner of his life who sympathized in his success. She was amiable and accomplished, had a taste for art and literature, was skilful in French and Italian, and, like her husband, had acquired some knowledge of the Greek. But what was better than all, she was an enthusiastic admirer of his genius—she cheered and encouraged him in his moments of despondency—regulated modestly and prudently his domestic economy—arranged his drawings—managed now and then his correspondence, and acted in all particulars so that it seemed as if the church, in performing a marriage, had accomplished a miracle, and blended them really into one flesh and one blood. That tranquility of mind, so essential to those who live by thought, was of his household; and the sculptor, happy in the company of one who had taste and enthusiasm, soon renewed with double zeal the studies which courtship and matrimony had for a time interrupted. He had never doubted that in the company of her whom he loved he should be able to work with an intenser spirit; but of another opinion was Sir Joshua Reynolds. "So, Flaxman," said the President, one day as he chanced to meet him, "I am told you are married; if so, sir, I tell you you are ruined for an artist." Flaxman went home, sat down beside his wife, took her hand, and said, with a smile, "I am ruined for an artist." "John," said she, "how has this happened, and who has done it?" "It happened," said he, "in the church, and Ann Denman has done it: I met Sir Joshua Reynolds just now, and he said marriage had ruined me in my profession."

For a moment a cloud hung on Flaxman's brow; but this worthy couple understood each other too well, to have their happiness seriously marred by the unguarded and peevish remark of a wealthy old bachelor. They were proud, determined people, who asked no one's advice, who shared their domestic secrets with none of their neighbors, and lived as if they were unconscious that they were in the midst of a luxurious city. "Ann," said the sculptor, "I have long thought that I could rise to distinction in art without studying in Italy, but these words of Reynolds have determined me. I shall go to Rome as soon as my affairs are fit to be left; and to show him that wedlock is for a man's good rather than his harm, you shall accompany me. If I remain here, I shall be accused of ignorance concerning those noble works of art which are to the sight of a sculptor what learning is to a man of genius, and you will lie under the charge of detaining me." In this resolution Mrs. Flaxman fully concurred. They resolved to prepare themselves in silence for the journey, to inform no one of their intentions, and to set, meantime, a still stricter watch over their expenditure. No assistance was proffered by the Academy, nor was any asked; and five years elapsed from the day of the memorable speech of the president, before Flaxman, by incessant study and labor, had accumulated the means of departing for Italy. They went together; and in all his subsequent labors and triumphs, the wife was his good angel.

For thirty-eight years Flaxman lived wedded—his health was generally good, his spirits ever equal; and his wife, to whom his fame was happiness, had been always at his side. She was a most cheerful, intelligent woman; a collector, too, of drawings and sketches, and an admirer of Stothard, of whose designs and prints she had amassed more than a thousand. Her husband paid her the double respect due to affection and talent; and when any difficulty in composition occurred, he would say, with a smile, "Ask Mrs. Flaxman, she is my dictionary." She maintained the simplicity and dignity of her husband, and refused all presents of paintings, or drawings, or books, unless some reciprocal interchange were made. It is almost needless to say that Flaxman loved such a woman very tenderly. The hour of their separation approached —she fell ill, and died in the year 1820; and from the time of this bereavement, something like a lethargy came over his spirit, although he, as his biographer remarks, was "surrounded with the applause of the world." He survived his wife six years.

THE POET'S COMPANION.

MRS. WORDSWORTH.

[FROM A SERMON PREACHED IN WESTMINSTER ABBEY ON THE SUNDAY AFTER HER DEATH.]

"There be some standing here that shall not taste of death."
MATT. xvi. 28.

LET us not imagine that these words are applicable merely to eminent saints and martyrs. They are realized every day and every hour, in the peaceful dissolution of all who depart hence in the true faith and fear of God.

Far be from us, my brethren, the spirit of irreverent curiosity, which pries into the sanctities of private death-beds, and reveals their secrets to the world. But when Almighty God takes to himself the spirits of just men and holy women, and when their mortal remains are consigned to the peaceful chambers of the tomb, in the hope of a glorious resurrection, then Christian piety loves to linger at their graves, and to ponder on the lessons of wisdom which may be learnt from their examples. Bear with me, therefore, my beloved brethren, in making here a *passing allusion* to one who departed this life in the bygone week, full of years and good works, and whose body now rests in peace by the side of a mountain stream, in a quiet country churchyard.

Let me be permitted to invite you to meditate for a few moments by the side of that grave. It is not the grave of a soldier, illustrious for heroic deeds, it is not the grave of a statesman, distinguished by political wisdom and brilliant eloquence; it is not the grave of any of the noble or great of this world; but it is the grave of an aged widow, who lived in retirement in a beautiful spot, in a fair region of our own land; and it is not for any personal purpose, but for the sake of the public lessons of religious wisdom which may thence be derived, that you are now invited to pause for a moment there.

She was the wife of an English poet, who appeared before the world at the close of the last century—one whose poems were at first received with cold indifference or disdainful scorn, except by some few prophetic spirits who acknowledged their value and augured their fame—one who, nothing daunted by harsh judgments and rash censures, not cast down by despondency, not irritated by obloquy, not brooding in sullen moodiness over his own ill-requited labors—but, conscious of the secret breathings of poetic inspiration stirring within him, toiled on calmly and quietly, devoting the intellectual gifts he had received from God to the glory of the great Giver, and to the welfare of human kind, in interpreting to the world the beautiful magnificence of nature, and in throwing a veil of graceful delicacy over the common concerns of daily life, and in elevating and purifying the thoughts by high and holy aspirations, and in enlisting the sympathies and affections of mankind in whatever is good and great, noble and lovely—especially when it is found in the life of the lowly-minded, the meek, the simple, and the poor.

He labored year after year, and he did not labor in vain. He scaled the hill of fame, and won his way to glory. The author of the "Lyrical Ballads" and of the "Excursion," the late Poet Laureate of England—for of him we now speak—received in his old age from the royal hand the noblest meed of praise that could be conferred by it on poetic genius; he was greeted by academic applause; the fame which he had earned in England was echoed across the Atlantic, with a voice of cordial assent, from every part of America; and at length, after his death, his memory was honored by a monument erected by public contributions, in this sacred Minster, in this mausoleum of national genius, amid the trophies of national glory.

And what now is our moral? what is our religious inference from these facts? How were they brought to pass? Where, let us ask, under God, was a mainspring of the comfort which cheered him in days of difficulty and of chilling neglect? Whence was the genial light which gleamed over his path?

It was—as he himself has declared in his published writings—it was in his marriage union. It was in his conjugal partnership with a holy and virtuous woman, whose price is above rubies. It was in his wedded life, in holy fellowship with one who was richly endued with "the ornament of a meek and quiet spirit, which (as the Apostle testifies) is in the sight of God of great price." (1 Pet. iii. 3.) This it was which gave consolation and joy to his hours of care and sadness, and ministered strength and courage for his noble intellectual work. This it was which conduced to impart a holy fragrance and a healthful tone to his writings, and made them more instrumental in the diffusion of public and permanent good in this and other lands. . . . . .

Blessed consummation! leaving a beautiful example of the salutary influence exercised by woman's love, by woman's faith, by woman's quietness, meekness, gentleness, holiness, over men of vigorous minds, endued with great intellectual gifts, and stirred by strong emotions, such as are generally found in those who are endued with poetic genius, and are fired with fervid imaginations. The influence of holy womanhood on such minds as these is like that of a spiritual gravitation. It is like that elemental influence of attraction, never seen, but always felt, which acts upon the heavenly bodies themselves, and controls those planetary luminaries, traveling in their rapid course, and keeps them in their proper spheres, and makes them ministers of light, of health, and joy to the world.

Here let woman see her privileges, here let her recognize her powers. Her might is in meekness. "In quietness shall be your strength." (Isa. xxx. 15.) It resides in the hidden springs of the heart, in holy instincts, and delicate reserve, and modest reverence, and tender sensibilities. . . . . .

THE CHRISTIAN HEROINE.

HARRIET NEWELL,

The first American heroine of the missionary enterprise, was born at Haverhill, Massachusetts, October 10th, 1793. Her maiden name was Atwood. In 1806, while at school at Bradford, she became deeply impressed with the importance of religion; and, at the age of sixteen, she joined the church. On the 9th of February, 1812, Harriet Atwood married the Rev. Samuel Newell, missionary to the Burman empire; and in the same month, Mr. and Mrs. Newell embarked with their friends, Mr. and Mrs. Judson, for India. On the arrival of the missionaries at Calcutta, they were ordered to leave by the East India company; and accordingly Mr. and Mrs. Newell embarked for the Isle of France. Three weeks before reaching the island she became the mother of a child, which died in five days. On the 30th of November, seven weeks and four days after her confinement, Mrs. Harriet Newell, at the age of twenty, expired, far from her home and friends. She was one of the first females who ever went from this country as a missionary;

and she was the first who died a martyr to the cause of missions. That there is a time, even in the season of youth and the flush of hope, when it is "better to die than to live," even to attain our wish for this world, Harriet Newell is an example. Her most earnest wish was to do good for the cause of Christ, and be of service in teaching his gospel to the heathen. Her early death has, apparently, done this, better and more effectually, than the longest life and most arduous labors of any one of the noble band of American women who have gone forth on this errand of love and hope. In the language of a recent writer on this subject, "Heroines of the Missionary Enterprise," Harriet Newell was the great proto-martyr of American missions. She fell, wounded by death, in the very vestibule of the sacred cause. Her memory belongs, not to the body of men who sent her forth, not to the denomination to whose creed she had subscribed, but to the church, to the cause of missions. With the torch of truth in her hand, she led the way down into a valley of darkness, through which many have followed. Her work was short, her toil soon ended; but she fell, cheering by her dying words and her high example, the missionaries of all coming time. She was the first, but not the only martyr. Heathen lands are dotted over with the graves of fallen Christians; missionary women sleep on almost every shore, and the bones of some are whitening in the fathomless depths of the ocean.

Never will the influence of the devoted woman whose life and death are here portrayed, be estimated properly, until the light of an eternal day shall shine on all the actions of men. We are to measure her glory, not by what she suffered, for others have suffered more than she did. But we must remember that she went out when the missionary enterprise was in its infancy—when even the best of men looked upon it with suspicion. The tide of opposition she dared to stem, and with no example, no predecessor from American shores, she went out to rend the veil of darkness which gathered over all the nations of the East.

Things have changed since then. Our missionaries go forth with the approval of all the good; and the odium which once attended such a life is swept away. It is to some extent a popular thing to be a missionary, although the work is still one of hardship and suffering. It is this fact which gathers such a splendor around the name of Harriet Newell, and invests her short eventful life with such a charm. She went when no foot had trodden out the path, and was the first American missionary ever called to an eternal reward. While she slumbers in her grave, her name is mentioned with affection by a missionary church. And thus it should be. She has set us a glorious example; she has set an example to the church in every land and age, and her name will be mingled with the loved ones who are falling year by year; and if, when the glad millennium comes, and the earth is converted to God, some crowns brighter than others shall be seen amid the throng of the ransomed, one of those crowns will be found upon the head of Harriet Newell."

"History is busy with us," said Marie Antoinette; and the hope that her heroic endurance of ignominy and suffering would be recorded, and ensure the pity and admiration of a future age, doubtless nerved her to sustain the dignity of a queen throughout the deep tragedy of her fate.

The noblest heroism of a woman is never thus self-conscious. The greatest souls, those who elevate humanity and leave a track of light—"as stars go down"—when passing away from earth, never look back for the brightness. A woman with such a soul is absorbed in her love for others, and in her duty toward God. She does what she can, feeling constantly how small is the mite she gives; and the worth which it is afterward discovered to bear would, probably, astonish the giver far more than it does the world.

Harriet Newell died at the early age of twenty, leaving a journal and a few letters, the record of her religious feelings and the events of her short missionary life. These fragments have been published, making a little book. Such is her contribution to literature; yet this small work has been and is now of more importance to the intellectual progress of the world than all the works of Madame de Staël. The writings of Harriet Newell, translated into several tongues, and published in many editions, have reached the heart of society, and assisted to build up the throne of woman's power, even the moral influence of her sex over men; and their intellect can never reach its highest elevation but through the medium of moral cultivation.

THE MISSIONARY'S WIFE.

SARAH LANMAN SMITH,

WAS born in Norwich, Connecticut, June 18, 1802. Her father was Jabez Huntington, Esq. Her biographer, Rev. Edward W. Hooker, says of her early years, after describing her sufferings from ill health during childhood, and also from the severity of a school-mistress, which circumstances, added to the death of her mother, had the effect to bring out great decision and sometimes wilfulness of character:

"But with these things in childhood, showing that she was a subject of that native depravity in which all the human race are 'guilty before God,' she exhibited, as she was advancing in the years of youth, many of the virtues which are useful and lovely; and probably went as far in those excellences of natural character on which many endeavor to build their hope of salvation, as almost any unconverted persons do; carrying with her, however, the clear and often disturbing conviction, that the best virtues which she practised were not holiness, nor any evidence of fitness for heaven.

"She was exceedingly attached to her friends. Her father was almost her idol. The affection for her mother, who was so early removed by death, she transferred with exemplary tenderness, to her step-mother; and it is believed the instances are rare in which the parties are uniformly happier in each other, in that relation, than were Mrs. Huntington and this daughter. Her warmth and tenderness of affection as a sister were also peculiar and exemplary. Her childhood and youth were marked with great delicacy of mind and manners; diligence, promptitude, and efficiency in her undertakings; love of system and fondness for study, improvement, and the acquirement of useful knowledge, joined with a great desire to answer the wishes and expectations of her friends. Dutifulness and respect for her parents and grandparents; reverence for her superiors generally; readiness to receive advice or admonition; a just appreciation of the good influence of others, and a spirit of cautiousness respecting whatever might be injurious to her own character, were also prominent traits in her habits. Disinterestedness and self-denial for the benefit of others were conspicuous. Long before she became a subject of divine grace, she took an interest in various objects of benevolence, particularly Sabbath-schools; and exhibited that spirit of enterprise, patience, and perseverance, in aiding the efforts of others, which constituted so prominent an excellence in her character in the later years of her life. Self-government; economy in the use of her time and pocket-money; tastefulness in dress, without extravagance; and a careful and conscientious consideration of her father's resources, also were observable in her early habits. These traits are not mentioned because they are not found in many other young persons, but because they appeared in her in an uncommon degree."

The virtues and graces of character enumerated do not, it is true, constitute the holiness of a Christian—that is, the especial gift of the Holy Spirit, to sanctify the heart; but they do show a state of feeling naturally inclined to the moralities of life, to which sin, acted out, would have been at "enmity." Her "moral sense" was refined and enlightened; she only needed the breath of divine grace to turn her heart to God; all her ways were in harmony with his laws; while converted men have, usually, the whole inner course of their lives to alter, or at least to put off the "old man with his *deeds*;" which is the struggle of a carnal nature women do not often have to undergo. Mrs. Smith is a true and lovely illustration of the noblest type of feminine nature. She commenced her office as teacher in a Sunday-school, at the age of fourteen, before she was a convert to Jesus; that is, before she had yielded her will to the convictions of her reason and the promptings of her best feelings, and determined to live the life of duty, and seek her own happiness in doing good to others. This change took place when she was about eighteen years old; from that time all was harmony in her soul; she had found the true light, and she followed it till she entered heaven. In 1833, Miss Huntington was married to the Rev. Eli Smith, of the American mission at Beyroot, Syria; and she went to that remote region as the "help meet" for a humble missionary. She was singularly fitted for this important station, having been a voluntary missionary to the miserable remnant of a tribe of the Mohegan Indians; she had thus tested her powers and strengthened her love for this arduous work in the cause of doing good. Her letters to her father and friends, while reflecting on this important step of a foreign mission, will be intensely interesting to those who regard this consecration of woman to her office of moral teacher as among the most efficient causes of the success of the Gospel. The literary merits of her writings are of a high order; we venture to say, that, compared with the "Journals" and "Letters" of the most eminent men in the missionary station, those of Mrs. Smith will not be found inferior in merits of any kind. Her intellect had been cultivated; she could, therefore, bring her reasoning powers, as well as her moral and religious sentiments, to bear on any subject discussed; the following is proof in point. The powerful competition which the missionary cause held in Miss Huntington's affections, with her home and all its pleasant circumstances, may be learned from two or three sentences in one of her letters written a few months before she left her country. "To make and receive visits, exchange friendly salutations, attend to one's wardrobe, cultivate a garden, read good and entertaining books, and even attend religious meetings for one's own enjoyment; all this does not satisfy me. I want to be where every arrangement will have unreserved and constant reference to eternity. On missionary ground I expect to find new and unlooked for trials and hindrances; still it is my choice to be there. And so far from looking upon it as a difficult task to sacrifice my home and country, I feel as if I should 'flee as a bird to her mountain.'"

Such are the helpers Christian men may summon to their aid, whenever they will provide for the education of woman and give her the office of teacher, for which God designed her.

Mrs. Smith accompanied her husband to Beyroot, and was indeed his "help" and good angel. She studied Arabic; established a school for girls; exerted her moral and Christian influence with great effect on the mixed population of Moslems, Syrians, Jews; visiting and instructing the mothers as well as the children; working with all her heart and soul, mind and might; and the time of her service soon expired. She died September 30th, 1836, aged thirty-four; a little over three years from the time she left her own dear land. She died at Boojah, near Smyrna; and in the burial ground of the latter her precious dust reposes, beneath a monument which does honor to America, by showing the heroic and holy character of her missionary daughters.

THE LABORER IN THE VINEYARD.

LADY WARWICK.

THE Right Honorable Mary, Countess of Warwick, was celebrated alike for her piety and accomplishments. She was born in November, in the year 1624, and died April 12th, 1677, aged 53. Her life extended over those years of the eventful seventeenth century which saw the splendor, the fall, and the restoration of the Stuart dynasty.

Lady Warwick's maiden name was Mary Boyle. She was the daughter of that Mr. Richard Boyle, born 1566, who, from the position of a private gentleman, rose by his merits to be the first, or great Earl of Cork. She had seven brothers and seven sisters, several of whom became illustrious; especially the Honorable Robert Boyle, who attained so much eminence as a Christian philosopher.

Lady Warwick had only two children, a daughter, who died young, and that promising young nobleman, Lord Rich, who died in 1664.

Her life affords us a conspicuous proof that there existed among the nobility and gentry of her period some persons of devoted piety who do not make much figure in our historical annals, as they purposely kept themselves as free as possible from the numerous political perturbations of the times in which they lived.

Her "Diary" furnishes a vivid and graphic picture—not only of her ladyship's character, but of the actual every-day life of her contemporaries; and also alludes to many events of the time which have been too little noticed by other writers. It affords us a peep behind the curtain at the secret history of the leading persons of the age, which is alike interesting and improving to reflective readers.

On the whole, Lady Warwick stands before us as an eminently devout and excellent character. Her life and writings present to our fellow-countrywomen—especially those in the higher classes—a noble picture of the true piety, dignity, and grace which the daughters, wives, and mothers of England should seek to cultivate and to display.

The most important biographical notice of her that has yet appeared is in a work of her friend and pastor, Dr. Anthony Walker. It bears this singular title: "The Virtuous Wom[illegible] Found, her Loss Bewailed, and Character Exemplified, in a Sermon preached at Felsted, in Essex, April 30th, 1678, at the funeral of that most excellent lady the Right Honorable and eminently religious and charitable Mary, Countess Dowager of Warwick, the most illustrious pattern of sincere piety and solid goodness this age hath produced: with so large additions, as may be styled, The Life of that Noble Lady. To which are annexed, some of her Ladyship's Pious and Useful Meditations: by Anthony Walker, D.D., and rector of Fyfield, in the same county."

The first edition of this work was printed for Nathaniel Ranew, St. Paul's Churchyard, A. D. 1678, and another A. D. 1687, and it is from this graphic memoir, written with so much of the old-world warmth, fulness, and directness, that the following picture of Lady Warwick's grave but winning character is taken.

God made use of two more remote means of her conversion—afflictions and retirement.

Like the wise man in the Gospel, Matt. vii. 24, she dug deep to lay her foundation on a rock. She made a strict scrutiny into the state of her soul, and weighed the reasons of her choice on the balance of the sanctuary. And, with the other builder of the Gospel, sat down and considered with herself what it might cost to finish her spiritual edifice, and whether she were furnished to defray that charge. And also whether the grounds of her hope were firm, and such as would not abuse and shame her, and her evidences for heaven such as would bear the test and Scripture would approve.

An account of this self-examination she drew up at large, with her own hand, judiciously, soberly, modestly, humbly.

Having thus put her hand to the plough, she

looked not back, but minded religion as her business indeed, and never gave suspicion of trifling in so serious a work.

Therefore, for her practice of it, it was her great design to walk worthy of God in all well pleasing, to adorn her professed subjection to the gospel by a conversation becoming it; and to show forth his virtues and praises who had called her to his marvelous light.

She was circumspectly careful to abstain from all appearance of evil. In all doubtful cases, it was her rule to take the surest side. Though, therefore, none were further from censuring others, or usurping judgment over their liberties, yet for herself she would never allow herself the addition of artificial handsomeness. She used neither paint nor patch, and was pleased with the saying of one of her spiritual friends, upon reading the book which apologizes for it: "O Lord, I thank thee that thou gavest me not wit enough to write such a book, unless withal thou hadst given me grace enough not to write it." Neither would she play at any games; because, beside many other inconveniences, she judged them great wasters of precious time, of which she was always very thrifty. And though she was known to be a woman of good understanding, yet there were three things that were too hard for her, and she would confess she could not comprehend them:

1. How those who professed to believe an eternal state, and its dependence upon the short inch

of time, could complain of time lying as a dead commodity on their hand, which they were troubled how to drive away.

2. How Christians, who would seem devout at church, could laugh at others for being serious out of it, and burlesque the very Bible, and turn religion into ridicule.

3. How knowing men could take care of souls, and seldom come amongst them, and never look after them.

And though, in the fore-named particulars, she was content only to give example of forbearance; yet from the playhouse, since the stage hath taken so great liberty, she would openly dehort her friends with the greatest earnestness.

She very many years since began to keep a diary; and consulted two, whom she used to call her soul-friends—and ever esteemed such her best friends—concerning the best manner of performing it. This "diary" she used at first to write every evening; but finding that inconvenient, by reason of her lord's long illness, which gave her many inevitable diversions and interruptions at that season, she changed the time into the quiet, silent morning, always rising early. And therein, amongst other things, she recorded the daily frame of her own heart toward God, his signal providences to herself and sometimes toward others, his gracious manifestations to her soul, returns of prayer, temptations resisted or prevailing; or whatever might be useful for caution or encouragement, and afford her matter of thankfulness or humiliation. By this means she arrived at such experience that she could conclude (at least make strong conjectures) of the events of things she spread before the Lord in prayer, by the frame of her own heart in the performance of it, as I could instance in particulars if it were convenient.

She used to call prayer, "heart's-ease;" as she often found it; and though her modesty was such, and she was so far from a vain affected ostentation of her gifts, that I cannot name one person with whom she prayed, yet can I say she was as mighty and fervent in prayer as constant and abundant in it: for she sometimes, using her voice, hath been overheard; and her own lord, knowing her hours of prayer, once conveyed a grave minister into a secret place within hearing; who, if I should name him, I suppose would not be denied to be a competent judge, and who much admired her humble fervency; for she, praying, prayed; and when she used not an audible voice, her sighs and groans would echo from her closet at a good distance.

But if she exceeded herself in any thing as much as she excelled others in most things, it was in meditation: this was her master-piece. She usually walked two hours daily in the morning to meditate alone; in which divine art she was an accomplished mistress, both in set times and occasional. In the first, choosing some select subject, which she would press upon her heart with intensest thoughts till she had drawn out all its juice and nourishment;

and in the second, like a spiritual bee, she would suck honey from all occurrences, whole volumes of which she hath left behind her.

After this consecrating of the day with reading the Scriptures, prayer, and meditation, a short dressing-time, and ordering her domestic affairs, or reading some good book, she spent the remainder of the morning till chapel-prayers, from which she was never absent, and at which she was ever reverent and a devout example to her whole family.

She was a strict observer of the Lord's day, which is truly called the hedge and fence of religion; and though some please themselves to call this Judaizing, to excuse the liberties they indulge themselves, I am sure our church hath enjoined us all to cry to God for mercy for the breach of, and for the grace to incline our hearts to keep the fourth commandment, as well as any of the other nine. And it is not hard to observe that the streams of religion are deep or shallow according as those banks are kept up or neglected.

She was a very devout communicant, seldom omitting to prepare her soul with solemn fasting to renew her covenant with God. And in the act of receiving, I cannot think of her without reflecting on St. Stephen, when he saw the heavens opened and Jesus standing at God's right hand, and his face was as the face of an angel.

She was a very serious and attentive hearer of the word, and constantly after sermon recollected what she heard—sometimes by writing, always by thinking, and calling it to mind—that she might make it her own, and turn it into practice; not content to be a forgetful, fruitless hearer only, but a doer, that she might be blessed in her deed.

And such she was for the external performances of religion.

And though this was beautiful and lovely, yet her chief glory was within, in the hidden man of the heart, in that which is not corruptible, in that dress of graces which adorned her soul. This string was all of orient pearls, and evenly matched, not one ill-watered or of unequal size. There was not one dried or withered limb, one member wanting or defective in the new creature; she was complete in Christ, all of a piece.

She avowedly designed to represent religion as amiable and taking, and free from vulgar prejudice, as possibly she might; not so as might affright and scare men from it, but that it might allure them, and insinuate itself into their love and liking. To this end she was affable, familiar, pleasant, of a free and agreeable conversation, unaffected, not sour, reserved, morose, nor disposed to melancholy, which presents religion most disadvantageously. She was naturally of the sweetest temper in the world; and grace, inoculated into such a stock, thrives even luxuriantly. Whereas, some crabbed, peevish, sullen natures starve the best scion they are grafted with. And she made grace and nature both subservient to the good of others.

As we say of some neat, well-fashioned persons, "whatever they wear becomes them, and sits well," I must do her this right to testify I never saw religion become any person better. And it was hard not to approve and love a dress so decent and adorning.

She kept herself free and disinterested from all parties and factions, that none might suspect her of a design of making proselytes to any but to God.

She was neither of Paul, nor Apollos, nor Cephas, but only Christ. Her name was Christian, and her surname Catholic. She had a large and unconfined soul, not hemmed in or pounded up within the circle of any man's name or drawing; a latitudinarian in the true commendable sense; and whoever feared God and wrought righteousness was accepted of her.

She very inoffensively, regularly, devoutly, observed all the orders of the Church of England, in its Liturgy and public service, which she failed not to attend twice a day with exemplary reverence; yet was she very far from placing religion in ritual observances. And I may not deny that she would sometimes warm her heart (though never with strange fire) at private altars in her own chamber or closet.

She would perfume the company with good discourse, to prevent idle or worse communication, not abruptly, upbraidingly, or importunely, which is very nauseous and fulsome, and spoils a good game by bad playing. But she was like a spiritual stove; you should feel the heat and not see the fire, and find yourself in other company amongst the same persons, and rather wonder than perceive how you came there. For she would drop a wise sentence or moral holy apothegm (with which she was admirably furnished, of her own making or collection) that suited with, at least was not far remote from what was talked of; and commending or improving that, she would wind about the whole discourse without offence, yea, with pleasure.

She kept a book of such wise pithy sayings, much valuing words which contained great use and worth in little compass.

I shall transcribe a few of many:

"The almost Christian is the unhappiest man; having religion enough to make the world hate him, and not enough to make God love him.

"God's servants should be as bold for him as the devil's are for him.

"What will make thee happy at any time will make thee happy at all times.

"O Lord, what I give thee doth not please thee, unless I give thee myself. So what thou givest me shall not satisfy me, unless thou give me thyself.

"O Lord, who givest grace to the humble, give me grace to be humble.

"He loves God too little, who loves anything *with* him, which he loves not *for* him.

"The true measure of loving God is to love him without measure.

"So speak of God as though men heard thee; so speak to men as knowing God hears thee.

"Seneca said, he was better born than to be a slave to his body.

"Luther said, Christ's cross is no letter; yet it taught him more than all the alphabet.

"We should meditate of Christ's cross till we be fastened as close to him as he was to his cross.

"By how much the more Christ made himself vile for us, by so much the more precious he should be to us.

"We need every day blood for our hearts, as water for our hands.

"He only can satisfy us who satisfied *for* us.

"He that takes up Christ's cross handsomely shall find it such a burden as wings to a bird, or sails to a ship.

"It is a great honor to be almoner to the King of heaven.

"Who would not starve a lust to feed a saint?

"To give is the greatest sensible delight; how indulgent, then, is God to annex future rewards to what is so much its own recompense!

"To be libeled for Christ is the best panegyric.

"Where affliction is heavy sin is light.

"God chastises whom he loves, but he loves not to chastise.

"Sin brought death into the world, and nothing but death will carry sin out of the world.

"If all men's troubles were brought into a common store, every one would carry back what he brought rather than stand to a share of an equal division.

"Though time be not lasting, what depends on it is everlasting.

"The best shield against slanderers is to live so that none may believe them.

"He that revenges an injury acts the part of an executioner. He that pardons it acts the part of a prince.

"Sanctified afflictions are spiritual promotions.

"Man is a pile of dust and puff of wind.

"Why are we so fond of that life which begins with a cry and ends with a groan?"

But I will not cloy you; knowing it is safest to rise with an appetite, even when we are entertained at a banquet.

It would require a volume to follow the biographer with his review of Lady Warwick, as a wife, as a friend, as a mother, a landlady, and the mistress of a great household—always affectionate, dignified, and charitable. The poor, the young children, and young scholars of promise were the objects of her special and unfailing care.

But methinks I hear it asked, says the worthy chaplain, "What! had she no spots, no scars, no real nor imputed blemishes? how could she live in such an age and not be corrupted, or at least traduced; neither scorched by the fire of infection, nor blackened by the smoke of revengeful detraction, for upbraiding the guilty by her innocence? This overdoing is undoing, if you make us believe she had no faults; we shall sooner believe you have no truth; and all that you have said hath more of romance and what you fancy than narrative of what she was or did."

I confess it is next to a miracle to consider both how divine grace enlarged her heart and established her goings, and restrained the tongues of others from reproach or showing dislike of that in her for which they deride and hate, not to say persecute others.

But since you are so inquisitive, and seem to deny me the just and civil freedom to draw a veil of silence over her imperfections, and your curiosity will be peeping under that sacred pall which should secure and shroud the worst of men from being pried into; and the vault and grave, that place of darkness and forgetfulness, which should bury all defects and render them invisible, must be ransacked: draw back the curtains, let in the light, survey its secret recesses; nor she, nor I in her behalf, fear the most piercing eagle-eye or scent. Not that I deny her to have been a sinner while I adore that grace that made her a saint.

But these two things I say and will adhere to.

First, that she was not notoriously defective in any grace or virtue.

Secondly, she was never stained with any scandalous deformity: another rare mercy; for though she did slip now and then, or stumble, if you will, she fell not, much less lay or wallowed to defile her garments; which I testify not only from mine own observation but her own pen. She says, "After God had thus savingly (I hope) wrought upon me, I went on constantly, comfortably, in my Christian course, though I had many doubts and fears to contend with; and did truly obey that precept of working out my salvation with fear and trembling; yet God was pleased to carry me still onward; and though I too often broke my good resolutions, I never renounced them; and though I too often tripped in my journey to heaven, yet I never forsook my purpose of going thither."

I never heard her blamed for more than two faults by the most curious observers and inspectors of her disposition or behavior.

1. Excess of charity.

2. Defect of anger, or what was reducible to those two. Two goodly faults! But even these admit apology more easily than they need it.

1. What was reputed the culpable excess of her charity was her credulous easiness to believe most people good, or at least better than they were. I confess she did bend a little to this right-hand error; but if it were a bad effect, it proceeded from a good cause. For, as it is observed, that as they who are conscious to themselves of some great evils, scarce can esteem any less nocent* than themselves; so they that have clear and innocent

* Noxious, injurious.

hearts are ready to judge the like of others. "Charity thinketh no evil," and she used this good opinion of others as an instrument to make them what she was so willing to signify she thought them. But though she would never despair of any men while she found them under the awe of God's authority and word—(for even those may receive some nourishment who eat against stomach, and the sieve under the pump may be cleansed, though it hold no water)—yet if she observed a person to scorn or deride the Scriptures, despise God's ordinances, and turn all that was sacred into ridicule, she used, as her phrase was, to set her mark upon that man. And I must further add, she was neither so often or so much mistaken in her judgment of persons as some supposed she was; they more misinterpreting her civility than she did the other's sanctity.

2. For her defect of anger.—This implies (if it be faulty) want of zeal against sin and sinners; and so it is an unjust charge; for though I confess she could not rage and storm, and discover her anger, as some persons do who verify the saying, "Anger is a kind of madness,"—for her sedate, composed, serene mind, and sweet and amicable disposition were scarcely forcible to what was so contrary to her nature; yet would she make deeper impressions of her displeasure for great faults, than those who appeared most curious; like a still soaking shower, which will wet more than a driving storm. And therefore it was observed, that if any

servants had been faulty, they had rather have passed the gauntlet thrice of their lord's most furious expressions than have once been sent for to their lady's closet, whose treatment was soft words, but hard arguments against their faults; and like that silent lightning, which, without the noise of thunder, melts the blade and singeth not the scabbard. Her reproofs were neither the frightful hissing, nor the venomed sting, but the penetrating oil of scorpions.

This little is enough to extenuate her almost commendable faults; and it is a great evidence of her goodness that these things were imputed as blemishes; for they who would not spare her in these little errors showed plainly that she was not chargeable with more or greater.

Never did bird take wing when disentangled from a net with greater cheerfulness, nor chirp out the pleasures of its unconfined freedom more merrily, than she did solace herself, when she had escaped the noise and crowd of affairs, which ruffled and turmoiled her quiet, and suspended the enjoyment of herself. And when her dearest sister was, in the beginning of the last winter, about to leave her, her last farewell she took was in these words: "Now I have done my drudgery (meaning her business), I will set to the renewing of my preparations for eternity; and she made it the repeated business of the last winter.

She on the Tuesday in Passion-week (March 26th, 1678) was taken with some indisposition, loss of appetite, and an aguish distemper, and had four or five fits, which yet in that season were judged both by physicians and her friends more advantageous to her health than dangerous to her life. And in this state she continued freed from her fits, in her own apprehension and in our hopes, till Friday, the 12th of April, on which day she rose with good strength, and after sitting up some time, being laid upon her bed, discoursing cheerfully and piously, one of the last sentences she spake was this, turning back the curtain with her hand:

"Well, ladies, if I were one hour in heaven, I would not be again with you, as well as I love you."

Thus lived, thus died, this right honorable lady, this heroic woman, this blessed saint, this incomparable pattern of flaming zeal for the glory of God and burning charity for the good of men, in the actual exercise of prayer, according to her own desire. For there are many witnesses who have testified that they have often heard her say, that if she might choose the manner and circumstances of her death, she would die praying, by which desire she so often anticipated heaven.

THE GUARDIAN ANGEL.

LADY MACKINTOSH.

[This noble tribute to a devoted wife is given in the "Memoirs" of Sir James Mackintosh, the "philosophical politician" and the humane and upright judge—one of the most able and estimable men ever intrusted with the administration of justice.]

ALLOW me, in justice to her memory, to tell you what she was, and what I owed her. I was guided in my choice only by the blind affection of my youth. I found an intelligent companion and a tender friend, a prudent monitress, the most faithful of wives, and a mother as tender as children ever had the misfortune to lose. I met a woman who, by the tender management of my weaknesses, gradually corrected the most pernicious of them. She became prudent from affection; and though of the most generous nature, she was taught economy and frugality by her love for me. During the most critical period of my life, she preserved order in my affairs, from the care of which she relieved me. She gently reclaimed me from dissipation; she propped my weak and irresolute nature; she urged my indolence to all the exertions that have been useful or creditable to me; and she was perpetually at hand to admonish my heedlessness and improvidence. To her I owe whatever I am; to her whatever I shall be. In her solicitude for my interest, she never for a moment forgot my feelings or my character. Even in her occasional resentment, for which I but too often gave her cause (would to God I could recall those moments!) she had no sullenness or acrimony. Her feelings were warm and impetuous, but she was placable, tender, and constant. Such was she whom I have lost; and I have lost her when her excellent natural sense was rapidly improving, after eight years of struggle and distress had bound us fast together, and moulded our tempers to each other—when a knowledge of her worth had refined my youthful love into friendship, before age had deprived it of much of its original ardor—I lost her, alas! (the choice of my youth and the partner of my misfortunes) at a moment when I had the prospect of her sharing my better days.

The philosophy which I have learned only teaches me that virtue and friendship are the greatest of human blessings, and that their loss is irreparable. It aggravates my calamity, instead of consoling me under it. My wounded heart seeks another consolation. Governed by these feelings, which have in every age and region of the world actuated the human mind, I seek relief, and find it, in the soothing hope and consolatory opinion that a Benevolent Wisdom inflicts the chastisement as well as bestows the enjoyments of human life; that Superintending Goodness will one day enlighten the darkness which surrounds our nature and hangs over our prospects; that this dreary and wretched life is not the whole of man; that an animal so sagacious and provident, and capable of such proficiency in science and virtue, is not like the beasts that perish; that there is a dwelling-place prepared for the spirits of the just, and that the ways of God will yet be vindicated to man. The sentiments of religion which were implanted in my mind in my early youth, and which were revived by the awful scenes which I have seen passing before my eyes in the world, are, I trust, deeply rooted in my heart by this great calamity.

THE END.

CPSIA information can be obtained
at www.ICGtesting.com
Printed in the USA
LVHW040434110522
718423LV00002B/334

9 783375 003562